Jack was on the phone with air traffic controllers in Kansas City, Kansas, when Jessi Bandison, her coffee-colored face suddenly pale, handed him the phone.

"Hang on," Jack said.

Jessi shook her head so vigorously it could have popped off. "Un-huh. It's the President. For you."

Jack hung up one phone and took the other. "This is Jack Bauer."

"Bauer, this is Harry Barnes."

"Yes, sir, Mr. President." He straightened automatically.

"I'm told you're the guy on the ground causing this crisis."

"*After* the guys who are causing it, yes, sir."

"Bauer, you understand the shit storm you are about to unleash with this? The kind of disruption this is about to cause? You're clear on this, right?"

Jack swallowed. "Yes, sir."

"You're sure what you're doing?"

"Sir, we know that the EMP was stolen, we know that eight—"

"Shut up, Bauer!" Barnes snapped. "Don't play that bureaucratic shell game with me. I'm not asking you to give me evidence so I can decide. You look at the evidence and *you* decide. That's what you get paid for. Is the risk worth the damage?" Barnes asked the last question slowly and clearly.

Jack didn't hesitate. "Yes."

"Then do it." Barnes hung up the phone.

24 DECLASSIFIED Books
From HarperEntertainment

24

DECLASSIFIED

VETO POWER

J O H N W H I T M A N

Based on the series by Joel Surnow & Robert Cochran

HarperEntertainment
An Imprint of HarperCollinsPublishers

HARPERENTERTAINMENT
An Imprint of HarperCollins*Publishers*
10 East 53rd Street
New York, New York 10022-5299

ISBN-13: 978-0-06-084225-3
ISBN-10: 0-06-084225-3

First HarperEntertainment paperback printing: November 2005

Printed in the United States of America

Visit HarperEntertainment on the World Wide Web at
www.harpercollins.com.

10 9 8 7 6 5 4 3 2 1

This book is dedicated to my friend and teacher, Darren Levine.

ACKNOWLEDGMENTS

I'd like to thank my original editor, Hope Innelli, for the chance to meddle in the world of "24," and my current editor, Josh Behar, for his patience and understanding!

24

DECLASSIFIED

VETO POWER

After the 1993 World Trade Center attack, a Division of the Central Intelligence Agency established a domestic unit tasked with protecting America from the threat of terrorism. Headquartered in Washington, D.C., the Counter-Terrorist Unit established field offices in several American cities. From it inception, CTU faced hostility and skepticism from other Federal law enforcement agencies. Despite bureaucratic resistance, within a few years CTU had become a major force. After the war against terror began, a number of early CTU missions were declassified. The following is one of them . . .

PROLOGUE—48 HOURS AGO

It was a lonely road, with no cars moving and only one car parked on the gravel shoulder, hunkered there like an unhappy drunk. There was one light in the distance, a single white industrial lamp hanging over a faded wooden sign that read AVILLA ELECTROPLATING. It had been hung there as a substitute for two large floodlights bolted over the sign. The floodlights did not work. The four men in the car had made sure of that.

All of them were slumped down in their seats as though sleeping, and three of them might have dozed off if it weren't for the fourth.

"He's gonna put up a fight. You think he's gonna put up a fight?" said this man. Boy, really. Old enough to skip a shave or two without anyone noticing. Young enough to get antsy waiting behind the wheel.

"If he does, he does," said the one in the passenger seat. Edgars. He was the pro in the group, which meant he'd done one job before. "Just take it easy, Heinny."

"Yeah, take it easy, Heinny," grunted Peterson, one of the two in the back seat.

"I don't like that," Heinny said. "It's not my name."

"We're just joking," Edgars said. "It's easier to say than Heinrich."

"I don't like it," Heinny said. "My friends never called me that."

Edgars shrugged. "Your friends liked to say things in German, that's why."

Edgars turned around in the passenger seat, still careful to stay low, and looked at the last member of their group. He was slumped in the seat next to Peterson, leaning away with his arms folded across his chest and his head rolled to one side, resting against the interior of the car.

"Looks like he's asleep," Edgars said. "Not that he looks so different when he's awake. Poke him."

"Why?" Peterson asked.

"Why not?" Edgars said. "You got anything better to do?"

Peterson didn't. And he wanted to do what Edgars said because Edgars had done this kind of work before. So he poked the sleeping man on the shoulder. When that didn't work he poked him on the chest.

The last of the quartet opened one eye. "Don't do that again."

"Are you asleep?" Peterson asked.

The man scowled. "Is it time?"

Edgars shook his head. "Ten minutes maybe."

The now-awakened man rubbed his eyes and stretched—not a big, long-armed stretch that would have put his body in view through the window, but a weird, low, bulging stretch, as though all his muscles swelled up in their places and then contracted.

In the front seat, Heinrich watched him in the rear

view mirror. He looked jealously at the man's white-blond hair and blue eyes. Heinrich himself had always been scrawny—170 pounds stretched drum-tight across a six-foot, three-inch frame. Heinrich's old friends would have praised the other man as a pure-blood inheritor of the Aryan mission, a natural soldier for the cause. Of course, the "cause" was different now—at least for the moment. Brett Marks had convinced him of that. Marks had shown Heinrich how to grow out of his skinhead beginnings and into the higher cause of the Greater Nation. Heinrich had to admit that a part of him missed the skinhead life. Going out in Detroit on a Saturday night, picking fights with the wetbacks at the bus stop or Christ killers walking home from the sin-o-gogue, that had been fun (except for the time they picked on the Heeb who'd been in the Israeli army; that one had broken his jaw). But at twenty he'd begun to sense that skinhead mayhem wasn't achieving its stated goal, and he began to search for something else. Something more.

He knew he'd found it the day he heard Brett Marks speak at the Christ Redeemer Church in Livonia. Marks was a true Aryan, but he never talked about race and he never even talked about religion. He didn't wear Doc Martens or shave his head or call down fire and brimstone. He wore a suit and spoke like a politician, and when he talked he used ten dollar words to explain how the government had usurped the Constitution and stolen away the rights of the states and the individual. He said it didn't matter if the current administration was dressed like the Rainbow Coalition or the Confederate flag, they were all attempting to steal the power of the people. Marks invited anyone who felt the way he did to join his political movement. Maybe it was the words, or maybe it was the message, or maybe it was just that twenty years seemed too old to be shaving his head and picking fights with ragheads, but Heinrich felt the message echo in his sunken chest. And so he found himself, a month later, joining the Greater Nation militia movement, and nearly one year to the day afterward he was sitting here on a dark rural street outside King City, California, waiting to strike his first blow against the tyranny of the Federal government.

He looked for something to say to the blond man. "You think it's going to go as planned, Jack?"

The blond man didn't talk much. He yawned a lot, which Heinrich thought meant Jack was bored, but Edgars said yawning was a sign of nervousness. Now Jack tipped his chin and said, "I hope so."

"Car coming," Edgars said.

They all looked at the rear or the side mirrors and saw car headlights blossom on the lonely road. Edgars checked his watch. "Four fifty-one. Timing's right."

The lights grew blinding in the mirrors, then the mirrors went dark as a Chevy half-ton with AVILLA ELECTROPLATING printed on the side cruised by them. On cue, the four men opened their car doors and got out. Their car remained dark—Jack had popped the tiny light bulb out of the overhead light so it would not go on when the doors opened. There was a dull thud as Heinrich closed his door too fast, but the sound didn't carry. Jack, Heinny, and Edgars drew handguns from their belts. Peterson slid a shotgun from the backseat. All four men hurried forward through the darkness toward the single light, where the truck had stopped.

Because the floodlights were out, it seemed to the

truck driver that the four men melted out of the darkness. The big, hard one who looked in charge, the one with the shotgun, the skinny one, and the blond one who hung back.

"Don't give trouble, you won't get trouble," said the one in charge, holding a gun up to his nose. "You're the foreman."

It wasn't a question, but the truck driver answered anyway, his voice filled with that hyper-alertness of someone who's just been shaken from sleep. "Yeah. Yes."

"Tell me your name."

"Javier. Garza."

"Okay, Javier Garza, you're going to take us inside and show us where you keep the sodium cyanide."

"Oh shit," Javier Garza said.

"Oh shit is right," said the man. "Now take us inside."

"You can't take that stuff," said the foreman. "It's a controlled substance."

"Don't worry, we'll control it," said Edgars. "Convince him."

This was directed to Heinny. The former skinhead clipped the foreman once across the jaw, just enough to hurt him. "Do what he says. Now!"

The foreman seemed to lose all his strength then, just as Brett said he would. Obediently he held out his keys to show them, then turned toward the gate in the chain-link fence of Avilla Electroplating. Heinny felt a shudder of pleasure go through him. He liked hitting people, and besides, everything was going as planned, and that also made him happy.

Then a moment later it all went to hell in the weirdest way. Out of nowhere, Jack grabbed the muzzle of

Heinny's semi-automatic with one hand and pushed the line of fire away from the foreman. With the other hand he smashed the barrel of his own gun against Heinny's temple. The single light over the building spun around several times and Heinny felt the ground jump up and knock the wind out of him. Somewhere far away Jack was yelling, "Federal agents! Drop your weapons!" At the same time, the floodlights that weren't supposed to work suddenly exploded in blinding light, and dozens of other voices were shouting things like "Down! Down!" and "Don't move!" and "Federal agents!" and "You're under arrest!" Heinny was pretty sure he even heard a helicopter whooping down from above.

His head was still swimming. He tried to get to his knees but someone kicked him in the stomach. Then the same person leaned in close to him, blocking out the blinding floodlights. It was Jack, but Jack was now holding a badge in his hand. "Jack Bauer, Counter Terrorist Unit. You are under arrest for assault, conspiracy to commit murder, and conspiracy to commit a terrorist act against the United States."

Jack Bauer knelt down even farther until his voice was a hiss in Heinrich's ear. "I spent six months listening to your Greater Nation bullshit. Now you're going to tell it to the prosecutors. And you're going to help me get Brett Marks."

At the same time, three thousand miles away in Washington D.C., three of the most powerful men in the world climbed into a limousine in front of the White House. Only one of them had been elected—President Harold Barnes, elected by the slimmest margin of the popular vote, which had not stopped him from turning a narrow victory into a powerful mandate. Across from him in the limo sat two men who also wielded immense power despite the fact that no citizen in any state in the Union had ever cast a single vote for either of them. One of them was Mitch Rasher, short, round, and brilliant, the President's political advisor since his days as a Florida governor. The other was James Quincy, the Attorney General of the United States.

Rasher glared at the AG with undisguised annoyance. His words, however, were directed at the President. "I don't like this," he said. "It's not the right call."

Quincy returned the glare. He was more intimidated than he let on—Rasher had the President's ear and could, essentially, make anything he wished into the law of the land—but like a man facing a pack of dogs, he understood that showing fear was a far greater sin than feeling it. "It makes perfect sense for me to come along," he replied directly to Rasher. "You're going to San Francisco for the Pacific Rim conference, and then you're heading to San Diego for the NAFTA discussion. Both of those items involve Justice."

"That's not why you're going," Rasher retorted. He had a way of leaning into his words that gave his rotund figure all the menace of an avalanche. "You're trying to get a boost for the New American Privacy Act. The whole idea of going to San Francisco was to put distance between us and NAP before the vote."

"You guys supported this bill," Quincy protested. "You guys helped me get some of the senior members in Congress to propose it."

"Well . . ." Rasher said, "that was then, Jim. Now,

even if it passed the Senate, I'm not sure we'd . . ." he trailed off.

The AG turned toward Harold Barnes. "You told me you were behind it, Mr. President. Don't tell me you're saying you'd veto it?"

Barnes stared at the window as though considering the AG's words. In truth, he wasn't doing much of anything. He had found this to be the surest type of politics—to surround himself with strong opinions and listen to those opinions wage war with each other. Leadership, he had decided long ago, meant presiding over those who had deep convictions.

Rasher ran interference. "There are degrees. There's fall-on-your-sword support and there's let-the-other-guy-fall-on-his-sword support. Guess which kind you get."

"No one is getting cut by this," Quincy argued, his eyes locked on Barnes's distant expression. "This bill helps us stop terrorists. Period."

Rasher raised his hands. "Preaching to the choir, Jim. But CNN tells me fifty-two percent of the people think NAP goes too far. We can score more points by scuttling it and looking good in the popular polls."

Quincy sneered. "We don't do what's popular. We do what's right."

Rasher laughed derisively. "Is that what we do?"

1 2 3 4 5 6 7 8 9
10 11 12 13 14 15 16 17
18 19 20 21 22 23 24

· ·

THE FOLLOWING TAKES PLACE
BETWEEN THE HOURS OF
3 A.M. AND 4 A.M.
PACIFIC STANDARD TIME

· ·

3:00 A.M. PST
Greater Nation Compound

It was three o'clock in the morning and Jack Bauer
was on his belly in a barranca in the high desert above
Los Angeles. He couldn't see his team or even hear
them, but he knew they were moving into position.
He could taste the dust in the air, kicked up by their
boots as they surrounded the compound. Bauer lifted
his head above the lip of the barranca and studied the
collection of one- and two-story houses surrounded
by a ten-foot wall. There were lights strung across the
top of that wall every fifteen feet. At the moment each
bulb gave off only a faint orange glow, like the ember
of a dying fire. But they were motion sensors—the

minute anyone moved within ten yards of them the lights would flare up and silent alarms would go off inside the compound, turning all his careful planning into chaos.

Jack stifled a yawn. He hadn't slept much in the past two days. After the sting operation in King City, he'd led the interrogation of Heinrich Gelb, the neo-Nazi turned Greater Nation foot soldier. They'd put the screws to Peterson and Edgars, too, of course, but Jack had known from the start Heinrich would crack first. His youth was against him, but there was more to it than that—Heinrich was a weakling. That's why the little Greater Nation hit squad had chosen him to be the heavy when they attacked the foreman— cowards always make the best torturers. So while Edgars and Peterson were stuck in their little rooms giving the cold shoulder to the other interrogators at the Counter Terrorist Unit, Heinrich sat in his metal chair under a bright light, pouring his guts out to Jack, the video recorder, and the Federal prosecutor. Heinrich was still talking when Federal prosecutor Martin Padilla gave Jack the nod he'd been waiting for.

On any other case, CTU satellites would have put Jack's quarry in an electronic vise. Not only would Jack have known where his target was, he could have known what he had for lunch and how many bites he took before he swallowed. But Jack's case was so low on the priority list that he'd had to rely on human in- telligence and a payphone to confirm his target's whereabouts. His request for a CTU special entry team was rejected, and his call for FBI or Alcohol, To- bacco, and Firearms units fell on deaf ears. All per- sonnel had been assigned to higher-priority missions. Jack had been forced to commandeer the local special response team. Local training was hit or miss. He just hoped that if rounds started going off, they hit what they aimed at and missed him.

His ear bud chirped twice: his Baker team was in position. Once the signal came in from Charlie, he'd broadcast the go tone, and the fun would begin.

The local special tactics team was out of Lancaster, California, which borrowed its law enforcement from the L.A. County Sheriff Department. The L.A. Sheriffs had provided him with their Special Entry Bureau, their version of SWAT. That was a good unit, but they'd gotten most of their experience serving high-risk warrants and laying siege to cornered bank robbers. He'd done his best to prepare them for the possibility of real resistance.

"These Greater Nation guys are militia," he had said during a midnight briefing. "Real militia, at least as far as they're concerned. They're probably well-trained and they're definitely well armed. They're anti-government types."

One of the SEB guys, with "Bastion" taped across his vest, laughed. "They're all anti-government when we kick down the door."

Jack didn't smile. "Most guys are only fighting to stay out of prison. These guys just might fight for a cause. I just spent six months with them. There are a lot of true believers on the other side of that wall. They've got just enough training to be dangerous but not enough to know when to give up. They're also weekend warriors. They'll need to get psyched up before they put any rounds down range. They won't put up a real fight if we hit them hard and fast."

"Hard and fast," Bastion said approvingly. "Just how I like my sex."

"Yeah," said another one, "that's what the captain told us."

Locker room talk. Cops doing an entry. Soldiers psyching themselves up for battle. It was all the same.

Three chirps in his ear. It was seven minutes after three and Charlie unit was ready. Jack moved his right leg quietly until it touched the leg of the agent next to him. He knew that man would do the same to the man beside him, all the way down the short line of cops. He waited until he was sure they were all prepared. None of them moved, but something changed— something electric in the darkness. Bauer thumbed a small transmitter in his hand, sending out an urgent five-burst signal.

Then he was on his feet, sprinting toward the soft glow of the sensors on the walls. He was vaguely aware of footsteps around him, but his mind was focused on the distance to the wall. Fifteen yards away the sensors kicked in and lights flared on so brightly they seemed to make sound. Anyone wearing night vision would have been blinded, but Jack had done his prep work and none of his people was surprised. Ten yards to the wall. Jack picked up his pace—inside the compound, alarms would be sounding, paranoid militia men would be trying to remember the drills they had learned, and someone somewhere would be chambering rounds into an automatic weapon purchased at a gun show in Orange County. Five yards to the wall. Jack gathered himself and jumped. He kicked off the wall with his left foot and went up, and for a moment he might as well have been in Kosovo again, or in Delta training, or even back in basic. Get your chest over the wall, but keep your head low. Hug the top like you want to hump it. Drop down with your feet under you and your muzzle down range.

His boots hit the ground under bright lights but nearly complete silence. There were four buildings—a two story main house and three one story ranch-style structures. One of them was a supply depot—Baker would secure it. Two were bunkhouses, but neither one should be full; Charlie would lock them down. Jack kept his eyes on the main house as his team came over the wall beside him, and together they charged ahead.

Lights were coming on now, upstairs and downstairs, and Jack knew that the next few moments would decide if someone had to die. He flew up the steps of the main house and flattened himself against the wall by the front door. The man behind him—Bastion—pressed himself against the other side. The third in line didn't even hesitate. Barely slowing, he lifted his knee and stomped his boot against the door. It boomed like a war drum, but didn't give.

"Reinforced," Jack said.

The SEB unit was ready. The fourth man in line slid a heavy metal rod from the third man's back. It had handles on either side and a blunt head like a medieval mace. The two agents gripped the handles, swung back, then slammed the rod forward. The battering ram smashed into the door. Wood and metal screamed in protest. The door frame shook. Two more blows sent splinters flying and the door swung open.

The SEB unit flowed into the house like an angry black tide. They were in a bare hallway with hardwood floors and small recessed lights in the ceiling. A room opened up on the left, and on the right broad stairs climbed up to the second story. Blueprints downloaded from the city planners had given them the floor plan, but it was Jack's six months under cover that really paid off. Half of Able team flowed left, where they knew six members of the Greater Nation would be sleeping in the living room converted to a bunkhouse. The other half rose up the stairs with Jack. At the top they broke left, down a hallway toward a heavy door that slammed shut as it came into view. The door was steel, as was the frame around it. Jack didn't bother with the battering ram.

"Charges," he ordered, stepping back. One of the black-armored SEB agents ripped open a Velcro pocket on his chest and produced a brick of pale, claylike C-4. He massaged it quickly, a sculptor on a deadline, into four thin ropes. Three he pressed along the steel door hinges, the fourth he wrapped around the handle. In seconds, all four were fitted with blasting caps connected by wires. By this time the rest of the team had backed down the stairs. In theory, the C-4 should blow inward, but no one cared about theory and everyone cared about keeping his parts attached to his body, so they'd all backed off.

"Three, two, one." BOOM!

Jack and the SEB team launched themselves forward again, hurtling through the smoke, trampling on the steel door that had been blown off its hinges and onto the hallway floor, and into the room beyond.

Jack scanned the room in an instant. It was a private study with a mahogany desk and shelves lined with books. Through an archway he caught a glimpse of an unmade bed in a room behind. In the next instant, Jack's eyes and gun sights settled immediately on the figure sitting calmly, with his feet up, behind a big mahogany desk. He was grinning. It wasn't the cocky grin of a bluffer who'd been called; it was more like the grin of a chess player who'd been outmaneuvered and was mildly amused that he hadn't seen the trap. The man's face was sharp-edged and handsome, with the squared-off angles of a disciplined youth overlaid with the crow's feet and laugh lines of an energetic middle life. His salt-and-pepper hair was short but annoyingly thick for someone in his fifties, and when he stood his back was straighter than a flagpole. He was wearing his pajamas and slippers, his arms behind his head. Jack's eyes soaked in details of the room—a zipped-up bag by the window; a pair of pants dropped on the floor beside the bag, shoes half-pulled from beneath the bed. Bauer had the distinct impression that, as soon as the alarms had sounded, the man had initiated an escape plan, then abandoned it as panicky and useless, choosing instead to weather the assault with serene indifference. That was more Brett Marks's style.

"Brett Marks, you're under arrest for conspiracy to commit murder, conspiracy to commit murder with a weapon of mass destruction, and conspiracy to commit treason against the United States," Jack said, moving forward behind the steady aim of his SigSauer 9mm.

The other man nodded and lifted his hands from behind his head to show that they were empty. "Jack Miles. Or what is it really? Agent, or Special Agent?"

Bauer let the rest of his teams swarm past him and pull Marks from his chair. They put him facedown on the ground and searched him, pulling a handgun out of a pancake holster inside his pajamas. Jack let them tag it as evidence, but he knew Marks well enough by now to know that the weapon would be completely legal. Though his goal was the overthrow of the United States government, the Greater Nation leader took care to stay just inside the law whenever possible. Jack studied Marks, looking for signs of annoyance or anger while they searched him roughly. These were clues he could use during interrogation. Brute force and sleep deprivation were sometimes unnecessary if you could find the key that opened someone's mouth. Often that key was something simple, a word or phrase that set him off, a certain posture that reminded him of someone he loved or hated. Jack had witnessed an interrogation in Bosnia where a tough Serbian assassin had resisted two days of beatings and headfirst baths in cold water, only to crack at the mention of his sister's name.

Jack had instructed his team to bang Marks around once the handcuffs were on. He was curious to see how the militia man would handle being knocked off his pedestal. The SEB team snapped cuffs on Marks's wrists. He grunted when they went on tight. Bastion used that as an excuse to slap his ear. "Stop resisting," he warned. Bastion grabbed Marks by his thick hair and pulled him up straight. Bauer studied his face. Marks looked uncomfortable. Jack would have been disappointed if he hadn't shown at least a hint of pain. But there was something missing, a sense of indignation that Jack would have liked to see. It would have told him that Marks didn't see himself as a prisoner; it would have indicated that he wasn't prepared for that abuse. Instead, Jack found Brett Marks staring back at him with a look of mild amusement.

"Good soldier, Jack," the militia leader smirked.

Jack clicked the radio mike at his throat, "Baker, status."

There was a moment of white noise, then a clipped voice broke back: "Baker here. Depot secure, over."

"Copy," Jack said. "Charlie, status."

There was another moment of white noise. "Charlie, status."

A burst of static chopped through the white noise, and someone cut in. "Able, Charlie. Be advised there's—"

"Freeze!" "Down!" "Down!"

A cacophony of commands around Jack overwhelmed the radio call. Four men had burst into the room, guns drawn. They looked half asleep and shocked. Most of them were clearly terrified.

"Drop your weapons!" one of them ordered. "You're trespassing!"

"Federal agent!" Jack said, holding up his badge and his gun. "Drop your fucking weapons now!" The speaker was the one to target, Jack thought. The others were shaking so badly they'd probably drop their weapons with or without the order.

"No," the newcomer said.

A half dozen fingers pressed triggers ever so slightly. The SEB agents didn't like having guns pointed at them.

"Frank."

It was Brett Marks. His voice was calm, the voice of a man who had led men in combat. Jack almost took his eyes off the militia men to look at him.

"Frank, calm down."

Jack hid his surprise. Six months of undercover work and countless hours of research had told him that under Marks's mainstream exterior lay the heart of a violent anarchist. He hated the Federal government, and he'd been preparing his true believers for a showdown just like this. Why was he striking his colors?

"Brett, don't give me this shit," said the other one. Jack knew him, though not well. He was Frank Newhouse, a lieutenant in the Greater Nation. Newhouse was Brett's colorless alter ego. Everything about him was flat, from his crew cut to his pale eyes to the permanent look of disinterest on his face. He had the lean, wide-shouldered body of a man who never worked out but also never stopped working. "This is what we're here for!"

Brett Marks shook his head. "This isn't worth someone's life, Frank. Not this. Whatever they want, we'll beat them in court. They don't have shit on us and we know it."

Only a witness who puts you in charge of a plot to steal ten gallons of sodium cyanide, Jack thought. Out loud, he said, "Listen to Brett, Frank. You don't want to die over this. Neither do those boys with you."

Frank grinned. "They don't want to die? Maybe you're right. What do you think, Danny?" He elbowed the man next to him, a carbon copy of Heinrich Gelb. "He's right, probably, isn't he? We might as well lay down our weapons when the Federal government can send liars and spies into our group, point guns at us, knock down our door whenever they want to, right?"

Danny said, "Hell, no."

"Frank," Brett said. "You've still got a mission to finish. Focus on that."

"Put the guns down!" Jack ordered.

Jack couldn't tell who fired first. If it was his own people, he couldn't blame them. A man can only stand under the gun for so long before he has to act. All Jack knew for sure was that the militia man's words were still hanging in the air when the room erupted in gunfire. Jack found his senses assaulted by the crack of handguns, the flash of muzzles, and the sharp stink of gunpowder. He flinched for only the briefest of instants before laying his sights across Frank Newhouse's chest and squeezing the trigger. *Front sight, trigger pull, follow through.* The mantra of an old combat firearms instructor scrolled through his memory as his Sig spat fire, but even as the flashes imprinted on his eyes, he saw the militia boy named Danny fall across his line of sight and knew that he'd missed. Danny hit the ground, along with his three companions. Frank Newhouse disappeared beyond the doorframe.

"Stay on him!" Jack ordered half his team. The other half followed Jack through the doorway into Brett Marks's bedroom. White sheets and a heavy comforter lay askew across the mattress. A bathroom door and a closet door were both open, and Frank Newhouse was nowhere to be seen.

"Shit!" Jack swore. He jabbed a finger at the closet, ordering someone to check it, and threw himself against the wall beside the bathroom doorway. He kicked the half-open door and burst in, following the arc of the swinging door with the muzzle of his gun. Nothing.

"Sir!" someone called.

Jack spun toward the closet as several of the SEB agents cleared an aisle. Shirts and pants on hangers had been pushed aside. A panel in the back had been kicked through, revealing a shaft that dropped down into darkness.

"Go!" Jack said. "Keep on the radio. Get that guy!"

Three members of the assault team went through the panel and down the shaft. Jack pointed to one of his team. "Stay with them by radio. I want to know what direction they're heading and where that tunnel comes out."

Bauer took a deep breath and assessed his situation. His primary target had been caught. His teams had captured the Greater Nation's munitions depot and rounded up most of the militia men. One target missing, but pursuit was in progress. He looked to the doorway, where SEB agents were huddled over the bodies of the three militia men. One of the agents looked at Bauer and dragged his thumb across his throat.

Jack checked his watch: 3:23. The whole operation had taken less than fifteen minutes. Three militia men dead, no casualties on his team. So far, so good.

"Where's he going to go, Brett?" Jack asked, returning to the outer room.

Marks smirked. "You're an agent of the Federal government, Jack," he said. "You have no authority to do or say anything against a private citizen like me."

Bastion laughed. "He's shitting you, right?"

Marks frowned at Bastion like a professor dealing with a naïve student. "Check the law, my friend. Read the Constitution. *Your* Constitution. Under 18 U.S. Code 242, it is illegal for anyone under the color of law to deprive any person of the rights, privileges, and immunities secured by the Constitution. And the Constitution allows Federal law to act on state territory only for treason, counterfeiting, piracy on the high seas—"

"Give it a rest, Marks," Jack growled.

"—crimes against the laws of nations, or civil rights violations by officials. You are violating the same Constitution you swore to protect. These men should be arresting you."

"He is shitting you," Bastion said in disbelief.

Brett shook his head. "It's a felony punishable by ten years in prison."

Bastion nodded his head sarcastically. "Oh well, in that case I'll just take these off and put them on Agent Bauer here."

Marks half-turned so he could look Bastion in the eye. "Officer, you are joking. But I'm telling you the truth. Look it up."

"Sorry, I don't subscribe to *Nutcase Weekly*."

"Then maybe you should check the Constitution. Or the United States Code published by the House of Representatives. What I'm talking about is right there in black and white."

"Move him out of here," Jack said. Guns and handcuffs aside, Marks was still on his home turf, in his comfort zone. He needed to change that. "Get him in the van and sit on him until you hear from me."

Jack's ear bud chirped. "Agent Bauer, this is Able, over."

"Able, Bauer. Go ahead."

"We're in the munitions depot. You want to come see this now, over."

"On my way. Bauer out." Bauer eyed Bastion. "If he keeps talking, shut him up. But keep your eyes on him."

Bauer spun toward the door. As he did, he started to take himself down from his assault status. He checked and holstered his weapon, then pulled the black skullcap from his head and tugged the gloves off his hands. He stopped in a bathroom and splashed water on his face, letting it rinse away the black combat paint he'd smudged there. Lastly, he slid his mobile phone out of a Velcro pocket of his black battle dress uniform pants and turned it on. Immediately it emitted an angry buzz.

3:35 A.M. PST
CTU Headquarters, Los Angeles

It was after three-thirty in the morning, and CTU Special Agent in Charge Kelly Sharpton's mood was as dark as the unlit hallway. He banged his toe against a chair and swore like a sailor. He wasn't a sailor, though, he was Air Force—eight years in, ending up in the Office of Special Investigations before leaving the Corps to join the FBI. He'd been a field agent in the San Francisco office before his computer skills—and a few personal problems—drove him off the streets. Now he mostly rode a desk, but he didn't mind. At CTU he had eyes and ears that saw the entire world. He was good at his job, and he liked it most of the time.

Not now, though. Now he'd been roused out of bed by the gravediggers—his nickname for the analysts who worked the swing shift from oh-dark-hundred until the sun came up. Sharpton was used to getting calls from the graveyard, so it wasn't the when that angered him—it was the who.

"Bauer here," said the gravelly voice on the other end of the line.

"Yousonofabitchwhatthehellareyoudoing?" Sharpton spewed. "I've been calling you for the last hour."

"Sorry, Kelly, I had my phone off. I'm in the middle of something."

"So I hear," Sharpton spat back. "Of course, I don't hear it from you. I hear it from the gravediggers, who happen to be monitoring police frequencies to keep themselves awake."

"I told you I had this militia leader—"

"That requisition was denied," Kelly said, lowering his voice. He'd reached the end of the dark hallway and entered the guts of CTU's operation—a war room lined with computer terminals, overlooked by a loft designed for several windowed offices. All of the offices and most of the computer terminals were dark at this hour. A few swing-shift analysts—the gravediggers—looked up from their screens, braced to weather the brewing storm. He gave them a nod and a wave as he passed them and climbed the stairs to his office.

"The denial was for manpower," Jack said. "No one said I couldn't arrest him."

"What the hell do you think you're doing authorizing the seizure anyway."

To Kelly, Bauer's answer sounded rehearsed. He'd prepped himself for the criticism.

Now at his desk, Kelly sat down, put his feet up, and rubbed his forehead. *Loose cannon,* he thought, although the sentiment wasn't entirely negative. Four years in military special investigations had taught him that loose cannons sometimes blasted through red tape.

But Bauer's current path seemed to be one of self destruction. Bauer's fall from grace was, in fact, the reason Kelly Sharpton had been transferred to CTU Los Angeles. The transfer hadn't been popular—certainly not with Bauer, nor with his second in command Nina Myers. Jack's star had been on the rise after the recent

"Hell Gate" case, only to fall precipitously in recent months after a botched arrest and interrogation.

"Does Walsh know?" Kelly asked, referring to their direct boss, Richard Walsh, head of operations at CTU Los Angeles. Jack was cut from the same cloth as Walsh, who gave him a little more leeway than most. If Walsh was on his side, then Jack stood a chance of getting through his current insubordination with some of his hide intact.

"Only if you told him," Jack replied.

"Jesus," Kelly groaned. "Chappelle's going to bust you down farther than he did last time." Chappelle was the capo de tutti capo, District Director, which put him even over Walsh's head. "All you needed to do was keep a low profile for a few more months. They'd send me out of here and you'd have your job back. Let everybody forget your screw-up on the Rafizadeh case."

He heard an edge creep into Jack Bauer's voice. "I'm not taking a six-month vacation. You put me on the militias and I look into the militias."

"Yeah, but you weren't supposed to find anything—"

"Well, I did. The Greater Nation militia was planning to drive a truck loaded with a cyanide bomb into Washington D.C. I've got testimony from a militia soldier, I've got the militia leader's orders on the raid to get sodium cyanide. Don't get in my face for doing my job."

Sharpton felt a knot form between his eyes. "I'm doing you a favor, Jack. You got in trouble on your last assignment for coloring outside the lines, and here you are doing it again."

"This is different. Requisitioning local law enforcement without filling out a few forms isn't the same as—as that other thing."

"Did you get him, at least?"

"Oh, I got him," Jack said, a smile in his voice. "We got—hold on." He heard a muffled voice off line. Then Jack's voice came back on, all the smiles gone. "Shit. I've got to go."

The line went dead.

3:45 A.M. PST
Greater Nation Compound

Jack had been talking to Sharpton as he left the main house and strode across the compound to the munitions depot. Around him, his team had quickly taken control of the entire compound. Every light in every building now blazed. A group of bleary-eyed Greater Nation wanna-bes sat on the ground, their legs out in front of them and their hands bound by rip-hobble cords behind their backs. As he passed them, Jack saw in some faces the righteous indignation of true believers. In most, though, all he saw was the frightening realization that playing soldier could actually get you into trouble.

The munitions depot was a single-story ranch house. Jack passed through the broken door—battered down like the main house door—and went inside. This building had been stripped down to beige walls and stained carpet. An SEB agent met him at the entrance. "Merrit, sir. Right this way."

Jack followed Agent Merrit down the main hallway, past several rooms where agents were busy cataloging racks of firearms. "It looks like a National

Guard armory in here," Merrit said. "They've even got a fifty caliber machine gun in the garage."

Another agent stepped out of one of the rooms holding a large metal bracket. "Hey, Merrit," the other man said. "We found boxes full of these. Any idea what they're for?"

"Search me," Merrit said.

"Swivel mounts," Jack said matter-of-factly. "They were made so you could mount an M-4 on top of a Humvee for better aim."

"Jesus," Merrit said. "What were these guys planning to do, invade the country?"

"Yes," Jack said. "What did you want to show me?"

Merrit led him to the end of the hallway, to a room that would have been the master bedroom in a normal house. Here it was a planning room. There were no weapons, but a large card table and several computer terminals. Two investigators sat at the computer terminals, scanning the files. Jack knew they wouldn't find much. Paranoia discouraged the Greater Nation from keeping too much information in digital form. They used the Internet for advertising and recruitment, but the juiciest details would be off the grid.

Sure enough, what Merrit showed him was a box full of three-ring binders, spiral notebooks, and frayed blueprints.

"This looks like it was their next target," Merrit said.

Jack nodded. "I know they were planning on building a cyanide bomb and driving it into Washington—"

"No, sir," Merrit interrupted. "We found that plan all right. It's over there." The agent jabbed a thumb over to another box being tagged by one of the investigators. "This is something else." He held out a notebook, but Jack didn't touch it—he'd taken off his gloves.

"Tell me."

Merrit opened the notebook. "According to this, the militia was tracking some kind of Islamic terrorist cell inside the country."

Jack felt something cold grope the inside of his stomach. "What terrorist cell?"

"I don't know—"

"Where is it located?"

"That's what I wanted you to see," Merrit said. "It's here in Los Angeles. And if these notes are right, these Islamic terrorists are going to make an attack. In the next few hours."

1 2 3 4 5 6 7 8 9
10 11 12 13 14 15 16 17
18 19 20 21 22 23 24

....

THE FOLLOWING TAKES PLACE
BETWEEN THE HOURS OF
4 A.M. AND 5 A.M.
PACIFIC STANDARD TIME

....

4:00 A.M. PST
San Francisco, California

The phone on Senator Debrah Drexler's nightstand
rang with a sense of urgency. Despite the early hour,
the Senator picked it up before it rang a second time.
She was still on East Coast time and she'd been awake
for an hour.

"Drexler." Her voice was like the crack of a whip.
She had spoken in softer tones, once upon a time, but
one abusive marriage and two terms in the United
States Senate had covered her softer side in armor.

"Senator Drexler, thank you for taking my call."
Drexler curled her lip at the mere sound of that

voice. "Not at all, Mr. Attorney General. What can I do for you?"

There was a pause on the line. The faint electric hiss of fiber optics and electricity sounded somehow ominous. Finally, Attorney General James Quincy said, "You and I both know what you can do for me. For the country."

"I work on behalf of my country every day, Mr. Attorney General. And it's early. You'll have to be more specific."

She knew this would irk him. The AG was famous for quick decisions and short conversations. He despised those who wasted time, especially his time. But since he was already quite public about his loathing for the female senator from California, she wasn't worried about losing points with him.

"Give me your vote on the NAP Act," he said with his legendary bluntness. "Then I'll carry Wayans and D'Aquino, and this thing will pass."

"Sir, are you calling on behalf of the President?" she asked.

"I'm calling on behalf of the country."

She almost laughed. "Ah, the cheery sound of jingoism in the morning is so pleasant. You should have "The Battle Hymn of the Republic" on in the background when you talk like that."

Even through the phone line, she could tell that his spine had stiffened at her remarks. "I expect a little more respect than that, Senator. I am the Attorney General of the United States—"

"Then stop acting like a politician," she snapped. She knew he hated to be interrupted. She'd done the same thing during his nomination hearings, and the press had had a field day with his apoplectic reactions. It almost made her happy he'd been approved, just so she could do it again. "Since when does the Attorney General get on the phone and lobby senators to pass a bill? Use the right wing media like all the other fascists."

She smiled, waiting for the volcano to erupt. She wasn't afraid of Quincy's vesuvian temper. She wasn't daunted by angry male voices. Her first husband had beaten those weaker tendencies out of her. He'd nearly lost an eye that last time he'd tried to rough her up, and the combination of a painful divorce court and a scar on his neck made her former husband relent. She got alimony and custody of their baby daughter. With her newfound freedom, she'd moved from New York to San Francisco decades ago. It was hard at the beginning— very hard—but with her newfound strength, she'd gotten on her feet and, after a few years, she'd entered local politics. Now here she was, arm wrestling with one of the most powerful men in the world. She loved it.

But Quincy didn't explode. His voice was, in fact, cold and calculated. "I may just use the media, now that you mention it. But I did want to give you one more chance. The New American Privacy Act gives us the power to root out terrorists no matter how they try to hide. The Justice Department needs to be able to dig into records, set up phone taps immediately when we identify a suspect—"

"The only problem with your theory—no, one of the *many* problems with your theory, Mr. Attorney General, is that the current administration and the FBI both seem to consider anyone who disagrees with them a suspect. If I remember right, last year you investigated people just for going to an anti-Barnes rally."

"The individuals we focused on had ties to—"

"If you want to debate, let's go on Sunday morning television," Drexler said impatiently. "Otherwise, accept the fact that my vote is going to be a no. And I'll tell anyone who listens to me to vote the same."

There was another pause on the line. Somehow, Drexler didn't like it. Quincy wasn't the kind to give up, and he certainly wasn't the type to let someone else get the last word in. His calm demeanor put all her empathic sensors on alert. He wasn't giving up. He was coiling like a cobra.

"Senator, I strongly recommend that you reconsider. Otherwise you may end up regretting your decision."

Drexler snorted. "You're not the first man to say that to me."

4:14 A.M. PST
Greater Nation Compound

As the Senator hung up her phone, five hundred miles to the south, Jack Bauer threw open the door of the black SUV. He grabbed Brett Marks by one handcuffed arm and pulled him out of the car. Marks grunted—he was belted into his seat. Bauer barked as though it was the militia man's fault. He unbuckled Marks, then pulled him, stumbling, out of the car.

"What the hell is this?" Jack said, holding up the notebook from the munitions house.

Marks squinted. There was just enough light from the houses around for him to see the cover of the notebook. He smiled. "Ah, that's Operation Backup."

Bauer tapped the notebook against Marks's head. "That doesn't tell me anything."

Marks looked amused by Jack's loss of composure. "It's not that complicated, Jack. There is a terrorist cell operating around Los Angeles. Since the Federal government wasn't doing anything about them, we decided that we would. After all, that's what the militia is for, if you want to read the Second Amend—"

"No sermons," Jack rumbled. "Tell me about these terrorists."

The Greater Nation leader nodded at the notebook. "It's all in there. We got a tip from some contacts overseas that some terrorists had slipped past the border. We started snooping around a little and we found out how they were connected here. We were going to take them out before they did any harm. See, Jack, it's like I was saying when you were pretending to be part of the cause. We are patriots."

"My hero," Jack mocked. "Wouldn't it have been simpler—and legal—just to inform the authorities?"

Oddly, for the first time in this whole affair, Brett Marks actually looked surprised. "We did. We called Homeland Security. We called the FBI. They wouldn't listen to us."

"Imagine that," Jack snorted. He flipped open his cell phone and speed dialed the office. "Bauer here," he said when the gravediggers answered. "Give me Sharpton."

Kelly was on the line in a moment. "Don't hang up on me again."

"Chew me out later," Jack growled. "I've got something here, maybe. There's some indication here that the Greater Nation was on to an Islamic terrorist cell here."

"The militia guys were working with Islamic terrorists?"

"No, they were targeting them. Marks claims they uncovered a sleeper cell or something in Los Angeles. He says they reported it. The notes say three months ago. It also says here that these terrorists were planning something soon. Can you check the Domestic Security Alerts?"

"On it. Call you back."

4:18 A.M. PST
CTU Headquarters, Los Angeles

In his office, Kelly pressed a button on his phone and Jack's call vanished. He flipped the intercom line and said, "Jessi."

The voice of Jessi Bandison, the most capable of the gravediggers, came on. "Here."

"I need you to scan the tip sheets for me. Check Homeland Security's DSAs for the last six months. Also the FBI logs from local and national."

"Kelly, I'm not cleared for—"

"When you get to the logs, buzz me and I'll code you through. I'm looking for anything about tips on terrorists in Los Angeles."

Jessi buzzed back quickly—she was good at her job—and Kelly half walked, half jumped down the stairs from his loft to the pit where the gravediggers worked. Jessi Bandison—mocha-skinned, curvy, and attractive in all the ways a fashion model was not—watched unblinking as lines of code flashed from bottom to top on her screen. "Nothing in our logs about Islamic terrorists. At least not here in L.A."

"Okay. Link up with Homeland Security and go through their servers and the FBI logs."

She did, and a moment later a password screen came up. Kelly typed in his i.d. and password, and a second later they were through to a new level of security.

"So what is this?" Jessi asked.

"The FBI puts out formal alerts to all departments associated with Homeland Security. But they also keep their own logs for internal use. It's an ongoing intra-net brainstorming session set up after 9/11. Everyone and anyone doing field work or receiving data is supposed to log information of interest here."

Jessi looked pleasantly surprised. "That's impressive."

"It's bullshit," Kelly said. He leaned over Jessi. There was a faint smell of jasmine on her neck. He was careful to stare at the screen. "It's just a CYA gimmick. Everyone's afraid to miss something, so there's so much garbage poured into the log all the time that it's impossible to study it in real time. All it really does is allow you to go back and see if anything was done in the past. That way, if the shit hits the fan, everyone gets sprayed."

"Thanks for that image."

At Kelly's direction, Jessi searched for key words that included *terrorist, Islam, Los Angeles,* and *militia.*

4:25 A.M. PST
Greater Nation Compound

At the Greater Nation compound, SUV engines were revving as the SEB unit prepared to take their prisoners away. Jack nearly missed the phone call.

"Bauer," he said.

"Jack, we've got nada. No reports, no tips, no nothing. If your weekend warriors told anyone, it must have been the post office."

"Thanks." Jack snapped his phone off and glared at Marks. "No tips. Truth is, that's what I expected. You're not the type to rely on the government."

Marks shook his square head. "You don't get us, Jack. I don't know why I didn't see that. We believe that protecting our borders from terrorists is one thing the government should do. Of course I'd tip them if I learned something. But no one did a thing. The only difference between me and you is that you think if you can't stop it, we regular citizens ought to just lie down and take it. Sorry, that's not my style."

"Is that where Newhouse went? You told him to focus on a mission. Was this it?"

Marks said nothing.

"All right. You're such a patriot, then tell me the plan. Tell me where I can find these terrorists."

"Absolutely." The immediacy of his answer surprised Jack. "There's a family in Beverlywood. A father and a daughter. One of the terrorists is linked to them and we're sure they know what he's doing. Our plan was to start with them."

Jack felt the same cold groping in his stomach, like an ice-cold eel swimming through his guts. "A father and daughter. What name?"

"It's all in there," Marks said. "The address and everything. The name is Rafizadeh."

The eel in his gut found its home and settled heavily. "Shit," Bauer said.

* * *

Six months ago. A holding cell inside CTU headquarters, with a bare steel lamp hanging down from the darkness and bright, directed bulb that illuminated an uncomfortable steel table and left the rest of the room in darkness. Jack Bauer stood at the edge of the light, staring down at the man handcuffed to the table. He was an older man, his hands softened by a scholar's life and his belly rounded by many comfortable meals. The handcuffs weren't necessary for security—this old man offered risk of neither fight or flight—but they added to Jack's psychological advantage. The man in the chair was a prisoner. Jack was the jailer.

"Stop protecting them," Jack growled. "We'll find them anyway. Then we won't need you anymore."

The old man blinked at Jack. His glasses had been taken away—another small part of the psychological war—and he could barely see past the bright lights in his eyes. His cheeks above his thin, gray beard were sunken with fatigue, and three days of questions had bent his back and slumped his shoulders. But his voice was still as firm as the day Jack had brought him in.

"I hope you do them find, whoever they are," said the old man with a gentle Farsi lilt in his speech. "In the meantime, I once again ask for my lawyer."

"No."

Jack let the denial hang in the air. He didn't explain that the Patriot Act gave him permission to detain suspected terrorists—even U.S. citizens—indefinitely. The denial held more power without the rationale behind it. Of course, he also didn't explain that even with the broadened powers the Patriot Act gave him, Jack's hold on this old man was tenuous, and based on little more than one email picked up by the FBI's Internet-searching

Jack straddled the chair across from his captive so that their eyes were level. He smiled. "Professor Rafizadeh, you've had a fairly unpleasant time here with us. But this is the honeymoon. I can promise that the marriage will be really ugly."

The old man shrugged his shoulders. "You are threatening me, sir, but with what? Do you think I don't know what is waiting for me out there? My job will be gone. My tenure, it is nothing now. My daughter will suffer from this also. You have already ruined everything I have, just with what you have done. What will you do, send me back to Iran?"

"At a minimum," Jack said. He stared at the scholar. He refused to ask again. Rafizadeh knew what he wanted.

The investigation had been fairly straightforward. A contact in Lebanon had pointed Israeli security to a training camp on the Syrian border. Israeli commandos had raided the camp a month earlier. There wasn't much there, but the commandos came across a few names that hadn't been deleted from computer lists. Some of those names turned up on Homeland Security's watchdog list of possibles who had entered the United States. Inside the country, they'd disappeared. That's where Bauer and CTU had come in. Like bloodhounds sniffing a cold trail, they'd tracked most of the names to dead ends. Only one lead had played out—the name of a suspected terrorist training at the Syrian camp turned out to be the son of Ibrahim Rafizadeh, professor of middle eastern history at the University of Southern California. From the moment he'd met the professor, Jack believed

Rafizadeh was a prime example of a criminal who hid in plain sight. He was an Iranian immigrant, naturalized in 1998, but who kept close ties in Iran. He had been an outspoken advocate for Muslim rights after 9/11 and a harsh critic of United States policies toward Muslims, including detainees held at Guantanamo Bay and other locations. At the same time, however, he published papers and had spoken on news programs lambasting fundamentalist Islamists as backward and dangerous. An Iranian ayatollah had even issued a fatwa against him in 2002 after his book, *The Divided Soul: A Study of the Heart and Mind of Islam* was published in the United States. What better cover, Jack thought, than to be a public figure speaking out for Muslim rights while denouncing terrorist activities.

But a month's worth of wiretaps, tag-team tails, and round-the-clock surveillance hadn't dug up a shred of evidence beyond Rafizadeh's connection to his son, whom he had apparently not seen in several years. It didn't make sense to Jack. He'd been in the Rafizadeh house several times—both with their permission and without—and the pictures on the walls, the scrapbooks, the framed report cards, all told Jack the story of a man who adored his children and would not, *could* not cut ties with them. So he'd brought the professor in under the Patriot Act, hoping to sweat the truth out of him.

The professor shrugged again. "If the fatwa is still in effect, it may be a short visit."

"Where is your son!" Jack yelled, slamming his fist on the table. He was surprised at the level of his anger, but he went with it. A change of rhythm might meet with success.

"I don't kn—"

"Yes, you do! He's here, in the U.S., and he's a threat to innocent lives. You tell me now or I swear I'll bury you so deep they'll—"

The door to the interrogation room had burst open. Ryan Chappelle had entered, flanked by two uniformed security men. Chappelle's face looked more pinched and angry than usual.

"Release this man," Chappelle wheezed. The two uniforms entered and immediately begun unlocking the old man. "See that he's escorted safely home. If he's hungry or thirsty, get him anything he wants. Mr. Rafizadeh—"

"Professor," the old man said, rising to his feet and rubbing his wrists. He looked uncertain, as though he thought this might be one of Bauer's tactics.

"Professor Rafizadeh," Chappelle restarted, "on behalf of this agency I sincerely apologize for any inconvenience we've caused. I hope you'll trust that we try to act in the best interest of the country—"

"Inconvenience!" Rafizadeh said.

"What's going on?" Bauer said, turning on Chappelle. Chappelle glared back, his ears turning slightly red. "He's clear, Bauer. The connection didn't pan out."

"How do you know that?" Jack said, growing upset as his only lead walked out the door. "That's what I'm trying to find out!"

"We found out for you," Chappelle said. He handed Jack a manila folder. "This got missed somewhere along the way. Rafizadeh's son died two years ago."

The fallout had been enormous. The press had a field day with it. "Scholar Learns Of Son's Death During Interrogation" made a great headline. Jack's name was never mentioned, of course, but the media sank their teeth into the story of the federal agent whose tunnel vision not only caused him to falsely imprison a known anti-fundamentalist scholar, but also caused the father to learn of his own son's death under the worst of circumstances. The Secretary of Homeland Security had been furious and had made his displeasure known. Jack had nearly been ejected from CTU, clinging to his job, much to Ryan Chappelle's disappointment, only by the tips of his fingers. As it was, he was taken off any and all high-profile cases and demoted as Special Agent in Charge. Jack's mentor, Richard Walsh, had brought in another agent, Kelly Sharpton, to head up the field teams temporarily. Meanwhile, Jack was assigned to the Domestic Threat Section, which was, considering the current world climate, the fetid backwater of U.S. counterterrorist work.

4:43 A.M. PST
405 Freeway Southbound

Memories of that investigation bounced around in Jack's mind as his SUV hurtled down the 405 Freeway in the predawn hours. It wasn't often that you could travel from Palmdale to Beverlywood in twenty minutes. From 7 a.m. to well after sunset the main artery from the West Los Angeles coast to the inland suburbs was a parking lot. Even at four-thirty in the morning there were cars on the road as suburbanites who had moved away to escape the grind now plunged back into it. In a few hours, Jack's drive would take two hours. But the dearth of cars and a speed of a hundred miles an hour made for good time. Jack reached the top of the Sepulveda Pass and hurtled down into the city, exiting at Pico and turning east, his car flying straight as a black arrow into the Beverly Hills-adjacent neighborhood of Beverlywood.

The Rafizadehs' address had changed in the six months since he'd investigated them. They had lived in staff housing provided by USC where the elder Rafizadeh had been a tenured professor. Now Jack pulled up to Spanish-style duplex on National Avenue that worked hard to keep its appearances up, but failed. Jack's habitual eye for detail absorbed information quickly—rusted rain gutters, badly painted eaves, dying grass. The Rafizadehs had moved down in the world.

They lived in the upper apartment. Jack took the stairs three at a time. He rang the bell and knocked on the door firmly. He waited a few seconds, knowing the first knock would only wake them into confusion, then he knocked again. He heard footsteps on the other side of the door. A light turned on inside, and then a muffled female voice demanded, "Who is it?"

Jack winced. "It's Bauer."

There was a long pause while Jack stared at the wood grains in the door. The female voice finally said, "Are you joking?"

"No," Jack said, trying to soften the habitual growl in his voice. "It's Jack Bauer. I need to talk to you and your father."

A bolt slid back and the door opened to the length of the security chain. A young woman looked furtively out from the space between the jamb and the door. Her dark, beautiful face was a mixture of sleep and anger. Her thick black hair was pulled away from her face by a terry cloth headband.

"Get the hell out of here," she said and slammed the door shut.

He pounded on the door again. "Nazila! I'm here to help you!"

"We've had about all the help we can take, thanks," the woman said from the other side of the door.

"Open the door, Nazila," Jack said, releasing the growl from his throat. "I'm not here to arrest you. I'm here to protect you."

The door opened again. The chain was still attached. Nazila's dark eyes studied him in the porch light. "From what?"

"Let me in, and I'll explain. I promise, I'm not here to arrest anyone."

"Do you know what you did to us?" she asked.

"Yes. And I think someone else is making the same mistake. I want to protect you. Open the door."

Jack wanted to believe it was his sincerity that made her open the door. More likely, it was her resignation. Months ago he had cajoled his way into their lives. He had first posed as a graduate student interested in learning more about the Middle East—one of the contrarians who sought to understand 9/11 by looking in the mirror. He had been charming and disarming, not only convincing Professor Rafizadeh of his desire to become a scholar of Islamic history, but also casting a spell over Nazila. She was a grad student at Cal Poly, working on her Ph.D. in applied mathematics. Like her father, she was brilliant, but unlike him, she'd allowed herself to become a little more westernized. They had shared dinners together, visited museums and concerts, and seen movies. Nazila Rafizadeh had just begun to wonder if she could fall in love with a non-Muslim when he appeared on their doorstep one day with a search warrant and a gang of federal agents.

Now Nazila unchained the door and stepped back, allowing Jack to slip inside. He recognized furniture he had seen in their previous house—there was a chocolate velvet sofa and chaise, a leather ottoman that doubled as a coffee table, a beautifully framed replica of a 15th-century map of the Persian Gulf and Indian subcontinent. All these items had been crammed into the tiny duplex. The boundaries of their lives had shrunk, but all the baggage remained.

Nazila stood in the middle of the cramped living room and smoothed the folds of her terry-cloth robe. She neither sat down nor offered him a seat, and she certainly would not offer him tea. She was short, but in that small room she seemed to gather size like a bird puffing up its feathers.

"After the problems with your case I was demoted to another unit—" Jack began.

"Good."

"I was investigating a militia group. They're nuts, but they're well-funded and active. They got hold of information similar to the intelligence that steered me toward you and your father. I believe they're going to act on it."

Jack delivered his information in the short bytes he would have used for another professional. Nazila was quick and, as he knew well, very strong. She absorbed the facts as fast as he could say them. "So you'll stop them," she said.

"We did stop them. We arrested their leader to-night. That's how we found out they had targeted you. But a few of them got away, and if I know these guys, they'll still try to finish their mission. I came here to warn you."

Now Nazila sat down, hugging her stomach and folding over like a flower closing up. "I feel sick. Why does this keep happening to us?"

"Bad luck," Bauer said. "Bad people."

He meant the Greater Nation, but her eyes bored into him. "Yes, bad people."

"Wake your father up. I want to tell him what's going on. I think we should move you to a safer location until we can find these guys."

Nazila Rafizadeh felt the tiny apartment grow even smaller. She stared at Jack Bauer, whom she hated more than a human being ought to hate someone. He had toyed with her feelings and terrorized her father. He could not have done more to ruin their lives if he had tried. She had no reason to trust him. But, then, he had no reason to be here. He had already taken everything from them, and as cruel as she believed him to be, she also knew that he did not waste his own time.

She unfolded slowly from the couch and stood up. She went into the cramped hallway and passed the single bathroom, toward two bedrooms. She felt Bauer's presence behind her. He moved very quietly, but she knew he was there. Her own bedroom door was thrown open. Her father's was closed. He was a heavy sleeper, especially these days. He did not sleep long, but when exhaustion overtook him, he slept the sleep of the dead. She knocked loudly. *"Pedar?"*

She opened the door into the darkened room. Jack leaned in over her shoulder. Even in the darkness he could see that the bed was empty and undisturbed. Professor Rafizadeh was not there.

"Where?" he asked.

"I . . . I don't know. He had plans this evening. He teaches English as a second language at the mosque since he lost his job. I'm always asleep before he gets home on Tuesday nights . . ."

Before Nazila had finished her sentence Jack was on his cell phone to CTU, and by the time her surprise had turned to fear, he knew two things: Professor Rafizadeh had left the Culver City Mosque just after two o'clock in the morning, and his car was last seen at the corner of Centinella and Pico.

He repeated the information to Nazila as it was relayed to him by Jessi Bandison.

"How do you know these things so fast?" she asked.

"Traffic cameras, security feeds, cell phone records . . ."

She shook her head. "The power you have is terrifying."

"You won't think so if it helps find your father. His cell phone placed a call here. Check your message machine."

Nazila went back to the living room. A silver cordless telephone stood upright on a stand that also contained the message system. She pressed play, the machine beeped at her, and her father's voice chimed in. "Nazi, I will be home a little late. Someone wants to see me about a research project for a movie. It's late for an old man, but if it is something, we could use the money. The name of the company is on a card on my nightstand. That's where I'll be if you worry."

"Movies?" Jack asked.

"He consulted on a movie once before, when they

needed an expert on Islam in the Middle Ages. A movie about the Crusades."

He followed her back to her father's room and scanned the room as soon as she turned on the lights. This was the room of a scholar—every flat surface piled high with books, magazines, and pages of notes. The nightstand was no different—Jack counted a stack of five books by the bed, plus two more that lay facedown and open, as though Rafizadeh had been reading both at the same time. On top of the stack was a precariously balanced pile of papers— brochures, business cards, junk mail, and letters. Nazila lifted a business card off the top, and the rest of the pile fell to the floor. She handed it to Jack, then hurriedly gathered up the papers that had fallen. He dialed CTU again, but his eyes were on her furtive movements.

"Bandison, Bauer again. Run a check on this company—" he glanced at the business card—"Minute Man Films. Based here in Los Angeles. I'm guessing it doesn't exist."

"Right back," Jessi Bandison said in shorthand, and put Jack on hold.

Nazila stacked the papers neatly and quickly—so quickly, in fact, that Jack almost missed her sleight-of-hand as she slipped one piece of paper into the pocket of her robe.

When Jack was taken off hold, Jessi Bandison was on the line. "Jack, there's no Minute Man Films."

"I figured. Thanks."

He snapped his phone shut. "Nazila, I'm sorry. I think your father's been taken by the Greater Nation. This company he was meeting doesn't exist."

Her faced paled. "Can you help him?"

"I'll do my best. I owe it to you," he said. "But first show me what you just slipped into your pocket."

Her hand covered her robes. "Nothing. It's personal."

"Show me anyway."

Reluctantly, defeated, she pulled the slip of paper from her pocket. It was a four-by-six generic greeting card with pictures of a watercolor of flowers on the front. Inside, spidery handwriting crawled from side to side. Jack didn't read what it said, because his eyes were drawn to two facts immediately.

First, the card was dated two months ago.

Second, it was signed by Nazila's dead brother.

1 2 **3** 4 5 6 7 8 9
10 11 12 13 14 15 16 17
18 19 20 21 22 23 24

•••

THE FOLLOWING TAKES PLACE
BETWEEN THE HOURS OF
5 A.M. AND 6 A.M.
PACIFIC STANDARD TIME

•••

5:00 A.M. PST

At five in the morning, the streets of San Francisco
lost all their romance. In another hour or two, the sun
would rise across the bay, and anyone with a good
view and a penchant for rising early could sit with a
cup of Peet's Coffee and watch the fog roll back out
the Golden Gate like a retreating army. But at this
hour, San Francisco was simply another dark and
quiet city, except with very steep hills.

The hour was, however, a convenient running time
for a U.S. senator whose circadian rhythms were still
set to East Coast Time and whose biological clock
kept sending all her weight into her hips. Debrah
Drexler, consummate feminist and liberal though she

was, was not above a little vanity. Her one self-indulgence in a hectic schedule was her three-mile jog every morning. She had been what was called a looker in her day, and while in her head she knew that the days had passed when she'd turn a man's head, in her heart she felt that one ought to at least make an effort.

She slipped out of her apartment in those first minutes after five onto the dark street spotted with street lamps. She started up the road at a slow pace, and a young man in an Adidas track suit fell in beside her.

"Bobby," she greeted.

"Senator," the young man said. She never said the word *bodyguard* out loud, but he wasn't a regular part of her staff—at least, he did none of the analysis or fund-raising work—but when she'd started her predawn runs a month ago, her staffers had gotten him from somewhere to make sure that she always returned home. He ran, and they talked sometimes, but more often she was involved in her own thoughts, and he just kept pace with her.

She kept silent for the first mile, running the streets that led to Golden Gate Park, trying to wrap her mind around Quincy's phone call. What had been the point of it? He knew which way she was going to vote, and it wasn't like the AG was going to twist her arm. Barnes might try—she could at least imagine him getting on the phone and using his President voice to intimidate her. That would have failed, too, of course. Barnes' party might have succeeded in cowing a lot of other members of her party, but not her. So if the President himself would have failed, why had the AG even bothered?

It had all started with the Patriot Act. Drexler had voted for it, too. Like everyone else, she'd been caught up in the emotions of 9/11 and her judgment had been clouded by the smoke of the burning towers. But Congress had possessed the sense, at least, to make the act temporary. She'd been appalled when the government had expanded it, and now she was furious that the Administration was attempting to replace it with an even more intrusive bill. The New American Privacy Act—the name itself was so Orwellian it sent shivers down her spine—granted the FBI and other investigative bodies powers that were tantamount to dropping the Bill of Rights into a paper shredder. Every time the politicians on her side of the aisle tried to sound the alarm, Quincy and the administration simply wrapped themselves in the flag and talked about the hordes of terrorists lurking in the shadows.

Of course, it didn't help that there actually were terrorists out there.

They reached Golden Gate Park, which wasn't nearly as big as Central Park in New York but had a beauty all its own, and started down the jogging path.

"Bobby, do you follow politics?"

The young man said, "I follow you, Senator."

She laughed. He was quick. "Seriously, I talk with the rest of my staff, I ask their opinions, I'm interested in their views." She was beginning her second mile. Her breath and her sentences were getting shorter. "I want yours."

"I'm not much on having opinions on the job, Senator."

"You'd make a good politician, then."

"There's no need to get nasty, Senator."

She laughed again. "So you're in security, or law enforcement, or something like that. I want to know what you think of the NAP Act."

He paused. She could tell he didn't want to talk about it. "I'm not really an investigator, ma'am. I mean, I only had a little training in investigation at FLETC."

She repeated it the way he pronounced it. "Fletsee?"

"Federal Law Enforcement Training Center. You get a little of everything there, but I focused mostly on the protective services area. I'm not really qualified to know what investigators need. This NAP Act stuff is over my head."

"No, it's not," she argued. "It's not over anyone's head. The bottom line is, do you want the government to be able to ignore all your rights if they think you're a terrorist?"

He considered. "I don't mind them ignoring the terrorists' rights when they catch them."

"But what if they catch the wrong people? What if they step on the rights of a hundred people to find one terrorist?"

"I'd say it's worth it."

"What if they step on the rights of a hundred people and don't find any terrorists."

"I see your point, ma'am."

She wasn't sure he did, but he was polite. Their jogging path joined another, and another jogger fell in beside them.

"Hey," the newcomer gasped. "Hope . . . you . . . don't mind some company . . . for a mile." He looked like a mile would kill him.

Drexler smiled. She'd been there a month ago, when she'd first started running again. "No problem. We're turning around in a minute anyway."

The man nodded and glanced ahead. She could see his face intermittently, illuminated and then lost as they passed under lamps on the park's jogging path.

He was on the far side of middle-aged (her age, she thought regretfully), with a bit of a paunch and thinning hair. He glanced at her once or twice, too, as though he was trying to place her. She got that a lot. Most of the electorate was, unfortunately, ignorant as to who their elected representatives were. Every once in a while she came across someone who'd seen her on CNN or the Sunday news programs. It always took them a minute to place her face.

"Don't I know you?" he said at last. "I've seen you somewhere before."

I'm your public servant," she said with a chuckle. "I'm Senator Debrah Drexler."

"No kidding?" the man said. He was still panting, but his voice had become more firm. "That's not what I was thinking. I was thinking I knew you from a long time ago. Maybe twenty years. I thought maybe I was a customer of yours back in the seventies."

Debrah Drexler stopped running. So did the other man, and so did Bobby. All three stood there panting for a moment—the Senator turning pale, the bodyguard trying to assess the threat, and the stranger smiling blissfully.

"What did you say?" Drexler asked. She ignored the sweat running into her eyes.

"I thought maybe you and I did some business way back when."

"Not unless you were selling shoes, my friend," she said coldly.

His smile widened into a leer. "There were lots of names for it back then, but I don't think we ever called it shoes."

"Bobby," Drexler said, "I don't think I like this man."

She was grateful when he stepped immediately between them. "You'll be going now," he said.

The man nodded. "Yes, I will. Just keep that in mind, Senator. I'm sure if I keep thinking about it, I'll remember exactly what kind of business we did together. See you later!"

And then he was off into the Park.

5:23 A.M. PST
West Los Angeles

As Debrah Drexler was slipping on her running shoes, Jack Bauer had stood in the Rafizadeh apartment. For one of the few moments in his life he was paralyzed by mixed emotions—anger, confusion, fear.

"Ramin Rafizadeh is alive," he growled. "Ramin Rafizadeh is alive."

Nazila stood before him, her back straight, her feet set slightly apart. The only sign of her nervousness was the quiver in her hands hanging at her sides. She was an island bracing for a storm. Jack felt that storm brewing inside him, the pent-up fury of six months banished to the backwaters of counterterrorism, listening to rednecks spew brainless bigoted curses at blacks and Jews when he should have been chasing down madmen who dreamed of killing thousands. Six months infiltrating a penny-ante gang of thugs led by a wannabe guru who'd read the Constitution backwards and wanted to relive his glory days as a soldier by starting a war on United States soil. Six months in exile . . . for the wrong reasons. He'd been right. Ramin Rafizadeh had been connected to a terrorist group in Lebanon and Ramin Rafizadeh was alive.

Ibrahim Rafizadeh was in contact with him. Jack had connected the dots. He'd done his job, and somehow the mission got screwed anyway. His sense of injustice at his exile was followed by the stinging irony that the weekend warriors and political radicals he'd been investigating for six months had been on the right track when his own people had gone astray. The Greater Nation, of all people, was still on the case while CTU was sitting on its ass.

He didn't say anything, but his face hardened into stone as he replayed these thoughts over and over in his head. Finally Nazila could not stand it anymore and said quietly, "He is innocent."

"Don't," he snarled, physically resisting the urge to strike her. "Sit." He pushed her so that she fell back onto the bed.

He took out his cell phone and dialed CTU. A second later he was connected to Kelly Sharpton. "I need a rundown on Ramin Rafizadeh. Everything we've collected."

He could hear Kelly's confusion. "Ramin? You mean the son? That's a dead file, isn't it?"

"Everything," Jack repeated.

"Hold on."

Jack waited for two minutes while Kelly called up the file and scanned it. He gave Jack a summary over the phone. Most of it was exactly as Jack had remembered it from six months ago.

Ibrahim Rafizadeh had spent years as a voice of moderation in Iran. He had cheered the downfall of the Shah—though he was a bit older than the students who helped overthrow the tyrant, he had applauded their passion. But he was dismayed a short time later when the Shah's corruption was replaced by a fundamentalist theocracy. Ibrahim himself had dreamed of a free Islamic state, guided by Sharia but not dominated by it. That dream had been naïve. Still, he remained in Iran, believing that as time passed and more moderate voices were heard, the government would relax. He raised his son and his daughter there, trying to strike the right note between a pure love of Islam as he saw it and obedience to the laws of the state. This was no easy task, and Ibrahim Rafizadeh would be the first to say he had gotten it only half right. His daughter had proved an apt disciple. His son, too, was a disciple—but one who'd turned toward a more absolute life than Ibrahim lived.

By the end of the 1980s, Ibrahim believed his patience had paid off. Rafsanjani was elected President, and although he was still conservative, he was a pragmatist who sought to improve Iran's reputation in the world at large. Reform, it seemed, could not be far behind. But by the middle of the 1990s, Ibrahim had grown cynical, and even with the rise in power of Mohammed Khatami, a true reformer, he believed little would change. By the time Khatami came to power in 1997, Ibrahim had already left Iran.

But Ramin refused to go. In 1997 he was eighteen years old, fiery, and passionate, with nowhere to sow his wilds oats. Finding no other outlet for his energy, Ramin had plunged into politics. He swirled like a leaf in the conflicting winds of reform and dogma, believing that Iran could and would become the ideal Muslim state for which everyone yearned. He refused to follow his father to America. From that moment on, Ramin Rafizadeh's life became a list of dates, places, and vague associations. He lived in his father's home near Tehran for another year, becoming active in Khatami's reform movement, then somehow leaving it in 1999 to work with more conservative voices attached to the Guardians Council. He popped up again in 2000 in Lebanon. This fact by itself immediately put him on American watch lists, since a young man's general route from Iran to Lebanon was through the terrorist group Hezbollah. But very little information came out of Lebanon about him, which meant he was either well-hidden, or not active. He all but vanished for two years, until, of course, the commandos had seen his name on a list in the remains of a terrorist camp near the Syrian border. That had been Jack's line of investigation, until it was cut short by the discovery that Rafizadeh had been killed in Lebanon, and Jack was accused of violating Ibrahim Rafizadeh's civil rights.

"There's got to be something more in there," Jack said when Sharpton finished his summary. "I've just found something that says Ramin Rafizadeh is alive."

"Jack . . ." The skepticism in Sharpton's voice was thick.

"I'm not obsessed with this," Bauer said. "I'm looking at a note written by Ramin to his father. It's dated two months ago."

That news hit Sharpton as hard as it had hit Jack. "Holy shit."

"Right. Keep digging, will you?"

"I'll see what we missed. Out."

Jack closed his phone and turned all the energy he'd been gathering for the last few minutes on Nazila Rafizadeh. He didn't have time for metaphysical mumbo-jumbo or New Age philosophy, but he knew that if you focused your whole self on another person, he felt it like a bullet come out of a gun. He focused on her now. He wanted to shout. He wanted to wring her neck for putting lives at risk by withholding information. He wanted to make her pay for the demotion he had suffered. But he didn't. He stuck to the most important question.

"Where is he?"

"He never had anything to do with those people—"

"Life in prison. Guantanamo Bay, or somewhere even less enjoyable. You'll be branded as terrorists yourselves."

Nazila shook her head, her eyes pooling. "You tried all those threats before, Jack. If I thought my brother was actually a terrorist, I would—"

"You would be the first person to hand him over," Jack terminated her sentence. "Bullshit."

There were tears forming in her eyes now. "You know why I won't tell you. All the reasons you just named. My brother has done nothing! But he's on someone else's list, so if you take him, he will end up one of those places you just talked about, and no one will see him again!"

"If he's innocent, he'll—"

"He'll what? Only stay in a prison for two or three years as an 'enemy combatant'?"

"Of course not," Jack said, although he knew he was lying. It happened. It was the price you paid sometimes to keep people alive. "But everything we know so far points to the fact that there are terrorists in this country, probably somewhere in Southern California. I thought so six months ago, and now I'm getting more proof. We may have gotten lucky that they haven't killed anyone yet. I need to find them, or people will die. And right now my only leads are your brother and those idiots in the militia. Tell me where he is."

She hesitated. Her lips parted, but no words came out. She nearly buckled under the pressure he exerted on her, but at the last minute, she shifted her feet, as though preparing for a fight, and said, "I'll tell you after you save my father."

5:31 A.M. PST
San Francisco

Debrah Drexler's hands were still shaking as she closed her apartment door behind her and slumped down in the wide leather chair in her living room. She remembered the first time her ex-husband had slapped her, all those years ago. There was pain, but mostly there was shock that such a thing could happen at all. That's how she felt now.

Who was that man? How could he know?

The first two years after her divorce had been a nightmare only slightly less horrible than her marriage. The friendships and the promises that awaited her in San Francisco were all broken. It was 1979, Carter was president, and Debrah had her own personal misery index: a little girl to feed, no job, and no money. What she did have was a body that had survived childbirth intact. And even in the depression of 1980, there were men with enough money and lust to allow her to pay the rent.

She'd never worried about her secret getting out. She was in and out of that business in less than two years, and she'd been nothing special. A middle-rate call girl using a fake name. No one paid much attention to her. If anything, the men wanted it kept secret more than she did. She was never arrested, never photographed. Since then, she'd been through five elections, and that period of her life had never even been a blip on her political radar.

The phone rang. Debrah took a deep breath to settle her voice and her hands. She picked up the receiver. "Drexler."

"Senator." Quincy's voice slid along the phone line like so much oil. "I hope you don't mind a second phone call in one morning."

"Why not," she said, switching on her business voice, "since our first one was so pleasant."

"I just wanted you to know that I am seriously considering your suggestion to use the media."

"Wonderful. You look very handsome on television."

"Oh, it won't be me. It couldn't be me. I'm not the one with the information."

She felt ice form in her stomach. "I don't understand."

James Quincy chuckled on his end of the phone. "Senator, I'm sure you've heard that politics makes strange bedfellows. But didn't they tell you you're supposed to get those partners *after* you enter politics?"

He knew. Of course he knew. He'd found out, somehow. The jogger was on his payroll.

"I take it from your silence you understand me. Now, let me tell you, Senator, that time is of the essence. The vote is not far off. Barely enough time for you to influence Wayans and D'Aquino. So I suggest something direct. A press conference. An early morning press conference, so that it hits the East Coast news cycle."

"I couldn't—"

"Yes, you can. You can say that you and I have had several phone conversations. These are logged, of course, so people will know we've spoken anyway. You can say that you're convinced the NAP Act is in the best interest of the country, which is true."

"No."

He laughed again. "I won't take that as your final answer. You have"—he paused—"a little over an hour until the 7 a.m. news cycle, which would hit the East Coast before lunch, which is perfect. If I hear that you've made your announcement, I'll know we have a deal. If I don't hear anything, then the next news I hear after that will be all about you."

The line went dead.

5:39 A.M. PST
West Los Angeles

"I don't know where your father is," Jack protested.

Nazila pointed at the phone in his hand. "Traffic cameras. Security tapes. Satellites."

"It doesn't always work like that. With a time and a place, we can scan particular cameras and routes. But just to look around randomly takes days and weeks, using everyone we've got. Just tell me where your brother is."

She hesitated, but this time it was not from doubt. She was shopping for a bargain. "We can make a deal," she said. "I will take you to him if you do two things for me."

"Only two?" he said.

"First, you have to promise that you will listen to his case. He is not a terrorist. And second, you have to promise that as soon as you find him, you will save my father before anything else."

Now it was Jack's turn to hesitate. He'd lied before in his job—in fact, it was often his job to lie—but something about Nazila gave him pause. He didn't want to lie to her, even though she'd lied to him. In the military and at CTU he'd dealt with all levels of evil—from petty criminals driven by greed to psychopaths driven to fill some dark hole in their souls. He knew that the devil had power to assume a pleasing shape. But when she said her brother was not a terrorist, she spoke simply and with conviction. Whatever might lurk in her brother's heart, hers was pure.

"I promise, I'll save your father," he said.

5:44 A.M. PST
CTU Headquarters, Los Angeles

Kelly Sharpton put his feet up on his desk and rubbed his eyes. It had been one of those mornings. His original daily sheet hadn't had much more than update meetings with three of his top field people, a video link with Homeland Security where all he had to do was listen, and a report on updating satellite link software that was supposed to improve their database searches by 5%. Instead, one of his field agents had raided a militia compound without permission and arrested a media-savvy, ex-military political radical, a terrorist investigation that had been closed six months ago was suddenly reopened, and a dead Iranian man had returned to the land of the living.

In this state of mind, he wasn't exactly surprised when the operator buzzed him. "Kelly, you have a Debrah Dee on the phone. She says it's important."

"Debrah Dee . . . I don't know the name. Will you send the call over to—"

"She says you'll know her from the Bay Area, but that she's moved to Washington D.C. since then."

"Washington—Dee?—oh, shit, put it through." In the seconds between the operator's click-off and the connection, he put it all together, and when the phone clicked in, he said, "There's a reason to be discreet, I'm guessing."

"Yes," said the caller. Her voice was measured—and not with the usual toughness of a female politician practicing her craft. Something was scaring her and she was trying to control it. Kelly knew firsthand that very few things scared Debrah Drexler. "I've got a problem."

"We should start a club," Kelly said. He had leaned forward in his seat, but now that he knew it was Debbie, he eased back again and put his feet up.

"I tried calling your cell phone, but I couldn't get through."

"It's off. New protocol they're trying out. No cell use permitted inside CTU. You know this call will be logged, too?"

"That's not a problem from this number. But I didn't want your secretary hearing the name. I need help. Real help, and you're the only person I could think of."

Kelly felt his face flush like a schoolboy. All he could think was *pathetic*. Twelve years later, and still the thought of being her knight in shining armor set his heart to beating. *For a guy who's supposed to be some top-notch field operative, you don't learn much from the facts, Sharpton.*

"Tell me what's going on."

She told him. When she reported her conversations with the Attorney General, and her encounter with the mystery man, her voice reacquired the crisp, direct tones of the Senator everyone knew from television. But as she concluded, the quaver returned. "I . . . I don't know how anyone could have known that, Kel. It was so long ago. No one knew me back then. You were . . . you were the only one I ever told."

Her words were part plea, part accusation. He could tell she couldn't—or wouldn't—believe he had betrayed her, but she was bewildered and desperate. She had to know, but couldn't bring herself to ask. He would have done the same thing in her place.

"It wasn't me, Deb. You know that. Besides, why would I tell the AG? You know how I feel about the NAP Act."

She stifled a sob. "Yes, I know."

Politics was all they could ever talk about anymore. This was ironic, of course, because it was politics that had driven a wedge between them a dozen years ago. She'd been the Mayor of San Francisco and he'd been head of the special response unit there. That made him the head of security and, ostensibly, her chief bodyguard. They'd danced around each other for several months. There was reason to hesitate—she was several years older than he was, for one thing; for another, a relationship, while technically permissible, was wonderful grist for the rumor mill. They'd finally taken the leap after a security briefing for a visit by the president-elect. She'd insisted on sitting in—even though the mayor had very little to say, and less to do, about the visits by the Federal government—and he'd enjoyed her biting style of questioning. In the general hubbub that inevitably follows one of those briefings, he'd managed to slide her a quick invitation to dinner. They'd each expected to be disappointed. How interesting could a law enforcement man be? How pleasant could a feminist politician be? And yet they'd each found a diamond in the rough and become fascinated. He had done undergraduate work at UC Berkeley, just across the bay, before chucking it all for a military career "just to see if he could hack it." She wasn't so much a feminist as an individualist, whose hackles rose whenever she perceived a person—any person—squashed by the system. The two years they spent together in the city by the bay were good years for both of them.

Good things end, though. No moss gathered on Debrah Drexler's career, and she used her Bay Area popularity to jump into the national game, winning a seat in the Senate on her first try. That had been the end. If a local mayor was allergic to gossip, for a U.S. senator it was deadly poison. Though Kelly grasped her reasons in an intellectual exercise, his heart remained baffled, and confusion led inevitably to pain. She threw sporadic communications his way, trying to maintain contact, but it was too hard, especially when the conversations turned to personal matters. So when they did speak, which was not often, it was only about politics.

That was how she knew that Kelly Sharpton opposed the NAP Act. He was one of the few in his agency who did—most agents in CTU, and most officers in other intelligence units, were grateful for every tool that helped them do their job. But the aggressiveness of this "New American Privacy" awakened in Kelly some of his old Berkeley sensibilities. He wasn't sure he wanted to live in a country so willing to sacrifice what it loved to save itself. It was his job to invade people's privacy, disrupt their lives, sift through their secrets, because sometimes those people were evil. But he had always appreciated the watchmen who watched him. But now the watchers had joined the party themselves praising and encouraging the very government operations that the Founding Fathers had sought to check.

"I don't really know the Attorney General," Kelly said. "Would he go through with it?"

Deb half-laughed, half-sobbed. "Oh, he'd do it just to hurt me. We aren't the best of friends."

"The confirmation hearings. I remember."

"This is just icing. It would ruin me. 'Champion of Women's Rights A Former Prostitute,'" she read the imaginary headline. "That's going to be fun."

"What do you need from me?" Kelly asked.

"He's got something, Kel. Some kind of proof, or he wouldn't talk about making it public. Twenty year old rumors would be useless. He's got something. I need you to find out what he's got and destroy it."

Kelly felt his chest tighten. A fist clutched his heart. "That's . . . you say it pretty easy. Do you have any idea what that means?"

"I'm desperate," she said.

Words like *felony, destruction of evidence,* and *breaking and entering* floated through Kelly's mind. "We're talking about the Attorney General here. And it's the digital age. And he's friggin' three thousand miles away from me. I can't just toss his apartment and look for the negatives."

"There's got to be something. I don't know anyone else—"

"You're on the Senate Intelligence Committee!" Kelly shot back. "You know everyone! You know the bosses of my bosses' bosses!"

"But I can't trust anyone. Not anyone in Washington. Trust me, anyone I ask will either expose me right away or they'll use the information themselves and I'll do this all over again in a year or two. No one there is stupid enough to—"

"But I am . . ."

"You're brave enough," she said. She paused, as though the enormity of her request was finally dawning on her. "Kelly, I barely know what I'm asking. I don't even know what you can do. I don't even know what he has, exactly. All I do know is that I've got an hour to make a decision. And I can't let that get out."

He sat up, almost getting to his feet. "You don't mean you'd change your . . ." he trailed off, not able to finish the sentence. "That's not you. You don't buckle under."

He could feel her stress through the telephone line. This was killing her, to have someone force her hand. Every politician makes compromises, of course, but Debrah Drexler had slogged through twenty years of politics without sacrificing her principles. He'd known her for years, and even when they weren't talking, he'd watch her career and the way she voted. She was Liberal with a capital L, an ACLU supporter, and an outspoken civil rights champion. She bucked trends in either direction when her bullshit meter sounded. Despite her liberal tendencies, she had championed welfare reform for years . . . only to vote against the bill at the last minute because it did not provide adequate child care provisions for mothers who found jobs. That had nearly destroyed her reputation among the moderates who chose her over the conservative alternatives. By the same token, she had nearly destroyed her image on the far left by voting to revise affirmative action because she believed it had become a quota system that looked at color alone, without considering economic status. She weathered every storm by declaring her intention to vote for what she felt was right, even if it meant losing her job.

"There's a lot of work to be done in the Senate," she replied. "I don't know who would speak up for women. The abortion debate is still going on—"

"You can't vote for that bill," he stated firmly.

"Then help me destroy his evidence. I need you to do it." She checked her watch. "And I need you to do it in less than an hour."

1 2 3 **4** 5 6 7 8 9
10 11 12 13 14 15 16 17
18 19 20 21 22 23 24

....

THE FOLLOWING TAKES PLACE
BETWEEN THE HOURS OF
6 A.M. AND 7 A.M.
PACIFIC STANDARD TIME

....

6:00 A.M. PST
CTU Headquarters, Los Angeles

The phone clicked off and Kelly wished nostalgically for the moment when his biggest problem was Jack Bauer. She would do it. He found it hard to believe, but he had heard the fear in her voice. She would sacrifice her vote for the sake of her career, and although Kelly was not privy to politics inside the Beltway, he guessed that her vote would influence others.

Blackmail. God, he hated politicians. He settled into his chair, wondering what the hell he could do about it.

"I hope you don't mind meeting early, but otherwise the day's full," Mitch Rasher said as he stepped out of the way and let the Attorney General into his hotel suite.

Quincy was wearing a two-piece suit and tie to Rasher's wrinkled polo shirt and jeans. "No problem," he said crisply, "I was up anyway. No thanks," he added as Rasher motioned to the pot of fresh coffee on the table.

The suite was big, but not opulent. Rasher habitually rejected any show of status. The man who had been called "Barnes's brain" lived like he had no body. Staffers in the West Wing called him "the Hermit" because he sometimes spent days closed up in his office, working on arcane political strategy, sacrificing sleep (which everyone admired) and personal hygiene (which everyone regretted). He would show up to strategy sessions with his shirttails half-tucked and his tie askew, three days' worth of beard shading his face. He cleaned up for the cameras when he had to, but he preferred to avoid the limelight altogether. Rasher derived some perverse personal joy from being the man behind the curtain, and wanted no media dogs exposing him as he tugged at the strings of power.

Rasher bit off a chunk of bagel and flopped down on the couch.

"Two days, Mitch," Quincy said, settling himself easily into a chair opposite. "That's not much time, even for you guys."

"It could be two hours," Rasher replied through a

mouthful of bagel. "We've done all the arm twisting we're going to do, Jim. I told you that before Frisco. No more going out on a limb for this one. We've already taken too much heat on military spending and the tax thing."

Quincy tugged at his shirt cuffs, fingering his cufflinks. "It doesn't make sense, you know. You've made this Administration all about homeland security. You told me to go after this bill. Now you guys are benching yourselves in the fourth quarter when you should want to win the game more than anyone."

Rasher liked sports metaphors as much as the next guy. "Yeah, but sometimes when the game is lost, you sit your starters down so they don't get hurt."

The Attorney General stared at Rasher, who just chomped his bagel and smiled back. Rasher's balding head gleamed in the light of the corner lamp, giving him an angelic aura. But the grin beneath it was from another place. It was the juxtaposition of the halo and the leer that bent Quincy's thoughts at just the right angle. "Oh shit," he said.

Rasher's grin widened. Quincy knew him for what he was, of course. He was Mephistopheles. He was Iago. He was Machiavelli. He was the engineer within the White House fortress who kept the hapless other side constantly in disarray. But Quincy hadn't considered, until that moment, that Rasher's formidable powers could be directed inward as well.

"You want the bill to get killed," he said.

"Come on, Jim, I never said that."

"No, you wouldn't say it. But it's true. You want it killed. But what if something actually happens? What if there is a terrorist attack and it turns out we could have prevented it with more powers of investigation. What then?"

Rasher examined his bagel and flicked away a sesame seed. "That's the good part. We just blame the other side for denying us the powers we clearly needed."

"But if it goes down right now, you'll look like—" He was going to say, *look like losers*. But of course, they wouldn't look like losers. *He* would look like a loser. He was the poster child for the NAP Act. He was its architect. Quincy shook his head. Like all good plans, it was too simple to be seen, and he'd fallen for it like a hayseed in a poker game.

Lucky for him, he had a few aces up his sleeve. He recovered himself. "It may not work out how you think. I think I'm going to get the bill passed." He checked his watch. Almost twenty after. "In fact, I can almost guarantee it."

Rasher shrugged. "Okay. Then when it passes we just take the country's temperature. If they're still against it, we veto it and look good. If they're for it, then we sign it and look good."

Quincy said, "Then you'll look like tag-alongs. My suggestion would be to let the President get out ahead of the issue. He needs to see which way the parade is headed so that he can get in front and lead it."

Rasher lost interest in his bagel. "Thanks for the political advice, but you can't guarantee squat. You're down fifty-two to forty-eight and that's *if* Robinson and McPherson don't break ranks and go to the other side. All our guys tell us that there aren't any votes to turn around."

"Your guys have been wrong before," Quincy said.

"No," Rasher replied coldly, "they haven't."

"Well, they are this time. I'm predicting a flood of last-minute switches. I think it'll surprise you, and you'll get caught flat-footed. I'll get this thing through, and I'll get the credit, and there's no way you'll consider a veto."

Rasher yawned. "Anything else?"

"No." Quincy stood up, willing himself to walk casually to the door. He opened and closed it without saying goodbye, and only in the hallway did he allow his face to collapse into a scowl of rage. That bastard. Quincy had known they were abandoning him on NAP, but he'd never considered that they were actually going to let him hang for it.

Well, he thought, he had some surprises for them. His first plan sounded like it would work. And if it didn't, Plan B was already falling into place.

6:18 A.M. PST
Beverly Hills, California

It had taken a few minutes for Nazila to throw on some clothes, then she and Jack had driven north from Pico into Beverly Hills. Beverly Drive took them up through the heart of the little enclave, and Jack followed Nazila's directions into the actual "hills" themselves—a group of low rises and high trees that managed to hide several hundred immense mansions north of Sunset Boulevard. Soon enough, as the sky turned from dark to pale yellow, they pulled up in front of an enormous, flat-fronted monolith, one of dozens that had sprung up in the past few years. Locals called them "Persian palaces" because they were the preferred residences of wealthy Iranian immigrants.

Jack stared at the mansion, then looked at Nazila. "You've got to be kidding me."

"He is not a terrorist," she said for the thousandth time. "He has friends who sympathize with his troubles."

"We searched for him for six months and he was living here." Ramin Rafizadeh, fugitive from justice, lying in the lap of luxury.

She turned toward him in her seat. "You don't understand, Jack. The people who live here came to the U.S. to get away from politics. None of them are terrorists. A lot of them are no more Muslim than you are. They don't feel any connection to the Taliban and they've never set foot in a madrassa. You show them a terrorist and the first thing they will do is turn the other way. The second thing they will do is call the police. But do you know what makes them more afraid? You. People like you who arrest their sons."

Jack's lip curled. "Don't start with that politically correct bull. I'm not going after some grandmother from Boise when most of the danger is coming from the Middle East."

"We know that!" Nazila said. "That's why we put up with the looks on the airplanes, and the double-takes in restaurants, and the questions from the police. But your laws go too far, and you know it."

Jack had stopped listening to her. Standard operating procedure had become second nature to him, and while they both talked he had been scanning the street. At first nothing looked out of place—wide lawns, quiet houses, a few cars and a satellite dish installation van parked on the street. The cars were mostly expensive, but there were a few low-end Toyotas and Kias. These would be housekeeping staff arriving to wake the household up for breakfast . . .

He stopped. It was so obvious he almost missed it. He'd been up all night and his circadian rhythms were screwed up.

A satellite van. There wasn't a dish or cable company in the world that came when you wanted them. There certainly wasn't one that made 6:30 A.M. repair calls. He started the engine.

"Where are we going?" Nazila asked.

"Around the back."

Jack rolled his SUV gently, even sleepily, away from the mansion. As soon as it was far enough up the block, he gave it more gas and made a quick right turn. Most of these Beverly Hills houses had wide alleys separating them from their backyard neighbors. This allowed the city to collect the garbage without the bins or the garbage trucks being seen. Jack made another right into the alley and hurried down as quietly as possible, counting houses until he came to a high cinder-block wall that was his target.

He drew his gun. "Stay here," he ordered, and slipped out of the car.

6:26 A.M. PST
CTU Headquarters, Los Angeles

Kelly Sharpton's heart had known, from the moment Deb had asked, that he would help her. But his head struggled with the idea for a full twenty minutes.

What he was contemplating was criminal. It was worse than anything Jack Bauer had ever done. Jack, for all his brashness, was just a field operative, and in the field you made decisions on the fly based on experience and most recent data and then you fought like hell to win. Despite the flak he threw at Bauer, Sharpton had always admired him for coloring even close to the lines in his efforts to see the big picture.

But this . . . this was suicide.

His phone rang again. "Same caller, Kelly," the operator said.

"What?" Kelly snapped when the line went live.

Debrah Drexler sounded like she was pacing. "I'm running out of time here, Kel. I have to speak to someone from the press in about half an hour. If I don't, that news goes public and I'm ruined. I need help and I need it now."

"Do you know what you're asking me to do?" he hissed back at her, forcing his voice down.

"No," she said, quite honestly. "I have no idea. But I do know that you're the only one with access to information like this, and the only one who might be able to stop it."

Kelly looked around. The walls of his office were glass. He could have darkened them with a switch, but it was still early and the gravediggers were the only ones on. They were down on the deck, manning their terminals. He continued. "You don't even know what 'it' is."

"Yes, I do—"

"It might be a live witness. It might be a hard copy of a photograph in a safe somewhere. I can't touch that, period. I certainly can't do it in thirty minutes."

"I know what it is," Debrah repeated. "I just got a

copy of it on my e-mail. It's a reminder to do what I'm told."

Sharpton had the queasy feeling that his stomach was sinking and his heart was leaping at the same time. "You got an e-mail? Send it to me."

He hung up.

The e-mail came through a few seconds later. Kelly went straight for the attachment and opened it, and there it was. A series of black-and-white photos of a man with a woman who was definitely Debrah Drexler, twenty years younger than today and probably ten younger than when Kelly had first met her. The shots were grainy but clear, and they told a simple story. Man and woman enter hotel room. Man puts money on nightstand and undresses. Man needs to lose weight and shave his back. Woman takes money and undresses. Woman needs to eat more. Woman lays a pillow on the floor and drops to her knees . . .

Kelly recognized the style. These were screen grabs from gotcha footage from a sting operation. The man was clearly the target, not Deb, and he could guess why it had never surfaced before. The man, whoever he was, had cooperated, or become irrelevant, or the law had just forgotten about him, and the footage was filed away for years. The man, most likely, never rose to prominence, and the hooker was just the hooker. Without Debrah's name attached to the file, there was nothing to find, even when digital databases replaced card files. The greatest danger to Debrah Drexler's career had lain dormant in some catalog in a local archive for twenty years. Until now.

Kelly turned his attention to the e-mail itself. It was a forward, from Deb's e-mail, naturally. She'd received it from "*oldfriend1604@hotmail.com*", which would be a blind, of course, but that didn't worry him. He was the Federal government.

Kelly fired up a search program on his desktop and sent the e-mail, forward and all, into it. The search software was nicknamed "Sniffer" and it was the nephew of the Carnivore program, the FBI's daunting powerhouse that could track and monitor any e-mail sent anywhere over the Internet. Sniffer wasn't nearly so powerful, but it was a lot more focused.

The first thing Sniffer did was easy—it broke open the IP numbers, including the one for "old-friend1604." Now Sniffer really went to work, a digital bloodhound on an electronic trail. Kelly sent him back upstream to find where this particular collection of bytes had first come from. As the minutes ticked by, Sniffer sent him regular updates: a server in Los Angeles had relayed from a server in Arlington, Virginia, which had in turn relayed from a server in Washington, D.C. After chasing its tail in circles for a while inside the Beltway, Sniffer finally straightened out and pointed its nose at a computer terminal in the Attorney General's office registered to "Bigsby, Shannon." Kelly looked up that name in CTU's (rather extensive) listing of government employees, and learned that Shannon Bigsby was the assistant to the Attorney General.

"Kim, Kim," Kelly muttered, "what are you doing sharing dirty pictures?"

He heaved a sigh, but it was not relief. Using Sniffer was the easy part. Sniffer could trace, but it couldn't hack into computers, any more than a bloodhound could both find a fugitive and put handcuffs on him. For that, Kelly needed help.

He punched an extension into his phone.

"Bandison," came the voice.

"Jessi, can you come up here. I've got an exercise for you."

6:33 A.M. PST
Beverly Hills

Jack pulled himself up over the top of a wall for the second time that morning. This one couldn't have been more different from the one at the Greater Nation compound. The inside of the wall was screened by twenty foot tall Italian cypress trees. Jack slid down between two of them, using them as a shield as he surveyed the backyard. To his right was a rectangular pool with a black bottom, and a cabana that probably doubled as a guest house, its windows dark. The left side of the yard was a wide expanse of grass sweeping gently upward to a marble patio and a row of glass doors leading into the three-story main house. He saw no movement in the house. If someone was watching him from a window, he was still and quiet.

Jack moved carefully behind the screen of cypress trees until he was even with the cabana, then bolted for it, staying low and moving in a straight line. He reached the cabana and pressed himself against its wall, which offered him cover from most of the windows of the house. He listened to the cabana wall. He couldn't detect any sound or movement inside. He hoped it was empty. There was a space between the cabana and the side yard wall and he crawled there, ignoring the cobwebs and the beetles scurrying on the wall, as well as the skittering sound that could only be a rat. Even Beverly Hills had rats—maybe more than its fair share. He reached the far end of the cabana, and now there was nothing but open ground between him and the doors. He watched again, looking for any signs of movement. There was none. He bolted.

He reached the main house itself and melted into the wall. Carefully he peeked inside the nearest set of French doors, eight square panes of glass set in a white wooden framework. It was a den of some kind, and it was empty of people. He tested the door. Locked, which he expected. He hesitated, wondering what to do next. He could call CTU, but he wasn't looking forward to convincing Ryan Chappelle or Kelly Sharpton that they needed to raid another Persian household because he thought Ramin Rafizadeh was alive. He could try to pick the lock, but that kind of work wasn't his specialty and even if he could do it, it would take time. He could break the glass, but that would make more noise than he could afford.

A sound from inside the house made his choice for him. It was a muffled scream, loud enough to sound urgent but not loud enough to carry very far. Jack turned sideways to the glass panes and jabbed his elbow sharply through the pane nearest the door handle. It shattered in what seemed to Jack to be a thousand screaming pieces. If someone was listening, he'd heard him. He hoped the screams upstairs covered his entry.

Careful to avoid the glass, Jack reached through the now-empty rectangle and opened the door. He wasn't worried about an alarm. Either the bad guys had disabled it and the rest of his entry would be quiet, or the alarm would sound, bringing the police. Either option was fine by him.

No alarm. He slid the door open enough to slip inside, then closed it. He heard one or two angry voices somewhere above him, and another short scream. They were on the second floor. Jack kept his gun in front of him as he moved through the house, clearing each room that he passed. A hallway led out of the den and past three or four other rooms—maid's room, laundry room, downstairs office, before opening up into the biggest entryway Jack had ever seen. The floor looked like a single enormous piece of green marble filled with white swirls and gold specks. A chandelier as big as a Lexus hung down from a ceiling fifty feet above him. A circling stairway rose up to the next floor. Jack leaned out of the hallway, trying to see upward. All clear, as far as he could tell. He made for the stairs as an angry word and a sob filled him with urgency.

The stairs were carpeted so he went up fast and quietly. He reached the second floor and another long hallway, this one probably bedrooms and bathrooms.

"Sit there!" A harsh voice and more sobs, coming from the end of the hall. Jack crept down the hallway pressed against the wall, his eyes and his gun trained on the farthest doorway. He took his eyes away only long enough to glance into each room—empty, as far as he could tell, although some of them contained hallways stretching deeper into the house and out of sight.

He reached the end of the hallway and heard two voices talking to each other.

"Get her fucking feet, she keeps kicking."

"Kick her back!"

He heard a thud and a squeal. Jack melted off the wall, "slicing the pie" as he rounded the corner so he could take in the whole room at once. His muzzle fell instantly on two men dressed in blue overalls who were kneeling over an old woman in a gray robe. They had bound her hands behind her back and were in the process of binding her feet. There were three others in the room—a woman and two men. One of the men was younger, and the others were the same age. Jack guessed: grandmother, husband, wife, and Ramin Rafizadeh.

"Federal agent! Get the fuck away from her!" Jack yelled, stepping fully into the room.

The two men in blue coveralls jumped like startled cats. They whirled around, reaching for guns that they'd laid to the side. "Don't!" Jack yelled, firing a round into the couch an inch from one man's hand. The people in the house shrieked at the sound of gunfire. Both men turned ghostly pale and froze. Jack recognized one of them from the Greater Nation meetings.

"Get down on your knees."

The two men obeyed. Jack saw the entire room now. It was a library. Every wall space, right up to the door he'd just entered, was lined with bookshelves.

"Where is Frank Newhouse?" he asked. He didn't know why he asked that, when Ramin and Ibrahim Rafizadeh should have been his immediate targets, but he went with the question.

"Fuck you," one of the militia men said.

"You can say that to the friends you make in prison," Jack growled. "Maybe you can finally get fucked by Brett Marks, because that's where he's at right—"

He saw it too late. One of the Greater Nation soldiers looked at him, then his eyes flicked over Jack's shoulders for the briefest instant. Jack spun around, but it was the wrong move. He caught just a glimpse of the third militia man pushing with his arms, just before the book case came crashing down on top of him. Something heavy and sharp slammed into his forehead, and the world went dark.

6:41 A.M. PST
CTU Headquarters, Los Angeles

Jessi Bandison skip-stepped up to Kelly's office. She didn't know why that man turned her on. She was twenty-five and fine by almost anyone's standards, and her taste ran toward dark men with a little bit of street and a lot of education. But she was different—a black girl raised first in Amsterdam by diplomat parents who then moved to the United States when she was in middle school. She had dated every type, from thugs to jocks to Oreos. She'd maybe played around with a white boy now and then in college, just for fun, but only because college was for experimenting. None of them gave her that tingle in her belly. And she'd never dated an older man. So why this one?

But there she was, reaching the top of the stairs to his office just slightly breathless, and not from the climb. He was sitting in his chair, back straight, shoulders thrust out to the sides like the corners of a triangle that tapered down to the small of his back. The man wore fitted shirts, which was good, because for a forty-something white man he had a fine figure. His hair had a little gray on the sides, but it didn't show much because he kept it short. It was only his face that showed his age, and he wore it well, with those wrinkles near his eyes that bunched up when he laughed.

"What do you need?" she asked. She was informal

at his request. She'd have preferred it if he wanted to maintain the command structure—it would have been easier to mask her desire—but Kelly Sharpton didn't stand much on ceremony as long as the job got done.

"Sit down," he said, removing himself from the seat and offering it to her.

She took his place and looked at the computer. The screen showed a log-in page—for the Department of Justice.

"Okay, what?" she asked again.

"We've got an assignment. We need to run a fire drill on the Justice Department."

"Fire drill" was Kelly's nickname for fake hacks done on friendly networks to test their security apparatus. "We need to see if we can crack the Justice Department database and crawl inside their files."

"Really?" Jessi said, genuinely surprised. "Doesn't Justice have their own anti-hacking team for that?"

"Someone over there's worried they're getting stale. They want fresh eyes on the problem. We got picked, and I picked you. See if you can get me in."

Jessi put her hands in her lap. "Well, I can tell you off the bat that I can't do it. The encryption on the DOJ system is too strong. You'd need to be past the firewall, and we can't even do that. You remember when someone came close to hacking the DOD system a few years ago? Since then, it's impossible to get past the first layer, and then of course all the other layers are—"

"I can get you past the outer wall," Kelly said. "My terminal's already logged in, just like I did earlier when I wanted you to sort the FBI logs. It's the outer ring, and we're supposed to go a lot deeper, but it's a start." He smelt that jasmine smell on her again.

Jessi still didn't touch the keys. "Kelly, I'm off shift in about a half hour. Can't you have someone on the next crew do it?"

"No, I need you," he said, placing special emphasis on each word. She felt her heart skip a beat. "Besides, the shift won't be a problem. I need you to crack it in—" he checked the terminal's clock—"fifteen and a half minutes."

"You're joking—"

"Fifteen minutes, twenty seconds . . ."

"Okay." Finally, she put her fingers on the keys.

Guilt pinched his heart. But only for lying to her when he knew she liked him. He wasn't exposing her to any trouble. It was his order, his terminal, and his access code.

His phone rang. "Debbie Dee again," the operator announced, sending the call through.

"I'm on it," he said without a hello.

6:47 A.M. PST
Senator Drexler's Office, San Francisco

In the half hour since they'd last spoken, Debrah Drexler had driven from her apartment to her San Francisco office, located across from City Hall. The office reminded her of the old days, when politics were simpler and the results clearer. She'd chosen a third-story office, rather than something higher, because when she gave interviews from her home state, her small conference room provided a backdrop of downtown San Francisco, which felt like "home" to her.

A news crew was there already, and two more were on their way up the elevator. She hadn't called them, of course. They'd received a tip—"someone on her staff" was all anyone could say—that Senator Drexler had an important announcement to make, something big enough to rouse remote cam operators and still sleepy morning news reporters from their beds. The Attorney General had laid it all out for her.

Debrah had locked herself in her office. "I've got media here. They're expecting me to say something at the top of the hour." Panic crept into her voice.

Kelly pulled the phone away from his ear. "How you doing, Jessi?"

"Interesting encryptions here," she murmured, in her own world. "Are they watching from their end to see how I do it?"

"Sort of," Kelly said, getting back on the phone. "We're doing our best over here. I'm not sure we're going to be able to get the job done."

"Don't be a cynic!" Jessi protested.

"Shit!" Debrah Drexler said in her best Bronx accent. "I've got to go do this, Kelly. I've got to. It's one vote out of thousand votes that will help people."

"I wouldn't recommend that," Kelly said, forcing his tones into neutral for Jessi's benefit. "This is an awfully important operation. Some things shouldn't be compromised."

"It's my goddamned career! It's my humiliation!" she said. He heard the anxiety in her voice. She wasn't talking to him. She was talking to herself now, talking herself into it. She'd told him about the nights, long ago, when she'd used that same tone to talk herself into selling her body.

He heard noise in the background. "I've got to go. Call my assistant Amy at this number if you get anything."

The phone went dead.

"Jessi?"

"I don't think—oh, hey, I got it." The girl sounded surprised. "That was easier than I thought. Those guys over there are really going to need to—"

"You're right, thank you," he said, checking the time: 6:52. "Okay, nice work. Can you excuse me, now? I've got to consult with them and it's classified."

"Classified?" Jessi said as he practically lifted her up and out of her seat. "But I'm the one that broke it, shouldn't I—?"

"If they have any questions on the keystrokes, I'll call you up," he said. "Please, I've got a hard deadline on this."

"Okay," she agreed, although by the time she said it he'd already ushered her out the door.

Inside his office, Kelly reached for his remote and pressed a button. The clear glass walls seemed to fill with smoke and he was shielded from prying eyes. He grabbed a disc from his desk drawer. Through the clear plastic case he could read his own handwriting on the disc itself. It read: "Override." He popped it open and practically rammed it into the E drive on his computer. As the disc booted up, Kelly scanned the

DOJ database for the Attorney General's personal drive. He found it quickly enough—once he was inside, he was inside, and nothing was hidden from him—and logged in. James Quincy's computer now belonged to him.

The time was 6:55.

This was Kelly's bloodhound program. It was designed to work like many other computer viruses, slipping into a computer undetected and wreaking havoc. This virus was particularly nasty because it not only wiped out all the data on the infected hard drive, it also had the capability of tracing the source of any data—the bloodline—to other hard drives, and going after them. As soon as the virus was ready, a crude query screen popped up. Kelly entered the data and properties of the pictures of Debrah Drexler, then hit go.

His bloodhound was on the scent.

6:58 A.M. PST
Senator Drexler's Office, San Francisco

Debrah Drexler straightened her back and opened her office door. There were two camera crews there and a couple of reporters—she recognized the local girl from Associated Press, and the *San Francisco Chronicle*'s political reporter. They all looked sleepy and just a little put out for having to come to her office so early.

Debra Drexler had faced much harsher audiences before. The national spotlight during confirmation hearings had failed to wither her. Scathing op-ed pieces in the *Wall Street Journal* and the *Nation* hadn't fazed her. But at the moment this tiny contingent of the Fourth Estate was the herald of her doom. It didn't matter if there was one or four or forty. Once they put her on the record, the news would get out, and everyone would know that Senator Drexler had backed off her hard line on the NAP Act.

"Thanks for coming . . ." she began. There was no sign of Amy.

6:59 A.M. PST
CTU Headquarters, Los Angeles

The bloodhound sent back information. There were two digital counters, one for files checked and another for matching files found. The "files checked" counter was racking up numbers faster than the eye could follow. The other one remained at zero.

Kelly checked his watch. She'd be talking to them now. It was over.

The right side counter changed from 0 to 1. Then, almost immediately, it seemed to skip 4 and 5 and go right to 6—the total number of pictures.

6 FILES FOUND. DELETE FILES?

"Yes," he said as he typed.

TRACE BLOODLINE FOR THESE FILES AND DELETE?

"Oh, yeah," he said again.

DELETE ALL OTHER FILES?

Kelly hesitated. That hadn't been his plan. It was just one of the evil features of the virus he'd written. He typed in yes with malicious grin.

He picked up the phone and dialed Debrah's office. "Senator Drexler's office," said a young female voice. He checked his watch. 6:59. "Tell her it's done. Tell her right now. Go!"

1 2 3 4 **5** 6 7 8 9
10 11 12 13 14 15 16 17
18 19 20 21 22 23 24

•••

**THE FOLLOWING TAKES PLACE
BETWEEN THE HOURS OF
7 A.M. AND 8 A.M.
PACIFIC STANDARD TIME**

•••

7:00 A.M. PST
Senator Drexler's Office, San Francisco

"I hope you don't mind the early morning statement," Debrah said. "You guys always get my quotes wrong after you've had your coffee, so maybe you'll do a better job before the caffeine kicks in." Her office door remained closed. No Amy.

They gave her a polite laugh behind their cameras and notepads. She could see the sleepy and impatient looks on their faces. They assumed that a U.S. senator would have some significant reason for giving a statement this early in the morning. They were waiting for it.

She swallowed her pride. "As you know, I've been

an outspoken opponent of the NAP Act, which goes up for vote in two days before the Senate. Probably the most outspoken. I'm flying back for the vote tomorrow. In the intervening time, I've had time to reflect on the current war on terror, and on our activities inside our own borders to keep our people safe. I've come to the conclusion that—" she choked. She'd danced around the truth, she'd withheld information, she'd reserved judgment. But in more than twenty years in politics, she had never outright lied. Until now.

"I've come to the conclusion that—"

Her office door flew open. Amy appeared. She gave two thumbs up.

Debra Drexler felt warmth and comfort wash over her, a rejuvenating mixture of relief and love and pure, unqualified gratitude. Her knees nearly buckled, but she held herself up. She took a deep breath and gathered herself again. These were cameramen and reporters, and she was a United States senator.

"I've come to the conclusion that," she repeated, "I was absolutely right in my opposition. The so-called New American Privacy Act is the epitome of doublespeak. It takes away the rights of our citizens. It violates due process and the right to privacy . . ."

The woman from the Associated Press groaned audibly. She might as well have gotten up to report that there was fog on San Francisco Bay.

7:03 A.M. PST
Westin St. Francis Hotel, San Francisco

In a hotel room not far away, James Quincy fumed at his television screen. That bitch. Did she think he was bluffing? Did she think he wouldn't release those pictures? Hell, he was planning on releasing them in a few months anyway, just for spite. Now, he'd make sure they were above the fold in every major newspaper in the country if he had to paste them there himself.

But that was for later. First he had to salvage his sinking ship. Quincy picked up a cell phone and dialed a number. It rang only once. "I'm watching the news, too," said a voice on the other end.

"I can't believe it," Quincy said.

"I can. She's got big balls. You gotta admire it."

"There's no other choice now but to make her irrelevant. Everything's in place for our other plan, isn't it?"

"Like I said it would be. I've been moving that little project along as though this one wasn't going to work. Which it didn't."

"Stop saying I told you so," Quincy said irritably. "Just get it done."

He hung up. He hit the mute button on his remote to silence Debrah Drexler, but that gave him only mild satisfaction. He picked up the phone to call his office. At least he could console himself with the release of the pictures.

7:09 A.M. PST
Senator Drexler's Office, San Francisco

"Thanks for coming. Thanks!" Drexler said to the tiny squad of reporters now grumbling and exiting the conference room. Her press people were going to hear some gripes about this, but she didn't care. She was giddy with excitement.

She practically floated back into her office and closed the door, then dialed Kelly Sharpton's number. When he answered, she trilled, "You, sir, are hereby granted divinity. You're a god. How did you do it?"

"It wasn't that hard." Kelly's voice was flat.

"What about—are there any other copies any-where?" she asked, some of the happiness leaving her voice. "I mean, if it's digital . . ."

"My bug will keep tracking down any links to those pictures and wipe them all out."

"What about hard copies?" she asked

"I doubt there are any. This was old stuff, and there was no one attached to the crime anymore. If it's from the San Francisco archives, which it probably was, they transferred all their data to digital years ago, ex-cept for forensics, of course. Odds are the actual pic was destroyed once they had a clean scan. They're even lucky they had this much."

"We should get together again. For a drink," she added quickly. "I owe you, Kell. God, do I owe you. So much."

He heard the euphoria return to her voice. He felt proud to have saved her, he had to admit—it was some kind of ridiculous digital age version of a cave-man protecting his mate. But he also knew that some-thing was missing. It wasn't just that he felt dirty, which he did. He had just exercised a gross abuse of power, and he'd done it with an ease and lack of con-science that horrified him. But no, it wasn't just re-morse for an ethical lapse that bothered him. It was personal. The clean sharp edge had been shaved off his longing for her, leaving a jagged scar. "You don't owe me, Deb. And I don't think drinks are a good idea."

The heavy tone of his voice dragged her out of the clouds. "What?"

"You were going to do it, weren't you? Give up your vote. Just like that."

She stammered, "I hoped you'd . . . I mean you always . . . I would have—" She stopped. This wasn't the press or the public. This was Kelly. "Yes," she said at last. "I was going to give in."

He nodded. "You definitely don't owe me, then. What I did just now, I did my job. Bye, Deb." He hung up on her.

7:16 A.M. PST
Beverly Hills

Jack never remembered his dreams. His wife told him that he often muttered in his sleep, and even jumped out of bed some times, but he never recalled what he'd said or why he'd jumped up. For him, unconsciousness passed by in a blink—the split second of darkness that separated one moment of awareness from the next.

That's how it was for him then, as his eyes popped open. He was lying on his side on the floor of the library. The bookcase was on its side, but at least it wasn't on top of him anymore. Books lay were they fell, scattered in ones and twos. Jack tried to move, and immediately he knew three things. First, his face had been bleeding and might still be bleeding. Second, he wasn't alone in the room. And third, his hands and feet were tied.

He pulled his knees up to his chest and rolled to a sitting position. The room shook back and forth before his eyes and his stomach twisted, and that gave him more information, none of it good. Nausea. Possible concussion. Worry about it later. There was another change in the room, aside from the fallen bookcase. Another prisoner. The old woman was now completely bound, as were the husband and wife. But the young man had been taken away, and Nazila Rafizadeh had joined them.

Jack shook his head. "I told you to wait."

She shrugged.

The man whispered, "They said they'd kill us if we talk."

"I bet they did," Jack replied.

The man and the woman were frightened. The older woman, probably the mother of the husband or the wife, looked the toughest. The man and woman were plump and well-fed, the man's salt-and-pepper hair so smoothed by hair spray that even dragged from sleep he looked well-coiffed. The grandmother was thin and sharp as a hawk, her nose bent like a beak and her small black eyes glaring at him as though this was all his fault.

"Are you okay?" Jack asked Nazila.

She nodded. "I'm sorry. I saw you draw your gun and I thought you were going in to arrest him . . ." She trailed off without finishing.

The wife, her eyes glazed with tears, whispered, "Are they . . . are they going to kill us?"

Jack said quietly, "I don't know. Just stay calm and don't make any trouble and you'll be okay. They don't want you. You've seen them, but they're not professionals. They might let you go."

He didn't tell them that they'd been professional enough to station a layoff man who'd snuck up behind him, or that that man had been professional enough to catch him by surprise. He also didn't tell them that on the sodium cyanide job, the one where he'd betrayed them, they'd planned on killing the plant manager. Jack mentally kicked himself. He'd been in too much of a hurry. He should have cleared the entire house before making contact with the first two. Then he shook those thoughts from his head. There was plenty of time for a postmortem later, as long as it wasn't *his* postmortem. Right now he had to focus on getting out.

He listened. They were in the next room, talking in angry voices. He heard a fourth voice pleading. That was Ramin.

"Where are your friends? Tell us where they are!"

"I don't know what you mean. Please, no!" The sound of a hard slap interrupted his words.

"Fucking raghead," said one of the militia men. "We know you know them. We know they're here. Tell us!"

Ramin sobbed.

"My hand's starting to hurt," said one of the Greater Nation men. "Let's try something else."

"Get him over to the wall," said another. "Cut the cord off that lamp."

Jack examined the bindings at his ankles. Rip hobble cords. He could feel the same tight plastic strips cutting into his wrists behind his back. Rip hobble cords were strong and unbreakable, a heavy-duty version of the plastic ties people used to seal garbage bags. Police officers used them during mass arrests when they'd run out of handcuffs. If you pulled them tight enough, they were nearly impossible to wriggle out of. There was no release mechanism—they had to be cut off.

He searched the room and made a mental inventory of its contents: four other prisoners, floor-to-ceiling shelves filled with books, one fallen bookcase, small couch, small desk with a reading lamp.

"How long has that lamp been on?" he asked.

"What?" the husband asked.

"That lamp. How long?"

The man said, "I don't know. I was in here doing work when they came in. It's been on for perhaps two hours."

That might be long enough, Jack thought. He lay down and straightened himself out, then rolled himself over to the desk. When he reached it, he curled back up, sat up, and slowly got himself to his feet. With his ankles fettered, it was hard to maintain balance. He leaned against the desk to keep from falling.

"They'll come back in here!" the woman hissed. The old lady, probably her mother, said something sharp in Farsi, but she said it to her daughter.

Jack hopped around the desk until he reached the lamp. It was a modern looking directional lamp, designed for reading. A brushed metal stand rose up from the base, and a flexible coil curved away from the top, ending in a bell-shaped metal shade that pointed down toward the desk top. The bulb inside was bright. Jack leaned his face near it and could feel the heat radiating off it. It might be enough.

He turned his back on the lamp and leaned over, raising his bound hands toward it. The heat singed his skin. He ignored it and touched the rip hobble cord to the bulb. A few seconds later, the faint, acrid smell of burning plastic filled the air.

The problem was, the heat wasn't intense enough to melt the plastic right away, but it was hot enough to burn Jack. The skin on his wrist began to blister, but it was better than a bullet in the brain.

From the room next door, he heard a crash and a thud. The Greater Nation thugs were prepping Ramin for some more intense questioning. They were going to torture him, Jack was sure. The irony didn't escape him—that these zealots who believed the government overreached its powers now far overreached their own. In the end, he thought, people were all the same. They wanted what they wanted, and they made and broke rules to achieve their own satisfaction.

The burning smell grew stronger, and he heard something pop. But it was taking too long. The plastic was thick and the lamp was weak. It would never cut through before the militia men thought to check on their captives. Jack began to pull and wriggle his hands. If the plastic had been heated enough to stretch . . .

In the next room, one of the militia men said, "This is your last chance—"

"Fuck it, no last chances," said another one.

A muffled scream of agony penetrated the wall. The desk lamp in the library flickered on and off. When the light became steady again, they could all hear a sob from the other room.

Jack slid his hands back and forth. The plastic had stretched. Now he needed lubricant.

Jack crouched down a little, which wasn't easy with his ankles hobbled, and pressed his wrists against the edge of the desk. Gritting his teeth, he slid the side of his wrist along the edge. It hurt, but he could tell he hadn't cut the skin. He rubbed his wrist up and down a few times, ignoring the pain, then he slid his arm across the desk edge again. This time the pain was sharp, like a sudden burn, then he felt warmth ooze down to his palms and fingers. Blood, until it started to dry, was very slick. He started to rub his wrists up and down again, letting the blood spread. He pushed his elbows as close together as possible, making a straight line up and down relative to the plastic strip, straightened his fingers and palms, and pulled. His right hand slid up and out of the rip hobble. He brought his hands around and rubbed his wrists. The cut he'd made was deep, and still oozing. He compressed it against his chest as he shook the hobble off his other hand. His legs would be easier. He searched the desk drawer, hoping for a letter opener. He was rewarded with a pair of scissors instead. He attacked the plastic binding on his feet—even though they were sharp, the scissors wore, rather than sliced, through the hobble. Nothing short of wire cutters would cut the cord in one snip. The scissors, in fact, broke at the hinge. Jack swore under his breath, sensing that his time was growing short. He picked up one of the scissors blades and sawed at the plastic. Finally it surrendered and he was free.

The others looked at him expectantly. "Now my wife," the man said bravely.

Jack shook his head. There was no point in trying to cut them all free. It would take too long. Besides, he didn't like being on defense.

Jack reversed his grip on the scissors and stalked toward the door.

"Tell me names, and tell me where they are," one of the militia men ordered.

"Aaghh!" The lights flickered again and a muffled cry followed.

They were electrocuting him. Jack knew the procedure—the cord ripped from an electrical appliance but still plugged into the wall, the protective coating stripped from the ends of the wire, and a little water splashed on the most sensitive parts of the victims' skin made for a simple but effective instrument of torture.

"You don't like it on your balls. I can always put it in your eye instead."

Jack started out the door.

"Okay, okay!" Ramin Rafizadeh yelled.

Jack stopped.

"I'll tell you what I know."

This is good, Jack thought. *Let them do the dirty work.* He listened closely.

"Tell us where your terrorist friends are. Tell us what they're going to do."

"I don't have any terrorist friends—aghh!—I'm telling the truth, please, I'm telling the truth. I don't know any terrorists. But I have heard some people talk, just talk, that's all—aghh!—about some Saudis coming up from South America."

There is a quality of sheer terror in the human voice that is hard for most people to imitate. The best counter-interrogation specialists can mimic it, but for most victims it is impossible to simulate. It swells up from the gut, rising through the body as it rises in pitch until it escapes from the mouth like the very soul is under pressure. And it is at that moment that the torturer knows, with his hands and his instruments only millimeters from an eye or a genital, that he has broken through the walls of defiance and heard the truth.

Jack heard that same quality of terror in Ramin's voice. He was telling all he knew.

Jack felt eyes on him and he glanced backward. Nazila and the others were all staring in horror—not at the sounds coming from the other room, but at him. He focused on Nazila and he read her thoughts through her eyes and her expression. *You monster,* she was thinking, *you're letting them torture him. You're torturing him through them to learn what he knows.*

Yes, Jack thought. *That's what I'm doing.* And he knew that in the world they came from, what he was doing was wrong.

"There's more," one of the torturers said. "That's nothing."

"No, no, no!" Ramin screamed as the lights flickered again. "That's all I know, and I don't even know if that's true. I just heard someone talking, I swear!"

Jack moved. He slid out of the library door, across the short distance of the hallway and into the room next door. When attacking it was best to use surprise, speed, and overwhelming force. Two out of three would have to do, Jack thought. He burst into the room and drank in data without stopping. Three men. Two of them leaning over Ramin Rafizadeh, who was tied to a chair. One closest to Jack, by the door, with his back to the entrance. Jack moved fast, and by the time one of the two torturers had looked up and shouted in alarm, Jack had buried the scissors blade upward under the base of the near man's skull. He jiggled it a little, scrambling the brains, and the man became a rag doll. He let the corpse fall, jerking the scissors blade out and lunging forward. It penetrated the throat of another militia man, who was just raising his weapon. The man shouted, but no sound came out except a gurgling from his throat. The third man, on Jack's left, had his weapon leveled. Jack's left hand shot out, grabbing the barrel of the pistol and pushing it off line. Two rounds thundered out of the muzzle. Jack ignored the deafening sound of gunfire close to his head and punched the scissors blade into the gunman's sternum. It stuck there, so Jack let go of it and, still pushing the pistol away, elbowed the man in the throat. He dropped to his knees. Jack snapped the gun from his grip and whirled. The second man, one hand still clutching his throat, shakily raised his gun in the other and fired. Jack dropped to one knee and the rounds punctured the wall behind him. He fired twice and red blossoms appeared on the militia man's blue overalls until he fell dead.

Jack waited on bended knee, listening for footsteps running toward them or away. He wasn't about to make the same mistake twice. But he could hear no one else in the house. Rising, he moved over to Ramin Rafizadeh and, with one eye still on the door, looked the young man over. He was thin, weak, and terrified. Blisters marred both cheeks, just below his eyes. His pants had been pulled down and his shoes had been removed. He'd been burned on the soles of his feet, his thighs, and his testicles. The gunfire had terrified him. He was sobbing.

Not a terrorist, Jack thought.

He moved back to the militia man he had elbowed in the throat. The scissors still protruded from his chest, but he was alive. He stared at Jack incredulously. "You stabbed me," he whispered hoarsely. "You stabbed me."

"Don't forget the elbow," Jack reminded him. "Right now your throat is probably swelling up like a grapefruit. In a few minutes you'll choke to death. I'm the only one who can save you."

The man's eyes widened. His rasping breath told Jack that he agreed with that assessment.

"If you want me to call for help in time, you tell me where Professor Rafizadeh is right now." The man started to shake his head. "Right. Now."

"Need . . . need me," the militia man rasped. "I call . . . eight—thirty . . . or he dies."

Jack put his hand on the protruding scissors blade and leaned gently. "Where?"

The man gasped. "C-Culver City!" He rasped out an address off of Sawtelle.

"Thanks." They'd taken his cell phone, so Jack ran to the bedroom phone and dialed quickly. When a CTU operator picked up, he said, "This is Bauer. Patch me through to Sharpton."

Kelly picked up seconds later. "Jack, wh—?"

"No time. I've got Ramin Rafizadeh. I've also got possible terrorists inside the U.S., and dead bodies. I need field agents and a medical team right away." He rattled off the address and hung up before Kelly could ask anything else.

He turned to Ramin. "You're okay, now. I'm a Federal agent."

Jack left the scissors in the militia man's body—pulling it out would only cause more bleeding—and ran downstairs. There was a spare room off the kitchen, and there he found a simple tool kit that included wire cutters. He ran back upstairs, past Ramin's room, and into the library. The four prisoners' terror turned to relief when they saw him enter.

He snipped them free one by one. "Ramin's okay," he said to Nazila as he freed her.

"You sick bastard!" she said in reply. "You let them hurt him!"

"You're welcome," he said sarcastically, cold and defensive and still adrenalized from having guns fired at his head. "They'd still be doing it if I hadn't stopped them."

Her hate-filled eyes lingered on him a moment, then she rushed past him to help her brother.

Jack checked his watch. Almost eight o'clock. He had a little over half an hour to save Nazila's father.

7:51 A.M. PST
CTU Headquarters, Los Angeles

Kelly slammed the phone down. Jack Bauer seemed hell-bent on pissing him off as much as possible today. Annoyed, he spouted orders at three different people to get medical team and law enforcement to the Beverly Hills address. He also ordered a holding cell to be made ready for Ramin Rafizadeh, the living dead man who was and was not a terrorist.

Kelly rubbed his temples. He felt a headache press against the inside of his skull like a dam wanting to burst. *I need food,* he thought.

Instead of getting up, he stared at his computer screen. He was still hacked into the Attorney General's computer, and his virus program was still deleting files. He had taken no small amount of pleasure in watching the files disappear one by one. He didn't know what they were, and he didn't care. Any files important to the government would be backed up elsewhere. This was just Kelly's own personal jab at the AG, who had tried to ruin the career of someone he lo—someone he liked very much.

His eyes meandered down the screen and tripped over the words *Greater Nation*. Kelly blinked. Greater Nation was the name of the militia group Jack had infiltrated. Why would the AG have a file on them?

Kelly clicked on the file. It opened up and he saw a list of notes— dates, names, times—all connected to the Greater Nation militia group. There was a lot of information recorded here.

"Holy shit," Kelly murmured. He glanced at the corner of his screen, where the progress report for his virus showed that complete destruction of all files was nearly complete. He couldn't stop it. He'd never built a stop command into his virus, not even a back door. It was going to eat that Greater Nation file along with everything else.

"Excuse me, Kelly?"

Jessi Bandison had come to his door. She was leaning against the frame, her head tilted slightly to one side. He smelled the scent of jasmine, freshly applied.

"Do you think—" she swallowed—"I'm off in a few. Would you want to grab a coffee before I go?"

"Not now!" he said. The anger in his voice had nothing to do with her, but it still hit her like a slap in the face. "I'm sorry," he said, no less sharply, "I just have a problem here. Can we talk later?"

"Okay," she said, and retreated out of view.

Kelly scanned the open document, his eyes searching for anything of value. Two phrases leaped out at him.

... *GREATER NATION TIP REGARDING*

POSSIBLE ISLAMIC FUNDAMENTALIST AC-TIVITY IN UNITED STATES . . .

and

. . . AGENT FRANK NEWHOUSE SUCCESS-FULLY INSERTED INTO GREATER NATION . . .

Then the screen went blank.

1 · 2 3 4 5 **6** 7 8 9
10 11 12 13 14 15 16 17
18 19 20 21 22 23 24

· ·

THE FOLLOWING TAKES PLACE
BETWEEN THE HOURS OF
8 A.M. AND 9 A.M.
PACIFIC STANDARD TIME

· ·

8:00 A.M. PST
Culver City, California

Culver City is a stone's throw from Beverly Hills—you can see it just to the south from the tops of some of the nicer mansions. But distance means nothing in Los Angeles. Los Angelenos do not measure distance by how many miles one location is from another. They measure everything by time. Beverly Hills is not fifteen miles from the ocean, it's about a half hour. UCLA is not ten miles from the airport, it's about an hour. Someone who lives over the Santa Monica Mountains, in the widespread San Fernando Valley, lives only eight miles from posh West Los Angeles.

But the miles meant nothing—it was the time it took to arrive that was significant.

And the time, of course, depends on the traffic.

In the 1970s, and even through the 1980s, there had been a rhythm to L.A.'s traffic—morning rush hour was from around 7:30 a.m. to 10 a.m., and then it picked up again around 4:30 p.m. to 7 p.m. or so. The times in between were, for the most part, free. But by the mid nineties all semblance of rush hour was gone—it was gridlock on the freeways and surface streets from early morning until late evening. If you wanted open roads in downtown Los Angeles, then you had to wait until 5 a.m. on Christmas morning.

So at 8:05 on Wednesday morning, Jack found himself shucking and cutting through Beverly Hills, headed toward Culver City and an address he probably could have hit with a stone if he had time to bend down and pick one up.

He had recovered his gun and his phone, then waited until the medical team and the additional field agents had arrived. As the adrenaline levels in his body eased up, he asked Nazila if he could speak with her. The girl was reluctant to leave her brother's side at first, but after a moment she relented and they went out to the front of the house. He wanted to speak to her there for two reasons. First, he'd know when his backup arrived. Second, she would be less inclined to make a scene on the front lawn.

"What do you have to say to me," she said softly but angrily. "How dare you sit there and let them torture him?"

Jack nodded. "Yes, I did. I admit that. But I did it because I knew he was going to be interrogated by someone. Nazila, whether you like it or not, his name ended up on a contact list used by terrorists in a terrorist training camp."

"But he's not—"

"I believe you," Jack interrupted. "I believe you."

Nazila's eyes widened like saucers. "You . . . do?"

"Yes," he replied. "But only because of what I heard in there." He thought again of the sheer terror in Ramin's voice, the fear that did not allow for lies. "I know you hate me, Nazila, but just for a minute put yourself in my position. Finding terrorists is my job. And all of them, and all the people associated with them, lie all the time. Every one of them lies, and some of them are dressed up like normal people, like professors and grad students and journalists. It isn't enough for me to have someone, even someone like you, say that he's not a terrorist. I need proof, and it's my job to keep working until I get that proof. Because if I stop too early, then somewhere in the world, maybe right here in Los Angeles, people die. If I had gone in there right away, then Ramin would end up right now in a holding cell being questioned by our people."

The girl touched her fingertips to her mouth. "Are you saying . . . are you saying that won't happen now? That he can go free?"

Jack shook his head. "I'm sure they'll want to question him. But they won't put pressure on him. I'll tell my people what I've learned, and he should be okay."

Nazila's shoulders dropped, and tension seemed to leave her as though exorcised from her body. But just as quickly, new worry filled her. "Am I . . . in trouble for lying? My father—"

Jack had considered that already. That would be up to Ryan Chappelle, not him, and Chappelle was a vindictive ass. He might pursue them for obstruction of justice simply for denying that they knew where Ramin was. But the truth was that the only person with a right to be angry was Jack himself. He'd pushed Ibrahim Rafizadeh to the extreme, sensing (correctly, it turned out) there was more to his story, only to get slapped down by his own department and sent into CTU exile. But of course during his exile he had already foiled an incident of domestic terrorism and come around full circle to the same leads that had made him an outcast. It was like a puzzle he'd finished by accident—completed but unsatisfying.

He struggled for something to say, caught unexpectedly in a maelstrom of emotions—compassion for her, anger at her deception, guilt in realizing that Ramin was probably innocent despite everything, primal anger at being shot at by the Greater Nation . . .

He looked at Nazila, who was already staring up at him, her dark eyes soft and deep. She watched him as though his emotional struggle was a drama played out clearly across his face. The warmth of her look gave him pause. He was a reader of looks and moods—it was vital to his profession. A poker player read bluffs, a psychologist probed for the secret release of emotions. Jack read the change of expression, the hardening of an eye that preceded the drawing of a gun or the start of a lie. In his career, he had read the looks of killers, madmen, and patriots. The expression on Nazila's face was one he had not seen, at least not in a long, long time. She offered him a warmth that was more pure than compassion or sympathy. It was understanding. And in that moment Jack, who had wanted only to alter her emotional state, found himself being altered. He had not had someone, not even his wife, bless him with that look of pure, unconditional understanding, in as long as he could remember.

"You have a hard job," she said at last.

Two black SUVs had rolled up at that moment, saving him from a response.

He pushed his emotions deep below the surface. "These guys will take you back to CTU headquarters. I'll phone ahead. They'll know what's going on by the time you arrive. I'm going to get your father." The words were a promise.

8:19 A.M. PST
Culver City

He reached Culver City at last, armed and ready to fulfill that promise. The field agent who'd picked him up had handed him a shotgun, which he checked quickly while she drove. She was a young agent named Lzolski, which was, for reasons inexplicable to Jack, pronounced "Wuh-zow-skee."

"Who's there?" Jack asked her.

"Two of our guys—Paulson and Nina Myers—and LAPD is rolling in quiet as back up. Our ETA is three minutes, give or take the traffic," Lzolski said. "Any idea what's in there?"

"Greater Nation," Jack said. "It's a militia group."

"Militia group?" Lzolski said. "That's so nineties."

They pulled to the curb a half block from the address. The street was a middle-class setting straight off a 1950 city planner's desk: a row of bungalows with trim lawns and walkways leading to front doors under small canopies, some of which were still made of the original painted aluminum. The two other CTU agents melted out of the shadows to join them.

"Nina," Jack said for a hello. "Ready to join the party?"

"I'm a party girl," she said with a grin.

Jack summarized quickly. "Unknown number of suspects are holding a hostage, an old man named Ibrahim Rafizadeh. Suspects will for certain be white males. Expect all of them to be armed, expect all of them to put up a fight. They're all Timothy McVeigh types," he added, referring to the notorious Oklahoma City bomber.

Nina asked, "Didn't most of them give up this morning?"

"A lot of them were weekend warriors who didn't like it when the shooting started. These here are the ones who put up a fight and got away." He was thinking of Frank Newhouse. "They're carrying out their mission even though their glorious leader is in the tank. Don't get me wrong, I want them all alive if possible. But I want all of you alive more, so go in ready to put them down."

Paulson, a field agent as short and wide as a fireplug, said, "Should we just wait them out? Call in the negotiators?"

Jack shook his head. "No time. I had it out with part of their team this morning. If this group doesn't get a call in—" he checked his watch—"five minutes, they kill their hostage. You two go up the back way. Lzolski, you and I will go in the front door. Okay? Go."

It was Jack's third combat mission of the morning. He was already tired and irritable. As he approached the house he nearly tripped over a broken section of sidewalk raised by a tree root. He swore to himself. No one should go this long without sleep or rest. He hoped he never had to do it again.

Jack didn't have a plan. But he also didn't have any time. In *The Art of War*, Sun Tzu had valued surprise as one of the greatest weapons in a warrior's arsenal. Several thousand years later, Napoleon, when asked what he valued most in his generals, answered, "Luck." Jack counted on both luck and surprise as he strode boldly up to the door and kicked it in.

"What the—?" Lzolski sputtered, since this particular tactic had not been presented in any academy she'd ever attended.

Jack entered the house behind the muzzle of his SigSauer as a big blond man with a shaggy mustache came lumbering from the hallway off the living room. Jack swept the muzzle toward him him and said, "Down!" The man pulled up short, practically filling the hallway. "Down," Jack cautioned.

"Company!" the blond giant said. He raised his right arm, and Jack fired three times. The first two rounds vanished in his chest. He fell fast for a big man, and the third round passed over his slumping shoulders and blew a hole in a door at the end of the hall. Jack moved down steadily, hoping Lzolski was right behind him. He slowed just long enough to kick the semi-automatic from the fallen giant's hand.

There were four doors on the hallway, two on the right, one on the left, and the one at the end with the brand new hole. Jack hadn't seen which door the big man came from. Wherever they were, they knew he was here now. His best bet was to keep making noise to give Paulson and Nina a chance to come at them from behind.

"Federal agents!" he shouted. "Come out with your hands up!"

There was a slight pause before a panicked voice shouted, "I've got a hostage!"

Only one bad guy, Jack thought.

"And we've got you!" he shouted back. "There's no way out. We've got your friends and we've got Ramin. Give it up."

"Back off!"

Two men stepped out of the second room. Jack recognized one of them immediately as Professor Ibrahim Rafizadeh, thinner than Jack remembered but still wearing his scholarly white beard. His hands were bound in front of him. Behind him, a Greater Nation soldier huddled low, his eyes barely visible over the professor's shoulder. When Rafizadeh saw Jack, his fear turned to disbelief and indignation.

"Back off or I'll kill him," the militia man threatened, shoving Rafizadeh forward. He clearly hoped to back Jack off.

Jack held his ground, snarling, "We'll see."

The door at the far end of the hall flew open and Paulson swung in, low even before he dropped to one knee. "Drop it!" he yelled. Nina, standing, leaned in behind him.

Jack steadied his aim, expecting the gunman to spin around in surprise, which would give him a clear shot. Instead the Greater Nation soldier half-spun, pressing his back against the wall and pulling his prisoner close, minimizing his exposure. Surprised, Jack adjusted his aim, favoring the wall to take out the back of the man's head. He exhaled and prepared to squeeze.

"Jack."

The voice came from behind Jack. He threw himself against the opposite wall, mirroring the militia soldier, and looked back down the hall. Lzolski was there, but someone had an arm wrapped around her neck and a gun to her head. Like the other milita man, this one huddled low behind his captive. Even so, Jack recognized him.

"Give it up, Frank."

"We're the ones with the prisoners, Jack," said Frank Newhouse.

"But nowhere to go," Jack said. He swiveled his gun to bear on Brett Marks's number two man. "We've got Brett. We've got Ramin. We've got you, too. You just don't know it, yet."

"I'll kill him! I'll kill him!" the other soldier yelled.

Jack stayed cool. Newhouse was formidable. He'd given the SEB team the slip and he'd gotten the drop on Lzolski. "Tell him we get the idea, Frank."

Frank Newhouse smiled over Lzolski's shoulder. "Thing is, I think he means it. Why don't you take a walk into that garage there and let us go."

"Bauer," Lzolski said apologetically.

"Your call, Jack!" Paulson shouted from the doorway.

"Good little soldier," Frank mocked. "Obedience without question."

Sirens wailed in the distance, which must have been LAPD's idea of "coming in quiet." Their arrival changed the nature of the standoff, and Frank Newhouse understood that immediately. "Shoot them!" Newhouse yelled.

A gunshot filled the hallway behind him. Jack squinted, ready to take Newhouse down even if he had to take off Lzolski's ear to do it. But Lzolski seemed to lunge toward him suddenly, her eyes wide as she charged the barrel of his gun. Jack shoved her aside, but by that time Frank Newhouse was gone. Jack raced after him, passing the entrance as two rounds chipped the doorframe behind him. Three more rounds whined past his ear and he tucked and rolled, finding cover behind a car. He came up searching for a target, but found none.

Frank Newhouse had escaped again.

8:31 A.M. PST
CTU Headquarters, Los Angeles

There was no such thing as a good visit from Ryan Chappelle. The Los Angeles District Director never appeared with good news. Thanks and congratulations, in his view, were the stuff of e-mail. Bad news and ass-chewing, however, deserved a personal touch. Chappelle prided himself on being one of America's watchdogs, even if his territory was the junkyard of bureaucracy. Growing up as the runt of the litter in Detroit, he'd learned to get tough fast. Knowing he'd never be the fastest or the strongest (or even the smartest), little Ryan had learned to work the system. He grew up a Pistons fan watching Isiah Thomas and Bill Lambier win games. They had skill and power he'd never have. But the younger Ryan Chappelle couldn't help but notice that the team owners were short, round, balding men. Most of them probably couldn't even bounce a basketball, but they *owned* the game. Chappelle needed no clearer lesson than this. While most of CTU's staff had come up through the military, Ryan Chappelle had gone to business school before joining the CIA. Unlike many of his colleagues, he'd never seen action in the military. Still, there was a place for the Ryan Chappelles of the world in every branch of government. He had a reputation for making the trains run on time, a service he knew to be far more valuable than the heavy lifting done by the action junkies he called the fence jumpers and door thumpers.

It was, of course, these same fence jumpers and door thumpers who usually caused the problems Ryan Chappelle had to fix, and this was why the terrierlike District Director appeared at Kelly Sharpton's door at 8:34 sporting a look that would have curdled milk.

"What the hell is Jack Bauer doing?" Chappelle demanded. This was his hello.

Kelly sat up straighter in his chair. He'd been staring at his blank computer screen, as though by will alone he could conjure up the words that had long since vanished.

"You heard?"

"Of course I heard!" Chappelle fumed. "You think I'm not going to hear about it when my agents requisition local law enforcement without authorization, raid private property without a search warrant—"

"Actually, he got an arrest warrant—"

"—and get into firefights in Beverly Hills?" the Director said, steamrolling over Kelly's comment. "I thought we sent this guy to Siberia. No wait, if we'd done that we'd be at war with Russia!" Chappelle's words and anger had carried him into the office, where he now passed like a small tiger in an even smaller cage. "Where the hell is Walsh?"

"Washington D.C.," Kelly said. "Testifying."

"Testifying? Oh, the NAP Act. God, I wish they'd just pass that thing and move on." Chappelle didn't bother to notice Kelly roll his eyes. The District Director continued. "Anyway, I want you to tell Bauer that he's going in front of the review board the minute he gets in—before he even changes his damned shirt but after I tear him a new asshole." Kelly, whose own anger at Bauer had diffused over the last hour, felt obligated to fill in for Jack's mentor Richard Walsh, in defending him. "He did get the guy. We've got Marks in the building. And you heard about the terrorist lead?"

"I don't care if he got Elvis—" Chappelle pulled up short enough to choke on his own words. "Terrorist lead? What lead?"

Kelly tapped his screen and the display lit up with CTU's internal report on Ramin Rafizadeh. "It's not all clear yet, but basically the Greater Nation had a lead on a terrorist squad on U.S. soil. They were going after it themselves. Jack discovered it, and it led right back to this guy, Ramin Rafizadeh. Jack was after him for a while until we heard that he was dead."

Chappelle smiled. "Right, we busted Bauer for that case."

Kelly nodded. "Well, get this. It turns out Jack was right. The Rafizadeh father did know where his son was and the son was—is—alive. Jack just rescued Ramin from the Greater Nation and he's going for the father now." Sharpton checked the chronometer on his computer. "Should be there already."

Chappelle rubbed his hand across his balding head. He never liked any statement that included the sentence "It turns out Jack was right." He sighed. "All right, when Bauer checks in give him to me. We have this Marks guy?"

"Holding room two."

"How'd he get hold of intel on terrorists in the U.S.?"

Kelly had been wondering that himself. "We don't know. But these guys are pretty well-financed. Most of them are rednecks, but their upper ranks are filled with a lot, and I mean a lot, of ex-military officers, Special Forces, like that. They have money and they're passionate about their cause."

"Yeah, well I'm passionate about my cause and I *don't* have money so I'm also very irritable," Chappelle said. "So let's make sure they pay. Add obstruction of justice to the charges. This guy should have reported the terrorists to us."

Chappelle started to walk away. Kelly chewed the inside of his cheek before saying, "Yeah, well, that's an issue . . ."

Chappelle said over his shoulder, "What, there's no space left on the booking sheet?"

"No," Kelly said, "I think he did report them to us."

Chappelle's shoes squeaked on the tiled floor and stopped. He turned around. "What do you mean?"

"Marks told Jack that he had passed on his tip. We can't find any record of it anywhere."

"So, he's lying," Chappelle said. "Bad guys lie."

"Except . . ." Kelly hesitated. He realized there was no way for him to describe what he'd seen on the Attorney General's computer without exposing himself.

"Except what?" Chappelle said.

"I may have a little information that suggests the Attorney General knew about the tip but didn't pass it on. And I also got a clue that the AG's office may have their own man inside Greater Nation."

Chappelle stepped back toward Sharpton. He

didn't like surprises. He didn't like them on his birthday, he didn't like them disguised as suitcases in train stations, and he especially didn't like them coming from his own staff. "What sort of 'little information'? Who gave you the clue?"

Kelly looked right into Chappelle's small eyes. "I can't tell you. It's a personal source," he lied.

"Proof?"

Kelly watched in his mind's eye as the data were destroyed by his virus. "No, it's gone. But I saw it with my own eyes. The Attorney General knew about the terrorists but didn't pass it on. And he had his own mole inside Greater Nation and no one ever mentioned it to us, even though we had our own man in there six months."

"No proof, no case," Chappelle declared, waving the issue off. "Especially when you're talking about the AG. Besides, Bauer got one bad guy. That sounds like plenty for one day."

Chappelle turned his back on the issue.

8:35 A.M. PST
Westin St. Francis Hotel, San Francisco

James Quincy bit into the last bit of cantaloupe on his room service breakfast, wiped his hands on the white napkin, and picked up the phone. He relished this call, and had decided to wait until after breakfast to make it. This act of vengeance would make the perfect dessert.

"Zelzer," he said. "Make the calls. *Washington Times*, *Wall Street Journal*, the *Nation*. Add the *Wash-*

ington Post and the *New York Times* as well. She's a hero over there, and I want them to choke on their own rags. Right, do it now. I'm sending the pictures."

Quincy hung up. He fired up his laptop and connected remotely. The laptop contained encryption software, and there were five or six hoops to jump through to reach his own desktop via the remote software, but eventually he arrived at his own terminal's log in. He typed his name and the password "winstonsmith" and waited. After a moment, his desktop booted up. At least the screen said his desktop had booted up. But there was nothing on it. He clicked on the icon for his hard drive and saw all his applications, and none of his files. None of them.

"Son of a bitch," Quincy muttered. He didn't know how his files had been deleted. But although he did not know how, he was sure he knew who. He had had no idea Debrah Drexler could be so formidable.

He picked up the phone again. "Zelzer, I need you to get someone from IT security over to my office. Someone's been tampering with my computer. I want to know who and I want to know now!"

8:37 A.M. PST
Culver City

Black and white patrol cars filled the street, their red and blue top lights spreading color over the scene. Uniforms were searching backyards and bushes, but Jack knew they wouldn't find anything. Newhouse was good. He was much better than a weekend warrior deserved to be.

Jack watched LAPD tape off the area, adding bright yellow ribbon to the rainbow. He ducked under it and went into the house. The body of the big blond militia man lay where it had fallen. The second Greater Nation goon, the one who'd held Rafizadeh, also lay where he'd died. Lzolski was pouting by the door, furious at having been caught. Paulson and Nina were arguing over whose shot had put the second militia man down.

"That was my head shot," Paulson said, raising his empty hands and aiming his fingers like a gun.

Nina rolled her eyes. "Get over yourself. You missed. That was my shot."

"Whoever shot him ought to be hanged," Jack said. "That guy was our lead. These militia nuts are after the same thing we are—terrorists—but they're always one step ahead of us."

Jack went into the living room. Professor Ibrahim Rafizadeh was sitting on the couch flanked by two paramedics. They were checking his vitals and giving him oxygen. Two more paramedics were pulling a stretcher into the house. Even through the oxygen mask, Jack saw that the professor's face was covered with bruises and blisters, the same kind of blisters that Ramin would have by now. The Greater Nation had tortured the old man.

Rafizadeh lifted his eyes to meet Jack's. Just as Nazila had felt compassion for Jack, Jack now empathized with her father. The old man had withstood intense interrogation from Jack himself not six months ago, and he hadn't cracked. This morning he'd been brutalized and broken down. He'd handed the torturers his own son. And then he'd been saved by the man who had apparently ruined his life.

"Ramin is safe," Jack said.

Rafizadeh nodded. He pulled the mask away from his face momentarily. "He is not a—"

"I talked to your daughter," Jack said. "She's pretty convincing." He smiled. He didn't see the need to tell the professor that he'd allowed Ramin to be tortured. "He's at CTU, but I've told them to use kid gloves. They'll just want background." Jack paused. "He did know something, you know. He heard a rumor about a terrorist cell here."

Rafizadeh shook his head. This time he didn't bother to lift the mask, so his voice was hollow and distant. "There are always rumors. Someone knows someone who knows someone whose cousin was in the madrassa, whose friend was killed by American bombs, and he mentioned . . ." The professor trailed off, rolling his hand over and over to indicate the unending pattern of gossip. "We are victims of a rumor."

"A rumor is just a premature fact," Jack said.

"No," Rafizadeh replied in scholarly tones. "No, that is not true. Rumor is a weapon."

Jack had no reply. The paramedics bustled around the professor for a moment, then asked him to lie on the stretcher. Once he was comfortable, Rafizadeh looked up at Jack. "These men. Did they get our names from you?"

"No," Jack said earnestly. "We don't know where they got them. We arrested their people for a different reason. It was coincidence that we found your name. It all happened early this morning. We learned that they thought you were terrorists and were coming to get you, so I came to . . . help."

Rafizadeh chuckled. "God is great. But he has a wry sense of humor."

8:42 A.M. PST
Department of Justice, Washington, D.C.

Brian Zelzer loved his job with a youthfulness that was out of place for a man approaching fifty. Pear-shaped with thin arms and thinner hair, he still bounced around the halls of the DOJ like a teenager. He couldn't help it. If someone had told him that a scrawny kid from Atlanta could bluff his way through UNC-Charlotte, learn to write succinct bullshit for a PR firm ("It doesn't have to be accurate, it has to be succinct," his bosses told him long ago), then grab the coattails of a few career politicians he'd met at Bible study once he'd gone on the wagon and end up in Washington, D.C., he'd have laughed. But here he was, the Department of Justice's interagency liaison, working a few doors down from the Attorney General himself. Of course, to Brian he wasn't the Attorney General, he was just Jim, with whom he'd commiserated for nearly twenty years. Brian had found that sobriety—he'd been sober since 1989—gave him nearly unlimited energy, especially when it came to griping about the sorry state of affairs in the country. He and Jim had griped about the secularization of the country and activist judges who added bricks and mortar to the imaginary wall between church and state, until one day Jim, who'd made a name for himself as a Kansas prosecutor, had offered Brian a chance to help do something about it. Next thing he knew he'd stopped writing press releases and started campaigning for Barnes, and now here he was.

He even liked dealing with the maze of interrelated agencies that made up the Justice Department and law enforcement and intelligence community. His official title was Deputy Assistant Director of Interagency Communications for the Office of Intergovernmental and Public Liaison, but privately he gave himself the same informal title he'd used as a PR man: shitslinger. His job was to manage the message that went out from the DOJ to the internal law enforcement community (FBI, ATF, etc.) and the external intelligence community (CIA, Department of Defense, blah, blah), and he found it exciting to ride herd on the rumors and innuendos that constantly threatened to trample his boss's agenda.

So when the phone rang, he picked it up with his usual aplomb. "Zelzer!" he said.

"Brian Zelzer, this is Special Agent Kelly Sharpton, CTU Los Angeles."

Brian frowned, not unhappily. CTU. Counter Terrorist Unit. Sometimes it took a minute to navigate the government's habit of creating trinomial acronyms (FBI, CIA, DOD, ATF, DOD, etc.). "Yes, Agent Sharpton, what can I do for you?"

"Listen, I'm hoping you can help me with something. We have a case on our end, a domestic terrorism case. A militia group that was planning some domestic terrorism. We took care of that, but during a raid we discovered that they had some information on Islamic terrorists on U.S. soil. They said they reported it to the FBI and to you guys."

Zelzer said with automatic brightness, "Sure, you might want to try the FBI's domestic terrorism unit. I can give you Cindy Fromme's—"

"I tried them. They say they never heard anything. I was thinking you guys had heard something."

"Oh, no problem, then let me connect you to our investigations dep—"

"I tried them, too. They didn't have anything, and when I kind of pushed it, they sent me to you."

"I see. Well. How can I help?"

"To be honest," said the Special Agent, "I have some reason to believe that this militia group did turn in a tip on Islamic terrorists. The militia group is called the Greater Nation. You may have heard of them, they've made a lot of noise lately. I've been told the tip went right to the top over there, and I'm trying to track it down."

"Told by whom?" Brian asked. The brightness in his voice had lost a bit of wattage.

"I can't say," the CTU agent said evasively. "Look, I'm not accusing anyone of anything. I'm just trying to track down a lead."

"I wish I could help you, Special Agent, but we don't know anything."

"I see. Well, thank you."

Brian Zelzer hung up. The minute the line went dead, he hit his speed dial. It was answered immediately. "Jim, it's Brian. I think I might know who broke into your computer . . ."

8:45 A.M. PST
CTU Headquarters, Los Angeles

The miracle of the modern age was the instantaneous transfer of information. A reporter speaks into a microphone in Kabul, Afghanistan, and her voice comes out of a television in Boise, Idaho. A man presses his thumbprint into a scanner at London's Heathrow Airport, and his name appears on a computer screen in

New York. And when a CTU agent makes a phone call from Los Angeles to Washington, D.C., he finds his own telephone ringing a few minutes later.

"Sharpton," he said.

"Special Agent Sharpton," said the caller. "This is Attorney General James Quincy."

Uh-oh, Kelly thought. He felt fear and anger churn together in his stomach. This man had just tried to blackmail the woman he'd loved for years. He was also one of the most powerful men in the country, and Kelly had just hacked his computer. "Yes, Mr. Attorney General?"

"I understand you were making inquiries regarding the Greater Nation. Something about a tip."

"Um, yes. Yes, sir," Kelly found himself totally unprepared for the AG's directness. Did he know that Kelly had tampered with his evidence? "I . . . I'm following a lead. According to some of our sources, the Greater Nation had information on a terrorist cell in the U.S. We were hoping you—your office had more information. Also, again according to our sources, we had information that you might . . . that your office might actually have assets inside the Greater Nation—"

"Assets," the AG said calmly. "You mean spies."

"Yes, sir."

"How did you come by this information?"

Kelly said, "I'd rather not say."

"Hmm. I'm not sure I can help you here, Agent Sharpton. I'm aware of the Greater Nation, of course. We incarcerated some of their people when I was a prosecutor in Kansas. But I wouldn't count on any tips from them. In my experience, they're a bunch of far-right zealots. They're certainly capable of doing damage to themselves and others, but I hardly think they know more about terrorism than CTU does."

"That's true, sir," Kelly said, "but it's our job to follow up on any leads—"

"Yes, it is. And if you did your jobs, this probably wouldn't be an issue," the AG said sharply.

"Excuse me, sir?" Kelly felt his neck heat up.

"I'm not attacking you, Agent Sharpton. I just think CTU, and many other agencies as well, could be more efficient. I'm working to give you the tools to make you more efficient. The NAP Act—"

"Yes, sir," Kelly said, sharpening the edge in his own voice. "Well, perhaps you should save the sales pitch for the Senators."

The phone line was deadly quiet for a moment. "What did you just—?"

"I'm not attacking you," Kelly said with just a hint of sarcasm. "I just think the DOJ, and many other agencies as well, could be more cooperative. I'm not sure we need less personal privacy. I think we need less interagency privacy. For instance, if you could tell me about Frank Newhouse . . ." He let the name hang in the air. A pause followed the name, but Kelly could not interpret it over the phone.

"You are insubordinate," James Quincy said. "I did you the favor of returning your inquiry personally, and you—you'll be hearing from me again." He hung up.

Kelly slumped back in his chair, filled with bewildered dread, like a healthy man who's just been told he has a month to live. It didn't make sense. Why would the Attorney General call him directly? Was the Greater Nation that important? Was Frank Newhouse? Or maybe it had nothing to do with the militia and the terrorists. Maybe the AG knew that Kelly had hacked his computer and helped Debbie. It wasn't impossible—phone taps, computer taps, and a dozen other surveillance devices allowed even the most secret information to leak out instantaneously, given the right conditions. Kelly put his head in his hands. Whatever had happened, one thing was sure: he had just bought himself a lot more trouble than he'd bargained for.

Jessi Bandison watched Kelly from her desk in the pit. Her gravedigger shift was long over, but the more ambitious analysts often stayed behind for overtime or for advancement. The security team noticed that she hadn't logged out or left the building, but once they confirmed she was all right, no one gave her any more notice.

She could still feel the heat that had risen into her cheeks. The flush of embarrassment she'd felt in asking him to coffee had turned instantly to anger. Why had he spoken to her like that? He'd flirted with her almost as much as she'd flirted with him. The way he stood so close to her when they worked a program together, the way his face lit up when he smelled that jasmine on her skin. He was more obvious than she was. He had no right to snap at her like that.

George Mason walked past her terminal. He was the Assistant Administrative Director of CTU. "Bandison, are you still on?"

"Oh," she said, halting her internal diatribe. "Oh, no, not technically."

Mason looked disappointed. "We need help running a simulated attack on the network. It's a slow day, so we're doing diagnostics and security checks. I knew you liked to hack, so I figured you might want to give us a run for our money."

Jessi shook her head. "If it's optional, I'd rather opt out, if that's okay. It was a long night and I've already done one test hack."

"Really, for them?"

"No. I did one for Kelly."

Mason shrugged. "I didn't know we were running anything else. It wasn't scheduled." Mason blew by her, forgetting his own comment as soon as he'd said it.

But Jessi didn't. "It wasn't scheduled," he'd said. Kelly was a top analyst, but he wasn't the administrative director. Why would he know about a fire drill when Mason didn't? Jessi bit her lip. What had she done? What had *he* done? She looked around the room, wondering what to do. Her eyes settled on District Director Ryan Chappelle.

She walked up to him. "Excuse me, Mr. Chappelle?"

"Yes?" he said in his normal voice, which was as sharp as shattered glass. Jessi almost retreated from it. She hesitated, which only seemed to annoy him further, so she finally said, "Can I—can I speak with you for a minute?"

•••

THE FOLLOWING TAKES PLACE
BETWEEN THE HOURS OF
9 A.M. AND 10 A.M.
PACIFIC STANDARD TIME

•••

9:00 A.M. PST
CTU Headquarters, Los Angeles

Jack Bauer pulled his SUV into the CTU parking lot
and yawned. The drive from Culver City had meant
downtime, which was the worst thing for him at the
moment. Lacking the adrenaline dump, he now felt
tired, dirty, and hungry. He was still wearing his
BDUs and equipment from the Greater Nation raid,
gear that had already served him through three gun
battles that morning.

He didn't care. He was right. He had been right all
along. There was a terrorist cell in the U.S. Rafizadeh
had known his son was alive. Jack could have been
furious and he probably would be furious in an hour

or two, but right now he was riding the wave of euphoria that accompanied vindication. His exile among the rednecks had been unjust. He had been right.

Jack passed through the CTU checkpoint with a swipe of his badge and a wave of his hand to the guards, and walked into the main room. He looked around for Richard Walsh before recalling that his friend and mentor was in D.C. Tony Almeida gave him a nod but didn't say much. Jack had a grudging respect for Almeida, but he wasn't sure it was reciprocated, and that nod was about as far along as their relationship had progressed. One of the analysts threw him a small wave.

"Another day at the office." He sighed.

He didn't have an office—that privilege was reserved for the Special Agent in Charge, who oversaw field work, and the administrative agent who oversaw the analysts and tech work. Jack went straight to the locker room and secured his weapons. He wished he had time to shower, but the best he could do was strip down, splash water on his face and chest, and towel off. He changed into black chinos, soft-soled black shoes, and a blue button-down shirt. He wrapped himself into his shoulder rig, removed his SigSauer from the thigh holster in his locker, and snapped it into place. He reviewed the result in the mirror.

"From Delta commando to peace officer in three easy steps," he murmured to his reflection.

He slapped his face a couple of times to wake up. He'd have to talk to Brett Marks sometime soon, and he needed to be fresh.

By the bottom of the hour he was walking out of the locker room toward his workstation. An urgent message alert was flashing on his screen. He opened it and saw a note from Kelly Sharpton to see him immediately. Jack, halfway to getting his butt into his chair, hauled himself back up and marched up the stairs. Sharpton had seen him and was waiting. He looked anxious.

Jack entered and closed the door behind him. "Look, if it's about this morning, I really do apologize, but you know as well as I do that sometimes this job is about taking initiative—"

"Forget that," Kelly said abruptly. "Have you worked on Marks yet?"

"No, I was about to—"

"Good. I have some news for you." Jack was surprised, but pleased. He'd expected to be dressed down, or at least given a warning. The last thing he expected was cooperation. Still, Sharpton had surprised him. He quoted the rule book like a Ryan Chappelle clone, but he demonstrated the competence of men Jack thought of as, well, like himself.

"The DOJ knew about the Greater Nation's tip on terrorists," Kelly said, forging ahead. "The Attorney General himself knew. But the tip was erased from everyone else's system, if it was ever there. The Attorney General knew, but didn't act on it."

Jack waited for more. "But that's nothing. The Greater Nation are paranoid schizophrenics. I wouldn't believe half the things they say, either."

"Would you believe the Attorney General's office had a man inside the Greater Nation at the same time you were there? His name is Frank Newhouse."

Jack froze, the habit of a stealth fighter assessing danger. Questions tumbled like an avalanche into his head, and he sifted them for the most pertinent ones.

"Why would the DOJ put its own man into something like that? Do they even have people of their own?"

Kelly laughed. "Well, they have the FBI, the DEA, the ATF, and the U.S. Marshalls Special Operations Group, but otherwise, they're pretty hard up."

"Yeah, no, but why would they send someone in there without telling us. Isn't there supposed to be some kind of new information sharing happening?"

"That's what I read in the papers," Kelly said humorlessly. "But they treat us like mushrooms—keep us in the dark and feed us shit. I can't even find a file on Frank Newhouse anywhere. Did you ever meet this guy while you were undercover?"

"Once or twice," Jack said dryly. "You should ask Lzolski what she thinks of him." Jack quickly summarized his two interactions with Frank Newhouse. The man certainly had training and skill. But he'd also put other people's lives at risk both times. "If he's undercover, he's really convincing. Are you sure he's a Fed?"

Kelly nodded.

"Thanks," Jack said. "I can use that."

As Jack left, Kelly picked up his phone and dialed. An hour ago he swore he'd never dial that number again. Of course, he'd made that same promise five or ten times over the last few years, and broken it every time.

"Drexler."

"Hey, Deb. Take off your business voice."

"Kelly!" Her voice sounded much lighter than it had two hours ago. "You sounded mad before."

"Yeah, well I was. I am. I think I'm up to my ears in this thing now. But if I'm in, I'm going to be in all the way, so now I need a favor from you."

She laughed. People rarely saw her laugh on television, which was a shame because her laugh was lively, like a fountain. "That's the Kelly Sharpton I know. What do you need?"

"I need you to get information on someone who works undercover for the AG. The name is Frank Newhouse. I'm guessing he works for the FBI, but with all the government overlaps right now, he could be working for anyone."

The laughter died away. "You can't be serious. You're with CTU! You can get anything on anyone."

"Not till the NAP Act passes," he said with a snort. "Seriously, I have nothing on this guy. I'm guessing he's got a closed file somewhere, he might even do overseas work for State. You're on the Senate Permanent Intelligence Committee. I'm guessing you know people."

"Kelly," she said. "That's illegal. It could be treason."

She regretted saying it as soon as the words left her mouth. "Don't start that!" he snapped. He realized that he was eager to be angry with her. "What the hell do you think I just did for you!"

"I'm sorry. I'm sorry. You're right," she said, backing down immediately. "It's just, that was for a righteous cause—"

"It was to save your skin, so don't bullshit me," he said. "We've never been that way with each other, Deb. This cause is just as worthy, if you need to dress it up to make yourself feel better. We've got Islamic terrorists and domestic terrorism and secret agents. It'll look great against the backdrop of the flag, if you're into that. Me, I just want to make sure no one dies, or at least that the right people die. I just need to know who this guy is and I need to know today." He hung up the phone.

This day cannot get any worse, he thought.

His door opened and Ryan Chappelle strode in, with two burly security agents behind him. "Special Agent Sharpton, you are under arrest."

9:38 A.M. PST
CTU Headquarters, Los Angeles, Holding Room 2

Name:	Marks, Brett J.
DOB:	11 November 1951
Birthplace:	Lansing, Michigan
Gender	M
Education:	Champlain Elementary School
	West Point Academy, 73
	Wharton School of Business, '90
Military:	U.S. Army
	Ranger School
	USASOC, 75th Ranger Regiment
Tours of Duty:	Grenada, Panama, Haiti, Somalia, Iraq

There was more of Marks's dossier, a lot more. Two Purple Hearts and a Bronze Star, pysch evaluations that described him as a natural leader, "Blah, blah, blah," Jack murmured.

"The thing is," Brett Marks said from across the metal table, "I'm right here, you could just ask me."

Jack looked up from the dossier. Marks looked none the worse for wear after his rough treatment (prescribed by Jack) and a few hours in solitude. His hair was too high and tight to get messy, and his eyes were as bright as they'd been at three o'clock in the morning. He sat upright in his straight-backed, unpadded chair, with his wrists cuffed together and the cuffs chained to the table frame.

"I know, but this is so well-written," Jack said. He didn't show it, but he was happy. He'd wanted Marks to speak first, and somewhat to Jack's surprise, he had.

"Doesn't it worry you," Marks said, pointing at the dossier with one handcuffed hand, "that your government spies on its citizens."

Jack put down the dossier and leaned back in his chair, clasping his hands behind his head. He shrugged. "We only spy on the ones who collect big guns and try to hijack sodium cyanide. Call us crazy, but we worry that people who go to the trouble of stealing huge quantities of poison might be tempted to use it afterward."

Marks nodded. He managed to look both guilty and set upon at the same time, his shoulders slumped with the burden of responsibility. "Some of my people may have gotten overzealous. It's true. But Jack, the government you serve is illegal. They're not allowed to do most of the things they do these days. This place we're in, Counter Terrorist Unit, is it part of the Federal government? Is it FBI, CIA, what?" Jack didn't answer. "See, it's unconstitutional for the federal government to have secret organizations that spy on its own citizens. That's what people fought and died for in 1776. People today forget that."

"So now you're George Washington?"

"We make a big deal out of the President of the United States," Marks said. "Look at the guy in the White House now. There's all this talk about the NAP Act, which side he'll take. Maybe he'll veto it, maybe he won't. Meanwhile, the majority of the people are against it! The media talk like it's government's decision. But it's not. It's ours. We have the ultimate power to veto anything the Federal government says or does. That's why the Founding Fathers designed the government the way it did. They didn't want a repeat of the government forced on them by the British."

Marks paused. "Take you for instance." Marks leaned forward, resting his chin on his overlapping hands. "Forgot whatever story you told us to get into Greater Nation. You're military, right? Or at least ex-military."

Jack didn't answer. Interrogators don't answer questions unless it suits their purpose. Marks, however, didn't seem to need an answer. "Right, I knew it. Probably ex-military. Moved right from some special unit right into a Federal agency, correct? So they take you out of a uniform to avoid the *posse commitatus* law, but they sic you on American citizens anyway. They figure that's enough to avoid any illegalities. But it's not. Have you ever read the United States Code? I have. I know what section 242 states. You should know, too."

This was what differentiated Marks from all the other domestic wackos. He wasn't a beer-swilling redneck in jackboots and suspenders, nor was he a wild-haired, polygamist pseudo-messiah. With his Boss suits and his easy recitation of constitutional law, Marks resembled nothing more than an evangelist whose message was freedom from the tyranny of the Federal government. When he spoke of *posse commitatus*, he referred to the law forbidding the United States military from engaging in police actions on United States soil. The law itself was an echo down the years of the Founding Fathers' abhorrence of redcoats marching through the streets of colonial America.

Marks demanded, and got, eye contact with his captor. "It was illegal for them to send you to spy on us."

Undaunted, Jack laughed. "If you think that was illegal, wait until you hear this." He leaned forward, bringing his face close to Marks's. Marks reminded him of his friend Walsh, but without the mustache. Jack said in a low voice, "Your friend Frank Newhouse was an undercover agent for the DOJ."

Marks's face executed a serious of pirouettes worthy of a prima ballerina. His eyes lifted, then collapsed into confusion. He smiled in disbelief, then frowned as he considered the possibility. Finally his face settled into neutral territory. "Impossible."

Jack felt immensely satisfied that he had cracked Marks's shell. "Not for a government like ours," he countered.

Marks studied Jack, his eyes roaming across the landscape of his face, the position of his hands and shoulders, the pace of his breathing. The militia leader appeared totally unselfconscious about his own staring, oblivious when Jack returned his gaze with a fierce glare. When his scan reached down to the tabletop, Marks's gaze ascended, restudying Jack's body until his eyes found Jack's. Nearly a minute of silence had passed.

"You're not lying," Marks decided. "You believe it's true."

"I know it's true," Jack said.

Brett's eyes widened. *That's the first time I've seen him actually surprised*, Jack thought. *That's the first chink in his armor*. Everything would flow from that moment. Interrogating prisoners was like chipping mortar off a wall. As a whole, the mortar is cohesive and strong, but once the mason breaks off that first piece, the whole section falls apart.

Sure enough, Marks's eyes fell to the floor, and when he looked up, he had something to say. But Jack was not prepared for it. "Then he's already reported everything we know to you guys. Are you going to stop the terrorists?"

Jack rolled his eyes. "Jesus Christ, the only terrorists here are you! Don't you get it? All Ramin knew was a rumor, the same kind of crap we get off the Internet every day. There is no terrorist cell." He shook his head. "You militia nuts need to leave investigations to the investigators."

Marks scratched his nose and sat back. "I guess you're right. Because you must know all about the safe house."

"Oh, yeah, we got your safe house."

"Not my safe. The terrorist one."

Jack felt a curve slide by him. "Explain."

"Safe house. Frank Newhouse must have told you if he's one of you guys. Right?"

Jack sat forward so fast his chair slid back from the table. "Pretend I don't know anything about this safe house. Tell me."

Marks tried to scratch his chin, but the chain wouldn't let him. He laughed at it. "You know, I think you're right about the terrorist sleeper cell. It's probably all a set up. Of course." Marks's eyes glazed over, and Jack could almost see the wheels spinning behind his eyes. "It's actually easy to do. The government creates the need; the people feel the need; the government sneaks in what it wants. Of course. You might as well forget about it."

"You can start making sense any time now," Jack growled.

The militia leader's eyes refocused on Jack. "You probably don't have to worry about it, Jack. The government was probably just setting us up. You're saying that this Iranian kid was a fake lead, so the hints we got of a terrorist hit this week are probably fake, too. Danger disguised inside a gift. The government sets up a fake terrorist cell to cause fear. Then they offer the gift of new legislation that's meant to save everyone. But hidden inside the gift is the very thing the people fear—the loss of their freedom."

Rising to his feet, Jack shook his head. "Why is it always a conspiracy theory with you people?"

Brett's answer was simple. "Because the government is conspiring against us."

"Tell me about the safe house. Tell me about the terrorist hit."

"Ask Newhouse."

"I'm asking you!"

The leader of the Greater Nation shrugged. "It's nothing to me, either way. This is where we found some of our information. It's where we got Rafizadeh's name. It also looked to us like they were planning a big hit soon. It's an apartment over near Exposition. You can check it out for y—"

Jack was already out the door.

....

THE FOLLOWING TAKES PLACE
BETWEEN THE HOURS OF
10 A.M. AND 11 A.M.
PACIFIC STANDARD TIME

....

10 A.M. PST
Senator Drexler's Office, San Francisco

Debrah Drexler spent twenty minutes on the phone in her office, canvassing her colleagues.

"I'm on the red-eye tonight," she said to Alan Wayans, the Senator from Illinois. "I'll be there in time for the vote. You're still on board, right?"

Alan Wayans had cultivated his public image as a stalwart standard-bearer of the moderate left, an image he owed far more to his handlers than to himself. Those who fought beside him in the political trenches knew him as a second-guesser and doubter whose private nickname was "Other Way Wayans." He wasn't spineless, but his backbone was frail enough that he often had to be propped up. Wayans, just shy of fifty, also had a weakness for strong-willed women, a fact that Debrah had discovered early and used often.

"Sure I am," Wayans replied in a flat, Northern Plains drawl. "You wouldn't believe the pressure, though."

Wouldn't I? Debrah thought.

"I had Latt from Tennessee drop hints that if I switched votes, they'd allow that rider into the appropriations bill for me."

"Don't go for it, Way," she said. "This thing's too important. And it'll all be over in twenty-four hours. Just hang tight. I'll see you tomorrow."

She hung up and checked the time. After one o'clock East Coast time now. She could make the call. She hesitated, her hand hovering over the phone on her desk. There was no turning back from the call she was about to make, and it frightened her. Debrah had defied riot police, locked arm in arm with other globalization protesters in Davos and Italy. She'd faced the bright lights of the media and the displeasure of opposing administrations in voting against war in other countries. But this . . . this was more dangerous than anything she'd done before. The morality of her goals could not mask the fact that what she was about to do was illegal.

She snatched the phone up and dialed before she could reconsider. It rang twice before her contact answered. "Gonzales," said a firm female voice, not unlike her own.

"Sela, it's Senator Drexler," Debrah said.

"Yes, Senator."

In a small cubicle in an office in Langley, Virginia,

Sela Gonzales's heart thumped. Drexler never called her for small talk. But she kept her voice impersonal and professional.

"I need information on someone. The name is Frank Newhouse. I'm not sure who he works for. All I am sure of is that he's doing something for the DOJ right now. Can you get me his file?"

Sela hesitated. She spoke in business tones, using everyday phrases, for the sake of anyone who might wander by her cubicle. "I'm not sure I can help you with that request, ma'am. We've had a . . . change in policy lately."

Debrah understood her to mean that there was an increase in security. The Barnes Administration was notoriously tight-lipped. Technically, the intelligence agencies worked for the entire government, not just the executive branch, but Barnes and his people considered all parts of government as theirs. They disliked prying eyes, and rejected congressional requests for information on everything from environmental impact reports to judicial nominees.

"This is important," Debrah said. "Very important."

"I suggest you try going through other channels," Sela said cautiously.

"I can't," Debrah said. "I have a contact at CTU that can't get the information. But it's life or death."

"I . . ." Sela abandoned her professional tone and lowered her voice. "If it's information like that, then I may not be able to help. And if I can find something, I can't copy it, I guarantee."

"Can I have someone meet you?"

Sela hesitated. Sela Gonzales had no illusions about herself. She had never imagined when she joined the CIA that she would become a national hero, or save the world, or even help overthrow evil dictators by traveling on camelback across arid deserts to support freedom fighters. She did not even pretend to know who was right and who was wrong in the endless internecine wars inside and outside the intelligence community. The issues were too enormous for her brain, and the political stakes were so high over her head that she did not even pretend to comprehend them. In an effort to find some solid ground in the whirls and eddies of politics, she had grasped one solid rock of understanding: the elected officials have a right to know. Beyond that, she made no claims, and she was perfectly willing to hide behind her credo and let those same politicians hang in the wind if need be. She was no martyr. But she would sing that credo to herself like a mantra: the elected officials have a right to know.

"Yes," she said at last. "Zachary Taylor Park in half an hour. Tell them to meet me by the stream."

10:08 A.M. PST
Westwood, California

He had been Frank Newhouse for so long that when he thought of himself (when he thought of himself at all), he used that name. But the truth was, when he looked in the mirror, as he did at that moment, he did not think of himself at all. He thought of the mission and his ability to accomplish it. He thought of the steps between where he was and where he planned to be. And he only felt satisfaction when those steps were clearly laid out before him. It didn't matter if they were difficult steps—he was no stranger to difficult missions. He cared only that the steps were clear, that the goal was quantifiable.

Frank Newhouse hated abstracts. Though not especially well-educated, he understood enough about art to recognize Impressionism, Cubism, and Surrealism, and to know that he despised them. He looked at his reflection and did not see squares, circles, triangles. He saw pale eyes and arched eyebrows under a protruding forehead and black hair short enough to spike out of his skull. He observed a face that no woman had loved and few had tolerated. He saw experience etched definitely into his skin with lines more accurate than memory could ever be. His eyes traced a thin scar along the ridge of his left eyebrow, a record of mortar fire more concise than any CNN report. He did not begrudge a single line or scar. They were real, they were honest. He had passed through the great museums of the world unmoved, but would pause appreciatively at any photograph of war and death. There was no pretense in pictures like these. They were real.

This mission was becoming real, at last. Frank was tired of the subterfuge. He tolerated it without complaint, of course, because it was necessary for the completion of the mission. But he was relieved now that the clandestine part of his task was near its end. No more pretending to serve a false master.

Frank's mobile phone rang. "What?" he answered. Only two people had this number: his superior and his contact. His superior, he knew, was otherwise occupied at the moment. His contact didn't rate much courtesy.

He listened to the voice on the other end, telling him what he wanted to hear. The plans they had carefully laid during the last six months were falling into place. But his contact ended with a warning: "Just be careful. CTU is getting warmer. They don't realize it yet, but they might."

Newhouse shrugged. "We expect them to sniff around. It's part of the plan. If they get too close, they get too close, and we'll deal with them."

"You might want to ditch that apartment, though."

Newhouse considered. "Yes," he said, and hung up.

10:13 A.M. PST
Downtown Los Angeles

Jack Bauer double-parked the SUV on Exposition near the campus of the University of Southern California, and the address Marks had supplied after a little more prodding. It was a six-story beige structure with dark brown trim on the railings of the tiny, unusable balconies outside each front window. Four broad steps climbed up to the glass double doors and the rust-framed intercom that served as security. On the way over, Jack had Nina Myers call the building for him, talk to the manager, and get the pass code. He beeped the code into the panel. The door buzzed and he entered a hallway with dark brown carpet, stained by two decades' worth of parties hosted by USC college students indigenous to this region.

Jack ignored the elevator and entered the stairwell, a stone shaft rising up, criss-crossed with stone steps and metal rails. Jack climbed as quietly as he could in the echoing shaft, until he reached the fourth floor. He slipped out into a hallway that smelled of mildew and Lysol and hurried to apartment 409. The door, like all the others, was eggshell white and dirty. Jack knocked once. When no one answered, he pressed his ear to the door. Hearing nothing, he stepped back and kicked the door hard. It didn't give on the first try. Hurrying before anyone came to investigate, he stomped on the door again. The deadbolt held, but the wood frame did not, and the door flew inward.

Jack drew his gun and moved inside. He really didn't expect to find anything, since the Greater Nation had been there before, but he preferred to enter any room with a gun in his hand if he could.

He was in a one-bedroom apartment with a tiny kitchen on his left, a dining table beyond that, and a living room, bathroom, and bedroom ahead. There was nothing on the walls and minimal furniture, causing Jack to reach three conclusions in sequence as he moved down the hall. First, that the Greater Nation had stripped the place; but that wasn't true because there were a few items left. Second, that he was in a typical college dorm, where cinder blocks and plywood served as bookshelves; but that didn't feel right, because it was missing the posters and Ansel Adams or museum art reprints that were typical of college students. Third, that whoever lived here had no interest in creature comforts.

The living room was decorated only with a futon, a few bookshelves, and a desk that, by the telltale signs of stray wires and plugs, had been stripped of its computer. Jack glanced into the bedroom, where he found four sets of bunk beds crowded into one small room.

The bathroom was bare except for a thin sliver of

soap left in a bone-dry soap dish in the bathroom. Even the medicine cabinet was empty. Jack opened and closed it, then stared at the mirror as though he might see the remnants of some previous reflection.

Jack went back into the living room. The desk was bare, but he guessed that the occupants had used a laptop computer there—there was a data port in the wall and a generic mouse pad sitting on the desktop. The drawers were empty, as far as he could tell, but he would leave the real investigation to forensics.

He activated his cell phone and called in. "Get me Sharpton," he said to the operator.

"I'm sorry, Agent Bauer, he's unavailable," the receptionist replied.

"What do you mean unavailable? Get him out of the toilet and—"

"No, sir, he's . . . he's been put on disciplinary leave."

What the—? Jack wondered. What had happened in the last forty minutes? "Where'd he go? I need to reach him. Is he on cell phone?"

"N-no, sir, he hasn't left the building. He's still with Mr. Chappelle."

Jack's felt the hair on the back of his neck rise. On disciplinary leave but not left the building was longhand for "under arrest." Kelly Sharpton was in some kind of trouble.

"Okay, Nina Myers or Paulson," he said. He'd worry about Sharpton when he had time.

After a series of clicks, Nina Myers picked up. "Another party?"

"Same party, different host," Jack said. "I need a rundown on the tenants for this apartment. And I

need a forensics team over here right away. Also . . ."
He scanned the room, trying to think of anything else
he might need at the moment. His eyes skimmed
across the spines of the books, spines with writing
that flowed up and down like an elegant scribble. *Oh,
shit*, he thought. "And also, I need someone who can
read Farsi and Arabic."

10:20 A.M. PST
Westwood

The name on the lease was Richard Brighton, a perfectly normal-sounding name until CTU's computers
chewed it up and spit back exactly nothing. No
Richard Brighton registered at USC, no Richard
Brighton attached to the social security number written on the lease. Landlords were required to take
photocopies of driver's licenses. Nina had a copy
faxed to CTU.

"I've got a photo of him. If this guy's name is Richard
Brighton then I'm Jessica Simpson," Nina said.

"Can you run face recognition?" Jack asked.

"We will, but the photo's not good. It'll take a
while."

"Okay, get going, and tell the forensics guys to
hurry up. Hey, what's up with Kelly Sharpton?"

There was a pause as Nina swiveled away from her
phone, then swiveled back. "He's not in his office."

"I know. I heard he was in some trouble."

"I don't know anything about it. You want me to
check?"

"No, stay on this. Just curious."

Debrah dialed CTU Los Angeles to give Kelly an update on the information he wanted.

"Special Agent Sharpton, please," she said, calling from her private line.

"I'm sorry, he's unavailable," said the operator.

"He'll take my call. Tell him Dee from D.C.—"

"I'm sorry, ma'am, but Mr. Sharpton is unavailable for any kind of telephone call. He can't be interrupted right now."

Debrah paused. It could be anything, of course. Kelly worked in a counter terrorism unit, for chrissakes. He could have been called out on an investigation, or in a meeting with the Joint Chiefs of Staff, for all she knew. But she did know. She guessed with the inerring talent of politicians who sniff out danger that Kelly Sharpton was not in a meeting, not on an assignment. He was in trouble. She hung up.

Juwan Burke hated being an errand boy. Star running back for his high school football team, second string receiver and academic all-American at Alabama, commencement speaker for the political science department, he was used to carrying much heavier and more important loads. He couldn't complain out loud, though—partly because this was how the system worked but mostly because all of Senator Drexler's support staff had both seniority over him and resumes that equaled his. Drexler was one of the most popular up-and-comers in the party, and everyone with plans for advancement wanted to get there riding on her coattails. Burke knew he'd go farther making lunch runs for Drexler than he would writing policy for half the representatives in Congress.

This wasn't a lunch run, he knew, but what exactly it was, he didn't know. He'd just gotten a call from the Senator herself telling him to get to Zachary Taylor Park over in Arlington by one-thirty, where he'd be met by a dark-haired woman named Sela Gonzales. She'd been given his description and she would find him.

He pulled into the parking lot at the park right at the bottom of the hour. At one-thirty on a Wednesday afternoon it wasn't crowded, although he saw a mother pushing a stroller and a groundskeeper picking up trash.

Juwan had never been to this park and he didn't know where the stream was, but water always flowed downhill so he followed the slope of the grass toward a line of trees. He found a path readily enough. It led down to the water, a small stream flowing east and south toward D.C., reminding anyone who cared to notice that D.C. had once been a swamp. He'd barely reached the water when he noticed a woman hurrying toward him. She was small, wearing a dark blue business suit. Her hair was glossy, like black satin, and her face was aquiline. She was not pretty, but she was striking. This became more apparent the closer she got, especially when Juwan noticed her sharply hooked nose. Juwan just had time to admire her bright eyes, like burning black coals, before she threw herself at him and kissed him full on the lips.

It wasn't often that a strange woman threw herself into a man's arms, even for a former college football star like Juwan. He was understandably surprised, but he wrapped his arms around her automatically. When he finally remembered to return her kiss, though, he felt the lack of passion in it. The woman continued for a few seconds, then pulled away just enough to press her nose affectionately to his. But when she spoke, she was all business. "So if anyone's watching, we're lovers," she explained.

"Uh, okay," he said. "What else are we doing here?"

"I have documents in my jacket," she said. Then she laughed as though he'd said something charming. "You have to photocopy them and get them back to me in—" she lifted his hand to her lips and kissed it, checking her watch at the same time. "Twenty minutes. The file needs to be back in its place by two o'clock."

"Okay," he said.

"Here." She kissed him again, her hands groping his back, even probing inside his suit jacket and running her hands along his chest. Breaking off from the kiss, she smiled sincerely for the first time. "Nice build."

"I . . . played football," Juwan said lamely.

"Okay, find a copy place and be back here in twenty minutes."

"Where are the documents?" Juwan asked.

"It's in your coat already," she said, patting his chest again. Only then did Juwan feel the file folder pressed between his dress shirt and suit jacket. This woman was either a nutcase or a spy. Either way, Juwan decided, this was definitely not another lunch run.

"Nineteen minutes," she reminded, tapping her watch.

10:41 A.M. PST
Westwood

Jack stepped out onto the tiny, unserviceable balcony to get out of the forensics team's way. They were dusting down the entire apartment, pulling up as many fingerprint samples as possible. Jack assumed they'd find a lot of Greater Nation prints, since Marks had already admitted that his people had visited the apartment, but he hoped to find additional prints as well.

There was a second reason he'd stepped out onto the balcony. He didn't want anyone on the team to see his anxiety. The truth was, Jack's heart was pounding harder now than it had during the firefight this morning. He thought his ribs would crack under the constant barrage of his heart against his chest. He needed to find solid evidence here. He was tired of conjecture, and he sure as hell was tired of looking like a fool at CTU. First there were terrorists, then it was all a big mistake, then there were militia men who knew about the terrorists, then there were no terrorists again, but Jack has to rescue innocent Iranians from the militia. Then it turns out a dead man is actually alive, and he has heard a rumor about terrorists, and the militia men know about an apartment. It was enough to drive a man insane, except that Jack was just too damned stubborn to go insane.

And the truth was, he hadn't even begun to tackle the mystery of Frank Newhouse. Why the Attorney General's office would have an undercover agent inside a militia group baffled him, especially when CTU followed policy and informed other departments, including the FBI and Justice, of any investigations that involved domestic terrorism. Jack had no doubt whatsoever that the proper authorities had been informed, since it was Ryan Chappelle's job to pass on the information. Chappelle might be an ass and a bumbler when it came to field work, but he pushed paper with the best of them.

In Jack's mind, there was a more important question than why the AG had inserted his own people: why hadn't Newhouse identified himself? The jig was up the minute Jack had raided the Greater Nation compound. And there was certainly no reason to keep up pretenses at the Culver City house, when Jack had rescued Rafizadeh. Not only had he not unmasked himself, he'd actually fired shots at Jack when he gave pursuit. Jack didn't take kindly to people shooting at him; if that guy really was an undercover agent, once this was over, Jack planned to take him outside and go round and round with him until the man explained himself.

Jack pulled his mind away from Newhouse. That was for later. He needed to focus on the task at hand. He stepped into the room, where five agents studiously dusted down surfaces, picked through the few belongings with tweezers, and ran a blue light over everything to expose biological tracings.

"Hey, something over here!" someone called from the bathroom. Jack hurried over to where a man in a surgical mask was swabbing sections of the counter and testing them in a portable scanner. He held a cotton swab under the scanner's sensor. A light on the side of the scanner had turned from red to green. "Traces of nitroglycerine. A little C-4, too. Someone was in here making a bomb."

"I've got something," said another tech from the living room.

Jack spun around and went back to the room, where the tech was thumbing through a book with gloved hands. This was Peter Ren, one of CTU's language experts specializing in the Middle East. He held up some scraps of paper inside the book. Jack looked at them, but they were also written in Farsi, which looked to him like so many elegant designs drawn along the page.

"Well?"

"It's poetry. Really old-fashioned poetry, I think," Ren said, perusing one scrap of paper and then another.

"You think?" Jack said sharply. He began to feel a small knot twist itself in his stomach. He sensed something with that sixth sense of experienced fighters. His enemy was out there somewhere, in the dark, unseen but near. The discovery of bomb making had increased his anxiety.

"Well, it's just scraps. It doesn't really make any sense." Peter Ren looked at Jack helplessly. "I'm a translator, not a scholar. I didn't even know that Muslims wrote poetry like this anymore."

"What makes you think it's important? Maybe it's junk."

Ren held out the scraps of paper he was holding. "Then there's a lot of it. I've got eight pages right here, and there are twenty or thirty more stuffed into another book. Look, if you really want to understand this stuff, you need someone who can do more than just translate the words. You need someone who understands medieval writing. I can call in, find someone for us."

Jack laughed, but the sound was miserable. "Don't bother. I know just the person."

"Who are you working for, Kelly?"

"I work for you."

"You're lying."

Kelly Sharpton and Ryan Chappelle had repeated that conversation, in different variations, six times during the last half hour. The variations usually came in the form of expletives and, once, a commentary on Kelly's parentage. Chappelle had also found different ways to ask the question, but it always came down to the same thing: assumption of guilt, gigantic leap to conclusions, and a question based on the conclusion, followed by Kelly's denial.

Kelly sat in the metal chair behind the metal desk. Chappelle had, for some reason, saved him the humiliation of handcuffs, but the smaller man kept the two big uniformed guards in the room. Kelly spent most of his time, during Chappelle's questions, wondering if he could take out both security guards and the District Director before anyone outside noticed.

"Kelly," Chappelle said, switching from bad cop to good cop with all the grace of a dog standing on its hind legs. "There's nowhere to hide from this. Jessi has already told us you told her to hack into the DOJ system. We know from Justice that someone went in and deleted all the AG's files. That's the Attorney General! We've done a keystroke log on your computer, and we know you futzed around in terminals over there. Why?"

It was a simple question, and there was a simple answer. Of course, Kelly refused to speak it. He had no intention of getting Drexler in trouble. He'd risked his career to save her, and if he was going to go down in flames, taking her with him would do nothing but make his crime an exercise in futility.

"That's all you're going to do, sit there?" Chappelle said. Standing, he was for once taller than Sharpton and seemed to enjoy the perspective. "The FBI will be here in an hour. You can talk to them."

1 2 3 4 5 6 7 8 **9**
10 11 12 13 14 15 16 17
18 19 20 21 22 23 24

••

THE FOLLOWING TAKES PLACE
BETWEEN THE HOURS OF
11 A.M. AND 12 P.M.
PACIFIC STANDARD TIME

••

11:00 A.M. PST
Zachary Taylor Park, Arlington, Virginia

Thank god for Kinkos, Juwan thought as he hit the
brakes and screeched to a stop at the edge of Zachary
Taylor Park. He jumped out and ran down the grass
slope to the water's edge.

"That took too long," she said.

"Fast as I could," he gasped. He reached into his
coat to grab the files.

"Kiss me," she said, throwing herself at him again.
He was more prepared this time, and caught her in his
arms and kissed her. Again, it was a movie kiss, full of
force but empty of passion. He was vaguely aware of

her hands on his body, just as before. When they separated, he felt an empty space where the files had pressed against his abdomen.

"You're really good at that," he said, knowing that the documents were now hidden under her own coat.

"You should see me fake an orgasm," she said. "Bye."

She turned and walked along the path without ever looking back at him.

Juwan hurried back to his car. The copies he'd made were on the carpet, half-stuffed under the passenger seat. He hadn't even had time to read them, but at a glance he could tell the pages contained someone's biography.

He left Arlington and was on his way into D.C. when his mobile phone rang. He popped his earpiece in and said, "Burke here."

"Juwan." It was the Senator herself. Juwan straightened in the driver's seat like a pupil at his desk when the teacher walks in. The Senator didn't call him very often.

"Yes, ma'am."

"Listen, you know that lunch I sent you for? Have you picked it up yet?"

Juwan was a smart man, and by now he was catching on to the clandestine habits of the others involved in this errand. To him it seemed as ridiculous as a spy movie, but he wasn't in charge, so he replied, "Yes, that lunch. I got it and I'm on my way back to the office."

"Good. There's someone who's really hungry for it. Starving, maybe. Hurry." She hung up.

That's when the Pontiac Bonneville slammed into him.

11:15 A.M. PST
CTU Headquarters, Los Angeles

Jack arrived at CTU with the the stack of papers and the two books in which they'd been hidden tucked under one arm. He marched straight past the analysts terminals and down the hall to the holding cells. There was a guard outside number two, where Marks was undoubtedly resting uncomfortably. There were also guards posted outside number three, where Ramin had been ensconced, and also number four, where Nazila and her father had been put. But to Jack's surprise, there was also a guard outside number one. He thought he knew who was in there.

He reached number four and told the guard to open up. The guard glanced worriedly at the bundle under Jack's arm. "Oh, get off it, I'm the one who brought them in. I'm not going to hurt them now. Step aside."

The guard hesitated, but then moved out of the way.

Number four was bigger than the other rooms, and better furnished. There were a couch and a reclining chair, and the walls were painted a soothing, if uninspired, gray. Number four was more of a debriefing room than an interrogation chamber.

Professor Rafizadeh lay on the couch and Nazila sat cross-legged in the chair. As the door opened she got to her feet. When she saw that it was Jack, her face turned purple with anger. "What are we doing here? You said—"

"Just questions," he said, holding up one hand both to show sincerity and to block her progress. "You are not suspects. Neither is your brother. I told you that before."

"But we can't leave," Nazila pointed out.

"Not yet," he admitted.

Professor Rafizadeh had risen slowly to a seated position. He rubbed his temples slowly, then the bridge of his nose. "Isn't that the definition of a prisoner?"

"Ramin—?"

"He's fine. Look, I need help right now," Jack said. He set the books and papers onto the one small table in the room. "I need these translated and understood. I think they are important."

Rafizadeh took his glasses off, wiped them, and replaced them. He stood up and leaned over the table, reading through the lines. He nodded in understanding, then turned to Jack and peered over the top of his spectacles. "I can read them."

"Why should he help you!" Nazila said, advancing on Jack. "You've done nothing but bring us misery!"

Jack waited a beat. "Well, I also saved your father's life. And your brother's life. And right now I'm trying to save a lot of other lives." He told them about the apartment and the bomb materials.

"Oh, please, not this terrorist story again," Nazila said. She paced back and forth. "Why are you focusing on Muslims? It seems to me you have your own brand of terrorists right here with this Greater Nation or whatever it is."

Jack sat down on the couch. Though she was spitting venom at him, Jack had nothing but compassion for her. He was angry, too, somewhere down in the dark chambers of his thought where he kept his anger when it served no purpose; angry because she had lied to him. But his compassion was closer to the surface. When he spoke, he spoke softly, the natural roughness of his voice softened to verbal caress. "Look, I've told you. You are not suspects in anything. But you move in certain circles, and you have to realize that you may have heard things that mean nothing to you, but could help us crack our case. It's the same with your brother. He's not wanted, but he was in Lebanon, right?"

Nazila hesitated, then nodded.

"Right. He may have heard something that is trivia to him, but a lead for us. So please, be patient. You both said to me that if there were real terrorists here, you'd love for us to catch them. Well, here's your chance to help." He turned to the professor. "Can you read those lines?"

Rafizadeh stroked his gray beard. "Well, of course I can read them. Anyone who reads Arabic can read them. But am I right in guessing that your translators didn't know what they were?"

Jack nodded.

"They are lines from three famous poems. Part of a collection called the 'Hanged Poems.'"

Jack felt a rush of relief and gratitude sweep through him. "Hanged poems. That sounds bad."

"They are called that because it is believed they once hung inside the Kaaba in Mecca, though of course that is no longer the case. They are old, from the fifth century. They are lines from the most famous three of the seven—the Poem of Imru-ul-Quais, the Poem of Antar, and the Poem of Zuhair."

Nazila had dropped herself back into the chair and crossed her legs and her arms. She occupied herself with casting irritated glances from Jack, to her father, and back to Jack again.

"So the guys who lived in that apartment were copying poems?" he said aloud. To himself, he began to wonder if the chemical tests had been in error.

Nazila said aloud what he was thinking. "Maybe your other tests were a mistake. Maybe these guys were just college students after all."

"They did not copy whole poems. Parts of poems. Lines of poems, not the complete text." The professor lifted pages and set them aside, examining each page to confirm his observation. "Yes, yes. Just lines."

"College students," Nazila said in an I-told-you-so voice. "Taking notes."

"Well, yes, there are a few notes here, along with the text. Did your translator tell you that?" Professor Rafizadeh asked.

Jack stood up. "No. What notes?"

"Numbers, along with the text. Sometimes just scribbles, but often a number written over a word."

Nazila had stood up when Jack stood. She went to stand beside her father, and her dark eyes went to the page in his hand. "Oh," she said.

"Oh what?" Jack asked. "What scribbles? What numbers."

Professor Rafizadeh put down the paper, which Nazila promptly picked up. As she studied it, her father said, "Agent Bauer, this is not my area of expertise, but I would say that what you have here is a message of some kind."

"A message," Jack repeated. "You mean a code?"

Rafizadeh shrugged. Jack had to admire his serenity. He had just been kidnapped and threatened with death, and nearly killed in the crossfire between the militia and CTU. Yet here he was, stroking his beard gently, reading ancient texts, and talking to the man who had ruined his life six months ago. Few, under those circumstances, would be able to control themselves, yet Rafizadeh seemed completely at peace.

"I can tell you," he said at last, "that the lines as they are presented make no sense. They are from three different poems, but the lines are jumbled together. The topics differ, even the themes are different. From a literary point of view, there is no purpose to them."

"Then why would they use them?" Jack asked. Why use the poems in some kind of code if—"

"Because the message isn't in the poems," Nazila said. "The poetry is just the key. This is a Hill cipher."

"Hill cipher?"

"A code," she said. "Not that complicated, but you have to know the source it uses for reference. It just transposes numbers and letters using some other source as the key." Jack's eyes shifted onto Nazila in surprise. *God bless the Cal Poly math department*, he thought. "You can translate this?"

"Maybe," she said, her eyes jumping from page to page. Then they lifted and settled firmly on Jack Bauer. "If you let all of us, including my brother, go."

11:35 A.M. PST
Washington, D.C.

Juwan hadn't seen the car, but he'd felt the impact rattle his head so that it nearly came off his shoulders. In the same instant his vision was overwhelmed by a huge white blur that scraped his skin, and he realized that the air bag had inflated. It began to deflate almost instantly. Juwan was practically standing on his brake pad. He slammed the car into park, though he wasn't sure it was still running anymore, and unbuckled his belt.

The other car had rammed into the passenger side.

Juwan was able to open the driver's side door and get out, standing on wobbly legs. He just had the presence of mind to reach back into the car and lift the copies he'd made. He stuffed them back into his breast pocket and stepped away from the car. He looked around. He was on a quiet side street in D.C. The other driver had knocked his car sideways, so that he was pointing from sidewalk to sidewalk. A few heads poked out of windows to see what had happened.

Juwan shook his head to clear the cobwebs out of his vision. The other car, a black Bonneville, was still connected to his side of his vehicle. People were getting out of both the driver and passenger sides of the Bonneville. They were two men.

"I'm all right," Juwan said from his side of the car. "I'm all right."

Only after he'd repeated it twice did it occur to him that the two men hadn't asked after his health. In fact, they hadn't said anything. They each walked around one side of the car, advancing steadily on Juwan. Their faces looked neither worried nor surprised. In fact, to Juwan Burke they looked very much like the faces of corners and free safeties who had tried to take his head off at the University of Alabama.

He backed up a few steps. One of the men growled, "Where do you think you're going . . ."

"Roll tide," Juwan murmured. He turned and ran.

They were chasing him. He could hear their footsteps, but he never looked back. That was the cardinal rule: never look back to see how close they are, because it only slows you down and lets them get closer. Keep your eyes front, focused on your goal, and fly.

"Fuck!" he heard behind him.

"Shoot him!" the other one yelled.

"Here?" the first yelled, angry and incredulous.

Juwan gritted his teeth as he ran, but no gunshot sounded. The footsteps faded a bit. He kept his eyes on the street ahead. He was only a few blocks from the Capitol Building. It was just two or three football fields away. He would make it.

11:43 A.M. PST
CTU Headquarters, Los Angeles

Ryan Chappelle paced the length of Kelly Sharpton's office, then he paced its width. He hated mornings like this—mornings when the trains derailed and the conductors were late. Of course, the real source of his anxiety wasn't just the disruption in the well-established flow of information in his domain; his fear was much more personal. If Kelly Sharpton was some kind of mole, the fact would damage Chappelle's own career. Soon the FBI would be here, and once they had Sharpton, the man was out of his hands. It would surely be the end of Sharpton's career, but other heads might roll. Chappelle was fond of keeping his firmly attached to his shoulders.

Jack Bauer appeared in the doorway. At any other moment, Ryan Chappelle would have leaped down the field agent's throat. Today he just said, "What?"

Jack saw that Chappelle was in no mood for small talk. He cut to the chase. "The Rafizadehs. I would like to release them."

"Okay . . . no wait," Chappelle said, distracted but

suddenly coming into focus. "Released? No, they just got here. They haven't even been questioned yet. We're letting them stew."

"They're already simmering," Jack said. "But I need them out. Nazila can help me get to a lead I need to find these terrorists."

"Now there are terrorists again," Chappelle said, as though the whole incident was a story Jack made up and discarded like a child's imaginary friend. "Will there still be terrorists if we let the Rafizadehs go?" It was a sarcastic question, so Jack didn't answer. Chappelle scowled and added, "How can she help? Is she part of the cell?"

"No. She has skills to help me break a code."

"We have teams—"

"It's in Arabic. Arabic poetry. Her father knows the poems, she's a math grad student at Cal Poly. You find me a better team."

Chappelle considered it. Jack saw the options spinning around inside Chappelle's bald skull. The two main options opposed each other: on the one hand, Chappelle was inclined to do his job when called upon, and that might mean releasing them; on the other hand, releasing them would please Jack, and that was something Chappelle tried to avoid.

"Not the son," he said. "We still have questions for the son. He was in Lebanon. His name was on that list. He needs to answer those questions."

"I've got a terrorist cell here in Los Angeles!" Jack said. "And these people can help me find them!"

Chappelle shrugged. "So let them help while he's answering questions. Oh, here's the FBI."

Two men had climbed the stairs. One was a middle-aged white guy in a gray suit, blue tie, and a bald spot atop his head. The other was a tall black man, over six foot five, with huge shoulders, wearing jeans and a windbreaker. Both were a little older than Jack, with the air of authority and suspicion that came from more than a badge. They looked at Jack and Ryan as though they both might be suspects. "Paul Meister," said the suit. "This is Londale Johnson. We're here for Kelly Sharpton."

"This way," Chappelle said. He led the two men down the steps to the holding area. Jack followed, his business with Chappelle not yet finished.

At holding room one, Chappelle had the guard step aside and opened up. Kelly was sitting alone inside. He looked annoyed at Chappelle, but when the two FBI agents entered, his face turned grave.

The suit, Meister, said, "Agent Sharpton, you are under arrest. Do you have anything you would like to say before we take you into custody?"

"That has got to be the tallest FBI agent I've ever seen," Kelly said. "And you have a very nice tie."

Behind them, Jack chuckled. He had to admit, Sharpton had style.

Meister grimaced. He and Johnson stepped forward and took out a pair of handcuffs. Kelly stood slowly, showing them that he meant no harm, and waited to be handcuffed.

"Mr. Chappelle! Mr. Chappelle!" Jessi Bandison ran at them, breathless. "There's a call for you."

"Later," the Director snapped.

"An urgent call!" Jessi said. "From the Attorney General."

Chappelle's already pale face turned white. He looked around for an extension and saw a phone on the wall. "Send it here."

Jessi disappeared, and a few seconds later the wall phone rang. "Chappelle."

"Director Chappelle," said James Quincy. "I understand that you have an agent in custody by the name of Kelly Sharpton. You are holding him on suspicion of some kind of sabotage against my computer system?"

"Er, yes, sir," Ryan Chappelle said. He looked at the FBI agents, as though they might have an explanation for the call. They offered nothing. "We have evidence that he—"

"Please release him, Director," Quincy said. "This man was acting on my orders. He's done nothing wrong. Is that clear?"

"Clear? Yes, sir, but I'm not sure I—"

"Release him," the Attorney General repeated. "There's no harm done."

Chappelle's head throbbed. He had yet to get a handle on any part of this day. "Yes, sir."

11:55 A.M. PST
Westin St. Francis Hotel, San Francisco

James Quincy placed the phone gently back on its receiver, willing his trembling hand to stop shaking with anger. It would not. To control himself, Quincy sat back in his chair and folded his arms. "Satisfied?"

Senator Debrah Drexler, accompanied by her man Bobby, stood on the far side of the hotel room's small coffee table. She was holding a faxed document in her hands, which she had just received a few minutes earlier from her Washington, D.C., office. She had already shown the documents to Quincy. She'd even offered to give him his own set, since she'd made a dozen copies and disbursed them to trusted associates in various parts of the country.

"No, I'm not satisfied," she said, waving the documents. "Drop the NAP Act."

Quincy snorted. "Don't push it. What you've got there isn't that strong."

"It will raise a lot of questions about why you sent your own private soldier into the Greater Nation. Those are questions you don't want to have to answer."

Quincy was unmoved. "I'll play this game because I tried to push you and you pushed back. Fair is fair. But you reach too high and I'll kick the ladder right out from under you."

Debrah hesitated, taking his measure. She rarely got this close to him. He was a handsome man, all in all, though she could have done without the annoyingly straight part in his hair. He was cool under pressure, she had to give him that. He'd hardly blinked when he presented him with the dossier on Frank Newhouse. He'd assessed the situation as coolly as a man judging a sale, and conceded dispassionately.

"All right," she said. "Your fascist bill is going down anyway."

"We'll see."

Drexler and her man left the office. As soon as the door closed, a side door opened and one of Quincy's men appeared. If Deb or Bobby had seen him, they'd have recognized him as the same man who had spoken with the Senator in Golden Gate Park that same morning.

"Should I have this taken care of?" asked the man.

"No, don't be ridiculous, she's a U.S. Senator," Quincy said. The man shrugged. People were people, and they all died about the same no matter what their title. "Besides, everything is going the way I expected it to."

11:58 A.M. PST
CTU Headquarters, Los Angeles

Jack resigned himself to defeat. He couldn't get Chappelle to release Ramin Rafizadeh. He toyed with the idea of breaking him out of prison, but discarded the effort as too drastic. He had no idea what those codes said, and he'd feel stupid sacrificing his whole career in return for a grocery list or a fundamentalist Islamic diatribe about the sins of the United States.

He walked down to holding room four and entered, his face downcast. "Look, I'm sorry. I argued my best, but they want to hold him for a day or two, just to—"

"Jack, forget that," said Nazila. He was so annoyed with Chappelle, he'd failed to notice her mood. The blood had drained from her face and her voice shook. "I mean, get him out, but I'll tell you what this says. I have to . . ."

"Naz, what is it?" he asked, his senses suddenly heightened.

"According to these notes, the terrorists plan to assassinate the President tomorrow. Right here in Los Angeles."

1 2 3 4 5 6 7 8 9
10 11 12 13 14 15 16 17
18 19 20 21 22 23 24

••

THE FOLLOWING TAKES PLACE
BETWEEN THE HOURS OF
12 P.M. AND 1 P.M.
PACIFIC STANDARD TIME

••

12:00 P.M. PST
CTU Headquarters, Los Angeles

Despite the rallying cry of 9/11 and the media's spotlight on interagency cooperation, it was often still difficult to bring law enforcement and intelligence communities together. The CIA and the FBI were like schoolyard rivals who had fought for so long it was habit. The National Security Agency had acted as an independent agency for its entire life, and simply did not know how to play well with others. Homeland Security was the new kid who wasn't sure how to fit in.

Still, there was one way to get them all talking together, and it began with the phrase, "There is a plot to kill the President tomorrow morning."

Jack Bauer, Kelly Sharpton, and Ryan Chappelle sat in CTU's video conference room as various monitors lit up around them. Jack saw station chiefs from the CIA and the FBI. The Attorney General was there, as was the National Security Agency's Deputy Director. So was the Assistant Secretary for Homeland Security. Benjamin Perch, head of the Secret Service, was there of course, and Jack was relieved to see the face of Richard Walsh appear on one of the screens. Having Walsh in the meeting gave him a boost of confidence.

Since the threat was directed at the President, it was Benjamin Perch of the Secret Service who ran the meeting. "Thank you all for attending on such short notice," he said in a deep bass. "This appears to be an urgent matter, so this is going to be a bit informal. You all know as much as I do: the Counter Terrorist Unit in Los Angeles has uncovered what it considers to be a credible threat to the President. I am going to turn this over to Jack Bauer at CTU."

Ryan Chappelle fidgeted in his seat. He disliked allowing anyone else to take charge of a meeting he attended; when that person was Jack Bauer, he felt like a passenger on a runaway bus.

"Thank you," Jack said. "I'll keep it short. We have evidence that a fundamentalist terrorist cell has been operating in the United States for at least six months. An hour ago we discovered an apartment in Westwood that contained traces of bomb-making materials and bunk beds suggesting at least eight members of the cell. We also discovered coded messages suggesting the terrorists plan to attack the President tomorrow morning in Los Angeles."

As concisely as he could, Jack described the Greater

Nation militia, the leads they had given, and the evidence he had compiled. He explained Professor Rafizadeh's credentials and Nazila's skills. The minute he was finished, the questions began.

"How long have we been tracking this terrorist cell?" demanded the Attorney General.

Jack felt Kelly Sharpton bristle. He had trouble hiding his own bewilderment. He and Sharpton both knew that the Attorney General already had a man inside the Greater Nation, one who clearly knew as much about the terrorists as they did. Jack gave a mental shrug. There was a game to play here, and he could play it if necessary.

"Well," Jack growled with a glance at Chappelle, "we caught hints of them about six months ago, but the trail went cold and we thought it was a false alarm. Recent events"—*my damned exile*, he thought—"led to the discovery of new evidence."

"Any leads on where the cell members are now?" asked Perch.

"No," Jack admitted. "All our information is less than twenty-four hours old. The leads on the actual attack are less than an hour old. We are cross-checking everyone who lives in the apartment building, and we're running the apartment's security videos through visual recognition software to see if anyone comes up."

"Likelihood?" asked Walsh, who spoke in a shorthand Jack could appreciate.

"Low," he replied. "The security cameras are erased and reused every forty-eight hours. But we'll check anyway."

There was a slight pause, then the deputy from the NSA, Margaret Cheedles, said, "Look, I respect the work Jack Bauer and CTU have put into this, but doesn't it seem a little far-fetched at this point to sound the alarms?"

No one else answered, so Jack said, "I'm not sure what you mean, ma'am."

"Well, you say this cell is communicating through codes left in poetry?"

"Yes, ma'am. Our working theory is that different members of the cell used the apartment at different times. To avoid electronic surveillance, and a possible raid, they left notes for each other through something like a Hill cipher, using the poetry as a foundation."

"Okay," Cheedles said, "but don't fundamentalist Islamists consider all poetry prior to Mohammed heretical? Why would they use it?"

"My expert tells me that these poems earn a certain amount of respect because they were once present in the Kaaba," Jack replied. "Besides, they had to use something, and they couldn't use the Koran itself. That would have been heretical."

"We're off track here," said Henry Rutledge, representing Homeland Security. "None of us is an expert on Islamic fundamentalism or literature."

"Agreed," said Richard Walsh.

"And I have to say the whole process has me confused," added Cheedles. "I've seen the Greater Nation mentioned in the daily security briefings, but never with this much of a presence. Aren't they a low-level threat? How would they have gotten so much information?"

"They are better funded you might expect," Jack replied. "And their leader is sharp."

"I agree with Agent Bauer," said the Attorney General. Kelly fidgeted again, but Jack was grateful to get support from any quarter. "Assuming they exist, these terrorists have had at least six months of planning time without being watched. Something went haywire back then and the trail went cold. If some nutcase militia that wants to take the law into its own hands picked up the ball we dropped, I say we say thank you, take the ball back, and start to run our own plays."

"I understand the concern, and I agree that CTU should continue to investigate," said Perch. "But there's one important part of this whole threat that everyone is forgetting."

"What?" Jack asked.

Perch shrugged. "The President isn't going to *be* in Los Angeles tomorrow morning."

12:16 P.M. PST
CTU Headquarters, Los Angeles

"Nice work, Jack," Ryan Chappelle drawled. "Really nice work in there."

The video monitors had all died down. Their last lights had burned into Jack's brain the looks of annoyance on each person's face. The one that had bothered him most was the look on Walsh's face. The tough veteran was far too disciplined to show any real reaction, but in his stony face Jack read a deep disappointment.

"That's going to really enhance CTU's reputation," Chappelle continued in a voice thick with sarcasm. "Not to mention your own."

Jack glared at him. "At least I spend my time out there fighting credible threats instead of arresting our own people."

Chappelle sneered. "Credible threats? Is that what

you call it when some mysterious group no one's ever seen uses poetry to plan an attack on the President in a city where he's not even going to be? No wonder we demoted you, Bauer."

Jack let Chappelle have the last word, then leave the conference room. He couldn't care less for Chappelle. He felt humiliated for stumbling in front of Walsh.

Jack felt a hand pat his shoulder. Kelly Sharpton had remained behind. "Happened to me once," he said. "I had done a threat assessment for a visit from the President of China, right about the time the Fulon Gong was active. I gave this whole presentation on Fulon Gong members in San Francisco and how they were likely to try something here. It wasn't till the end of my presentation that one of my own people mentioned that we'd already arrested the local Fulon Gong members."

"Great," Jack said, "so we're both a couple of asses." He sat down on the tabletop. "Look, I think you and I agree that something's going on here. This cell pops up every few months and somehow gets swept aside. This Frank Newhouse is some kind of wild card out there doing who knows what. I don't know about you, but I've got to keep looking into this."

Kelly grinned. "Who says I was going to stop. Let me work on the Frank Newhouse angle."

Jack raised an eyebrow. "You get a little lust in your eye when you mention him and the Attorney General. What was the story there?"

"Not sure it's worth telling at this point," Kelly said. "Let's just say that the AG tried to strong-arm someone and I helped them out, and I'm not done with the payback yet."

"Strong-arm . . ." Jack murmured. He generally

avoided cluttering his mind with politics that did not involve his work, but some current events had a direct impact on him. "The New American Privacy thing?" he asked. "Was it about the Senate vote?"

Kelly nodded.

Jack scratched his head. There were too many pieces to this puzzle, and he was starting to worry that two different jigsaws had been mixed together. He made a mental list of the absolute connections: Greater Nation and Frank Newhouse; Frank Newhouse and the Attorney General; Attorney General and NAP Act; Greater Nation and terrorist clues; terrorist clues and threat to President. The stories seemed to spin off in two different directions.

"Okay," he said, "do you have anything to chase down with Newhouse?"

Kelly nodded. "There's an old address in the file. At least it's somewhere to start."

"That's more than I've got with these terrorists," Jack admitted.

"No it's not . . ." Nina Myers stood in the doorway of the conference room with an enormous grin on her pixie face. "You are going to want to make out with me when I show you this."

"I'm a married man, Nina," Jack said.

"Married to your work." She laughed. Jack felt a pang. He hadn't called his wife since last night. He felt a second pang when he realized that he hadn't even *thought* of his wife since last night. He sensed vaguely that his marriage was in rough water and heading for the rocks, but he had no time to steer that ship at the moment.

"What've you got?"

Nina strutted forward and handed him a printout.

On one side of the page was a photocopy of the driver's license they'd picked up from the lease on the apartment building. On the other side was a mug shot and a rap sheet from LAPD. The name on the driver's license was Richard Brighton. The name on the mug shot was Julio Juarez.

"Am I not the sexiest woman alive at the moment?" She grinned.

And the truth was, she was right.

12:29 P.M. PST
Senator Drexler's Office, San Francisco

Debrah Drexler closed her office door and gathered herself. She had a few minutes before her next appointment, and once her afternoon started it was a long slide down to a red-eye flight. On days like this, she found it advantageous to grab a minute or two of private time.

She was grateful that she'd been able to help Kelly. The man had stuck his neck out for her (again) and nearly gotten it chopped off this time. She made a mental note to find some way to repay Sela Gonzales, and another note to promote Juwan Burke. She hadn't gotten all the details yet, but she understood that someone had smashed up his car and chased him onto Pennsylvania Avenue before giving up.

Worry still gnawed at her. She had stopped the AG from blackmailing her, it was true. But if he was using strong-arm tactics on her, who else was he after? What else was he planning? She and the Senate leadership had already made their rounds of calls, and everyone was still on board. Unless something drastic happened, the NAP Act would go down to defeat in the Senate, and the Congress would, at last, slow the erosion of civil liberties.

Debrah Drexler rubbed her hands together, mentally pushing the issue aside. She was worrying too much. There was nothing left he could do. He'd played his hand and lost.

She opened her door and went on to her next item of business.

12:35 P.M. PST
CTU Headquarters, Los Angeles

The door to Ramin Rafizadeh's room opened and two uniformed security guards stepped inside. "You're free to go," one of them said briskly. "We'll escort you outside."

He stood and walked unsteadily into the hallway, where his sister and father greeted him with hugs. "Is it . . . is it over?" he asked, clearly unconvinced.

"I think so," his father said. "At least for us."

The guards led them down the hallway and past the main room. Nazila caught a glimpse of Jack Bauer sitting at a computer. He was absorbed by some information on the screen, and she slowed her footsteps to study him. It was the first time, she realized, that she had been able to look at him when he was working on something other than her. She saw in the hunch of his shoulders, the intensity of his gaze, and the rapt look on his face, that he was consumed by his work; he had entered a state she could only call passion. She could never decide how she felt about him, not six months ago, and not six hours ago. He seemed truly worthy of both hatred and love, and she had not been able to choose between them. Now, from a distance, with his attention directed elsewhere, she made her choice. "God bless you," she whispered.

12:46 P.M. PST
Holmby Hills, Los Angeles

Kelly Sharpton insisted on visiting the address himself. Although he wasn't a field agent anymore, he was field trained and certified. Before leaving CTU, he visited Jessi Bandison, who had remained at her desk long after her shift had expired.

"Kelly, I'm sorry—"

"Forget it," he shut her off. "I pulled you into something that was way over your head. It's my fault, not yours." As he leaned against her workstation, he rested his hand on the countertop so that it touched hers. "I'm also sorry about snapping at you earlier. I was under a lot of time pressure and I didn't explain myself well enough."

"Okay," she said, her face burning.

"I know you're way past your shift and you're probably exhausted, but could you stay a little longer. I need intel on an address and you're the best."

She smiled, but her face burned even hotter. He scribbled down the address of a condominium on Wilshire Boulevard. "Call me in my car," he had said.

Now his cellular buzzed. He pressed the Bluetooth earpiece in his ear. "Sharpton," he said.

"It's Jessi. The condo is owned outright. There are no loan papers on it. According to the tax assessor's office and the condominium's community council, the place is owned by a Patrick Henry."

A few minutes later he pulled into the condominium, one of several dozen that formed a "condo canyon" along Wilshire Boulevard just to the east of Westwood and UCLA. It was a posh building. The circular drive curved under the building structure and there a valet waited to take the SUV Kelly had signed out. The lobby was two stories high with a waterfall in the middle. The floor and walls were inlaid with travertine. A concierge stood behind a marble counter. Kelly crossed the lobby and flashed his badge. "I have a few questions about the condominium owned by Mr. Patrick Henry."

The concierge was a slight young man in his twenties with perfectly messed hair. His skin was as smooth as a woman's. His gold name tag read "Alexander." "Yes, Agent Sharpton. I hope I can help you."

"Me, too. Is Mr. Henry at home?"

"One moment." Alexander lifted a phone to his ear and dialed. He smiled and nodded at Kelly, then put the phone down. "I'm sorry, there's no answer."

"I'm sure you don't mind if I go up and knock."

Alexander wrinkled his brow, something he clearly did not do often. "It's against house policy, I'm afraid. No unannounced guests on the floors."

"Oh, I'm the United States government," Kelly said. "We're very informal."

He made for the elevator. He sensed Alexander behind him, distraught, trying to get his attention, but he ignored it. What was poor Alexander going to do, call the police?

It was a short elevator ride up to 12F, Patrick Henry's condominium. The twelfth floor was as sumptuous as the lobby. By the design, Kelly guessed that there were only four to six condos on each floor, which meant they were huge and expensive.

The entrance to 12F was a set of beautiful teak doors ornately carved in chevrons, eagles, griffins, and other creatures that reminded Kelly vaguely of Europe. He lifted his foot and stomped on a griffin in the center of the door. The door rattled on its hinges, but held. The eagles and the griffins held on stubbornly for three more kicks, but eventually they surrendered and the fractured doors swung inward.

Kelly walked in, not really expecting to find Frank Newhouse or anyone else in the apartment. But he was hoping for evidence, so he started to walk around. There wasn't much to see. The carpet was expensive, and the crown molding gave the expansive rooms the look of luxury, but all the rooms were empty. He went to the kitchen and looked for dishes. The first two cabinets he searched were completely empty, and looked as if they'd never been used at all.

When he opened the third cabinet, he saw the bomb.

It was counting down to detonation, and if the digital readout was correct, he had about five minutes left.

1 2 3 4 5 6 7 8 9
10 **11** 12 13 14 15 16 17
18 19 20 21 22 23 24

• •

THE FOLLOWING TAKES PLACE
BETWEEN THE HOURS OF
1 P.M. AND 2 P.M.
PACIFIC STANDARD TIME

• •

1:00 P.M. PST
Westwood

Kelly sprinted for the broken front doors and ran into
the hallway, but he had no illusions about leaving. In
a building this size, there was no way to evacuate
everyone in time. In the hallway, Kelly found a fire
alarm. He shattered the glass and pulled the lever. A
whooping alarm filled the hallway instantly, and ceiling mounted lights began to flash.

He ran back to the apartment, pulling out his cellular and dialing CTU. The phone was ringing by the
time he reached the bomb. "Get me Chappelle, and
get me someone who can defuse a bomb. Right now!"

"Agent Sharpton, this is Glenn Schneider, LAPD Bomb Squad."

"Hey, Glenn," Kelly said. He was sitting in front of the bomb, watching the digital timer tick down. "You better be a good conversationalist because you may be the last person I ever talk to. Hopefully, you can make small talk about bombs."

"Describe it to me."

Kelly had been rehearsing his speech for the last three minutes. "The timer is a digital stopwatch like they use at a track meet, but it's hooked up to a battery. The battery wire runs off in one direction, I think back toward the front door. The timer itself is taped to several very large plastic containers of powder. The powder looks like sugar."

"Solidox bomb," Schneider said. "How many cartons are there?"

"I'm looking at six," Kelly replied. "While I was waiting for your call I checked the other rooms. There are a couple wired to the heating system. There are wires running to the other rooms as well. The timer itself has at least fourteen wires leading from it to the C-4. I think it's fourteen, but they're all jumbled together so it's hard to tell. And by the way, I have one minute and forty-three seconds left."

"Most of the wires are dummies," Schneider said.

"There's also, believe it or not, a tennis ball sitting on top of the battery. It's got a piece of tape over part of it."

Schneider made a sound like someone had just poked him in the eye. "This guy took everything right out of the Anarchist Cookbook. Listen, that tennis ball is probably filled with matchheads and gasoline. If you pick the wrong wire, it's probably going to heat up and pop all over you."

"No problem," Kelly said. "Just tell me which wire is the right one."

"You need to find a wire that comes off the timer and into a heating source."

Kelly looked around the timer. "I don't see a heating source. Just the timer and the plastic tubs."

"Look around. It's probably the battery."

Kelly looked again. "No, the timer's connected to the battery, but the battery isn't connected to the tubs."

"Okay, it feeds back, then. The timer triggers the battery, but also keeps the circuit open. If you stop the timer, it automatically closes the circuit between the battery and the Solidox."

"So I need to get rid of the battery."

"Yes."

Kelly jumped to his feet and looked around. There was nothing in the apartment he could use. And the timer read fifty-eight seconds. He thought about backing up and shooting the tennis ball off the battery. But he didn't want to think about what would happen if he missed.

"Schneider, what exactly is this tennis ball thing supposed to do?"

There was a pause. "Well, it depends on what's inside. Sometimes tennis ball bombs are just big firecrackers. They're like a joke. But nasty ones have gasoline or napalm inside. They spread burning rubber that keeps burning whatever it lands on."

Kelly looked at the tennis ball. It was an innocuous, ridiculous little thing to be afraid of. "Fuck it," he

said. He stepped forward and kicked the tennis ball
and the battery.

The battery flew away from the timer, wires popping
out of it. The tennis ball didn't fly. It exploded with a
sizzle and pop. Kelly had instinctively covered his face
as he kicked, which was wise. Liquid fire splashed
across his forearms, and he felt his palms start to burn.

"Son of a bitch!" he yelled, dropping to his knees
and pressing his hands into the carpet. He didn't see
any flames, but his hands were still burning. It felt
like someone was pressing fiery coals into his palms.
He jumped to his feet again and ran to the sink. He
pushed the faucet on with his forearms and stuck his
hands under the running water. It didn't help. His
hands were burning on the insides now.

He ran to his cell phone, which he'd dropped on
the floor. He couldn't pick it up. Kelly lay down next
to it and pressed his cheek to the device. He could
hear Schneider on the other end calling his name.
"Get someone up here!" He yelled. "This shit is burning my hands off!"

1:16 P.M. PST
East Los Angeles

Jack Bauer had taken the 10 Freeway past the gathered skyscrapers of downtown Los Angeles and into
East L.A. He turned north and entered Boyle Heights.
The address matched a rundown duplex with dirt for
a front yard, cracked plaster, and a car on cinder
blocks settled in the driveway. As he drove, he noted
the faces he passed were brown, and the style of dress
tended toward baggy black pants and wife-beater

T-shirts. The billboards and storefronts were exclusively in Spanish. In this neighborhood, blond Jack Bauer and his SUV stood out like white socks with black shoes, but there was nothing to be done now.

He parked half a block away from the house and walked back. Heavy drapes hid the inside from view, and heavier iron bars protected the windows from the outside. Julio Juarez did not keep a very welcoming home. The whole place was still, and gave the impression that it was deserted. But Jack knew Julio was home. At least, Julio's cellular phone was home. The LAPD printout had given Jack access to all kinds of information about Julio, including his cell phone number. Jack had the mobile number's signal traced—as long as the phone was on, CTU's satellites could find it—and sure enough, the eyes in the sky had pinpointed Julio inside his own home.

Jack walked up the cracked blacktop driveway to a green door splattered with yellow paint and knocked.

"*Hola?*" someone yelled from behind the door.

Jack knocked again without saying anything. To the right of the door was a window, again with heavy curtains on the inside. Jack pressed himself against the door just as that curtain was drawn back. Someone was trying to see who was knocking. Jack was also careful to duck below the little peephole in the door front. But he knocked again.

The door opened to the length of the guard chain and someone whined, "Who's fucking with me?"

Jack drove his shoulder into the door, his weight snapping the chain. The man inside stumbled backward. He slipped inside and closed the door behind him.

The room inside was the complete opposite of the building's exterior. It was painted cool blue, and one whole wall was devoted to a graffiti-style painting of zoot suiters and tattooed esses in Ray-Bans and plaid flannel shirts. The carpet was plush gray and the furniture was leather. Ranchero music tripped out of unseen speakers and a fifty-inch plasma screen was broadcasting "Sports Center."

"What the fuck—?" the man on the floor said.

He looked like the mug shot. He was small and wiry, somewhere between twenty and forty, with a pathetically thin mustache, pockmarked skin, and short, dark hair. He picked himself up and puffed out his chest, but he didn't advance on Jack.

"What you doing?" he challenged. "You know who I am?"

Jack nodded. "You're Julio Juarez. You're a two-bit coyote who makes a living smuggling illegals over the border at San Diego and sometimes up through the desert in Arizona."

Julio scowled at Jack. His face seemed set into a permanent glare, with one side of his mouth drooping lower than the other. The eye on that side also looked eternally tired. "Yeah, that's me. I got friends in MS-13, bitch, so unless you want you and your family to end up in someone's trash can, get the fuck out."

Jack recognized MS-13 from CTU's daily threat assessments. It was a street gang that had started in El Salvador and quickly spread to the United States. They were active in California and Maryland and Virginia. The situation had gotten so bad that those three states had formed special task forces to deal with them. The fact that Julio was connected to MS-13, and MS-13 was active near the U.S. capital, bothered Jack some-how, but he couldn't figure it out at the moment.

"Relax, Julio," Jack said. "I'm just here to ask you a couple of questions. I'm a Federal agent, and I have a lot bigger problems to deal with than a chickenshit like you. You answer my questions, I leave, and you get to go about your business."

Julio's weak eye drooped even farther. "Okay, ask your question."

Jack nodded. "First, I want to know if you've ever smuggled anyone—"

He didn't finish the question, because Julio Juarez kicked him hard in the groin. He moved fast for a man with a droopy eye, and the kick caught Jack almost square. He felt his midsection explode and the air went out of him. The edges of the room turned black for a moment, and Jack barely saw Julio bolt down the hallway. Ignoring the pain, Jack sprinted after him.

1:40 P.M. PST
CTU Headquarters, Los Angeles

Ryan Chappelle sat in Kelly Sharpton's office, think-ing of ways to distance himself from Jack Bauer's blundering activities. He had a promising career ahead of him, but unfortunately he'd been linked with that heavy-handed ex-soldier who thought the only way to deal with a wall was to knock it down. Chappelle preferred to build a door.

His phone rang. "Chappelle," he said.

"Chappelle, this is Walsh," said Walsh from Wash-ington, D.C. "What the fuck is going on?"

"I'm sorry?" Ryan looked around as though the problem might be right there in the room with him. "What?"

"It's all over the news! Who leaked it?"

"I'm sorry, I don't—"

"Turn on your news, then figure out who leaked this story!" Walsh slammed the phone down.

There was a television in Sharpton's office. Ryan searched for the remote, found it on top of the television itself, and fired it up. He flipped on CNN. The main story was something about an earthquake in Tunisia, but the running banner told Chappelle what he needed to know: "Intelligence officials acknowledge credible threat to President Barnes. Sources suggest foreign terrorists on U.S. soil."

Chappelle felt the blood rise up into his cheeks. It hadn't been an hour, and the story was already in the press.

1:45 P.M. PST
Boyle Heights

Julio Juarez had gone out the back door and over the fence. Jack followed, nearly vomiting as his gut and groin bumped against the fence top. He made it over and sprinted down a dusty alley after the coyote.

His quarry turned left at the street, and Jack rounded the corner twenty feet behind him. He slammed into an old lady and spun around her without apologizing, trying not to lose sight of Julio. The wiry little smuggler ran two blocks down, dodging the cars. Jack gained on him slowly—Julio might have been quick with a kick, but he wasn't all that fast. Jack gained enough ground to see Julio duck into a yellow adobe building with faded writing across the top.

Jack entered the doorway right behind him, racing out of the sunlight into a cool, dark room, very wide and scattered with small tables and benches. There was a stage at the far end of the room, over which hung a banner that read "Viva Ranchero!"

Julio was right in front of him. Jack dived, catching the coyote by the backs of the knees and bringing him down in a tumble of chairs. Julio squealed and struggled. Jack caught him by the waist and rolled him backward, slamming Julio's head into the tiled floor. Some of the life went out of him then. Jack grabbed him by the hair and lifted his head off the tile, drawing his gun and putting it to the coyote's temple.

At the same time, he heard four or five hammers click back. Jack looked up. Five gang-bangers stood around him, their faces turned down in angry frowns and their weapons all pointed at him.

"What the fuck, esse?" one of them, a heavyset man with a thick black mustache said.

"Cesar, shoot this puta!" Julio squealed. "He's a cop!"

Jack rolled onto his back, pulling Julio on top of him and keeping the muzzle of his Sig pressed against the little man's temple. He didn't have to say anything. The big man, Cesar, was smart enough to understand.

"You got nowhere to go, white boy," he said.

"They kill you!" Julio said, trembling.

"But I'll kill you first, Julio," Jack replied.

1 2 3 4 5 6 7 8 9
10 11 **12** 13 14 15 16 17
18 19 20 21 22 23 24

••

THE FOLLOWING TAKES PLACE
BETWEEN THE HOURS OF
2 P.M. AND 3 P.M.
PACIFIC STANDARD TIME

••

2:00 P.M. PST
Boyle Heights

"Listen, I don't want to arrest him. I don't care about any of you. All I want is to ask Julio a couple of questions and I'm gone."

"We don't give a shit what you want," one of the other gang-bangers said.

"I bet Julio wants to live, though," Jack said. His heart was racing, but he kept his voice calm.

The second gang-banger said, "I don't give a fuck about Julio. This white boy comes into our place with a gun? He's dead, esse!"

But Cesar shook his head. "No, *tio*, we like Julio.

He brings my people up when I need him to. I don't want to lose him."

Jack slid out from under Julio, careful to keep his finger on the trigger and the muzzle on Julio. He stood slowly. Some of the gang-bangers clearly wanted to fire, but Cesar waved them off.

"Listen, Julio, this is all I want from you," Jack said, moving to keep the little man between him and the other guns. "I saw your picture on a driver's license by the name of Richard Brighton."

"Never heard of no Brighton," Julio said, his eyes straining to their corners to see him. "But if he looks like me he must be a handsome bitch."

"I'm thinking you helped some people cross the border a while ago. Maybe about six months ago, maybe a little longer. Maybe you helped some men cross over, guys who weren't Latino. Jog your memory?"

Julio hesitated. "Yeah, I did that. But it wasn't no six months ago. Maybe two."

"How many guys? What'd they look like?" Jack was inching backward toward the door. The gang-bangers sauntered after him.

Julio said, "Eight, I think." Jack pushed the muzzle into his cheek. "Eight, eight! They were Arabs or something like that."

Jack stifled a desire to blow Julio's head off right there. The U.S. spent billions of dollars to protect itself from enemies that wanted to tear it apart, rooting out terrorist training camps in Pakistan, buying off weapons-grade uranium in the former Soviet bloc, and spending countless man-hours snatching cell phone calls and radio signals out of the airwaves using the most complex technology on the planet. And here was Julio from Boyle Heights, tearing their carefully constructed fences into shreds with a beat-up van and a path through the mountains.

"Where'd you take them?"

"Shit, I don't rem—okay! I dropped them off downtown. At a building on Flower. One of those new renovations with the apartments on top. I don't remember which one. But the guy who paid me was named Farrah."

"Thanks, Julio," Jack said, reaching the door. "You're a real patriot."

He shoved Julio back toward the gang-bangers and bolted out into the street.

2:13 P.M. PST
Westwood

Kelly kept sobbing until the Demorol kicked in. The paramedics had arrived fifteen minutes after his plea for help, along with Nina Myers and several other CTU agents. By the time they treated him the pain had made him delirious, and all he could imagine was hot, burning coals entering his bloodstream and coursing through his body.

The medics poured some kind of powder on his hands to snuff out the burning material. Then they washed his hands with some kind of antiseptic that stung like hell, and finally they wrapped his burned hands and shot him full of Demorol.

Glenn Schneider had arrived with the CTU team. He was bald, with wide shoulders and a wide belly, too. Spaced out on pain and painkillers, Kelly imagined him to be a human shield against bombs.

The bomb squad leader looked at Kelly's bandaged hands and said, "Whoever did this is a real bastard. That's homemade napalm they used. I guess they didn't want anyone messing with their bomb. You know, if you'd tried to pick it up instead of kicking it, it would have burned your hands and your face right off. It's also lucky it didn't hit the Solidox."

"Oh, I feel lucky," Kelly said dryly.

Nina Myers sat down beside him. "Nice work," she said. "You know they found more of this Solidox planted in the heating system in the hallway. This bomb would have taken out this whole floor, and probably started a fire that would have killed more people."

"We find anything here?" Kelly asked. He didn't mind saving lives, but he was hoping his burned hands had helped to advance their case.

"One thing," Nina said. "Bits of wire. Looks like someone tried to clean it all up, but they were in a hurry—"

"Yeah, well, they needed time to leave me that present."

"Right. Anyway, they missed some. The wire is just wire, same as you'd use in a computer or stereo. But the insulation is weird, and there are a couple of connectors that are also weird. We're taking it back to study."

"Bits of wire," Kelly said grimly, staring at his bandaged hands. "Well, I guess it's better than bits of me."

2:29 P.M. PST
Westin St. Francis Hotel, San Francisco

President Barnes never got angry in public, and he rarely lost his temper even in private. His self-control had nothing to do with temperament and everything to do with self-preservation; when Harry Barnes lost it, he lost it completely. The Presidential Suite at the Westin bore witness to that fact.

Barnes began with the telephone on his desk and progressed to the wooden guest chair. Those two objects and several others struck the desk with force, courtesy of Harry Barnes's temper.

"What the goddamned hell does that asshole think he's doing!" Barnes raged.

Mitch Rasher weathered the storm better than the shattered chair (it helped that he was neither the object nor its target). He stood to one side, serene as a stone, letting the storm blow over him.

"Who leaked the fucking story!" Barnes demanded.

"Well, offhand, I'd say it was him," Rasher said.

"He wouldn't dare!" the President said. His initial rage was passing. He felt it drain away, emptied into the sacrificial pieces of furniture. Everyone thought Mitch Rasher's greatest contribution to his presidency was his political strategy. It wasn't; it was this—this ability to manage Barnes as he passed through these infrequent but dangerous rages.

Barnes straightened his tie and smoothed his dress shirt. He picked up the remote and rewound, replaying comments from Attorney General Quincy at a press conference. "I assure you that the FBI and other agencies are investigating these threats and taking them quite seriously. I would like to point out that I have spoken directly with agents in charge of this investigation and I was told in no uncertain terms that these potential terrorists were under surveillance six months ago. However, the case was dropped due to an inability to gather evidence. If the NAP Act had been enacted back then, I'm sure these terrorists would have been apprehended long before they became a threat."

Barnes took one more deep breath. Drained, calm, he returned to the stone-faced deal maker everyone outside that room believed him to be. "He's using a terrorist threat against me to scoop up a little more power."

Rasher nodded. "But a little more power for him is a little more power for you."

Barnes waved that off. "If I don't have enough power now then I'm a sick man, and so are you. This privacy act is either good for the country or it's not."

Rasher smiled. He put his fingers together in front of him, adopting that strange angelic pose so out of sync with his schemes. "Jim seems to believe in it enough to use this so-called threat against you as a soapbox."

Barnes leaned against his desk. "There is no threat, right? That's confirmed."

"None," Rasher said. "The source itself is questionable, and they don't even have the right city."

"You know, he's forcing our hand. If I don't get out in front of this thing, I won't get any of the credit if it passes. I'll look like I sat on the sidelines while important legislation was enacted by him."

Rasher walked over to the coffee table and began to pick up pieces of broken chair. "Mr. President, do you recall who wrote the much ballyhooed campaign finance reform bill that proved useless?"

"McCain-Feingold."

"Exactly. And, by any chance, do you recall who wrote the Personal Responsibility and Work Reconciliation Act, commonly called the Welfare Reform Act, that was so popular a few years ago?"

Barnes searched his memory. "No."

"Exactly. When it comes to issues like this, people don't remember successes, they remember failures. Let Quincy be the pioneer, sir. Either he'll get shot full of arrows or he'll found a city. Then you'll come in and run it. Or if the people don't like it, you can veto the whole thing and be the people's champion."

Barnes frowned. He was too competitive to enjoy that advice, but he couldn't deny its logic. He decided to make a short list of replacements for the office of Attorney General.

2:40 P.M. PST
Downtown Los Angeles

The last half hour had been a frantic one for Jack Bauer and the support staff at CTU. Two minutes after reaching his SUV, Jack was driving on surface streets into the downtown area and receiving a detailed description of Babak Farrah. Farrah was a legal emigre from Iran, working in the import/export business, and information from Customs suggested that while most of his business was legal, Farrah had a taste for the illegal, from exotic antiquities to Prada knockoffs to drugs. He didn't seem to need the money. He enjoyed being a gangster.

Jack ordered CTU's clandestine operations team to build him an identity. He needed to be someone Farrah might want to work with—no one large enough to be a rival, but not so small that he was beneath notice. By the time Jack pulled to the public parking lot at Pershing Square, he knew who he was: Jack Knudson, low-level businessman who'd made some money trading weapons for cash. It wasn't a great cover, but it was the best they could do in fifteen minutes. Dummy phone lines were set up, and calls were made to several dealers who worked both sides of the fence, cooperating with CTU when the cash or the circumstance was right. They would back Jack's story.

Jack left his car and crossed the street, walking up toward Flower.

2:42 P.M. PST
Farrah's Loft

Babak Farrah was cutting the ring finger off a thief's hand when the intercom buzzed.

"What?" he barked.

"There's a guy here to see you. Says he knows Tamar Farrigian and that you should do business with him."

"Get his name."

"Jack Knudson."

"Tell him to wait."

Farrah turned back to his victim. The thief's hand was bleeding, but not too badly. Farrah had tied a rubber hose around his wrist. One of Farrah's two thugs—a big Armenian who could have been the twin of the other—had lain his substantial body weight over the victim, while the other one held his right arm extended.

"You understand now that it is not in your best interest to steal from me," Farrah said calmly.

The man, immobilized under the guard's weight, could only sob, "Yes, yes!"

"Wait a moment and we'll discuss this further." He walked around the pool of blood spreading across the plastic sheet they had carefully laid down. He didn't want blood in this apartment. The developers were charging an arm and two legs for these new lofts they were renovating downtown. He didn't want his ruined by some idiot's blood.

Farrah reached his desk, dialed a number, and waited to be patched through by a secretary. "Tamar, it is Babak. Yes, good, how are you?" He did not know Tamar well, but they moved in similar circles and had done some business together, and Babak trusted Tamar as far as he trusted anyone.

"Listen, do you know someone named Knudson? Yeah, Jack Knudson. He's okay? Okay, thanks. Keep your head down." He hung up. He walked calmly past the sobbing man, buzzed his intercom, and said, "Okay, let him come up."

He had put his knife down gently on a glass coffee table nearby. He picked it up now and signaled his men to hold firm. They bore down on the thief's arm and body. Farrah gripped another finger and laid the knife edge against it. The blade sank through the first millimeter like it was butter. After that, he had to work, just like with the last one. He was still sawing away when the elevator doors opened.

Jack walked into Babak Farrah's loft just as the second finger came off. One of the bodyguards stood up quickly and intercepted Jack, searching him. He pulled Jack's SigSauer off and tucked it into his pants. Then he nodded to Farrah and resumed his position over the victim. "So you take from my inventory and think I won't notice," Babak said. "You think because I have money now I don't count what I have. You did not grow up where I did. A man who has nothing counts everything, my friend. You, I think, will count fingers for the rest of your life." He reached down and patted the victim on the head. "Keep him there," he said to his bodyguards.

Farrah raised himself up to his full height, which was not impressive. He was five and a half feet tall and nearly as wide, with a thick, short mustache and a head of hair that nature never intended him to have. His eyes were dark and wet—disturbingly, they reminded Jack of Nazila's—and his mouth was small. He was wearing an expensive Ermenegildo Zegna suit. He nodded at Jack. "So, why do I want to meet with you?"

Jack said, "Tamar Farrigian said—"

"Yeah, yeah, I know you know Tamar, so what? Why are we talking, you and me?"

Farrah's loft was beautiful. One entire wall was a window that looked out on the city. By day, the view was ugly—the browns and grays of the city set beneath smog-shrouded mountains—but at night it must be breathtaking. The loft was one gigantic room divided by Japanese screens. A set of gleaming mahogany stairs rose up to the loft itself, which served as Farrah's bedroom.

Jack sat down on the couch as though he belonged there. "I'm here because I'm new in town and I want to work with the best. You're listening because I'm the best."

"Best what, my friend?" Farrah said. He looked amused, which told Jack he'd struck the right tone.

"Jack of all trades, master of none," Jack said. "But

I'm good at putting people who buy weapons together with people who sell them without my name getting on anybody's lips, and I know how to use a little muscle when I need to. You can ask Tamar about that."

"Well, it just so happens I could have an opening." Farrah laughed. "Stumpy there was one of my guys, but I caught him stealing. Didn't I catch you stealing?" he said, raising his voice. He tapped the man's head with the toe of his shoe.

"Y-yes," the man sobbed. The stumps of his fingers were still seeping blood onto the plastic sheet all around them.

"You're not a thief, are you?" Farrah asked Jack. "Tell me you're not a thief."

"If I do a good job for you and you pay me well, there's no need for stealing."

"Ah," Farrah said, still amused. "You are a closer. That is worse than a thief!" He laughed. "Okay, okay, look, maybe I hire you, maybe I don't. I have to check with some people. But for today, stay with me. A friend of Tamar's is a friend of mine, at least for this afternoon. Okay?"

"Okay," Jack said.

"Good. Just one thing. Let him up." He motioned to his two big bodyguards. The guards obeyed and got off the man, pulling him to his feet. He was bigger than Farrah, smaller than the two Armenian giants. His face was pale and contorted with pain. Farrah went to a desk half-hidden by one of the Japanese screens. He opened a desk drawer and took out a handgun, a very nice Kimber 1911, Jack noted, and walked back. He offered the Kimber to Jack. "Shoot him. Then we go."

• •

THE FOLLOWING TAKES PLACE
BETWEEN THE HOURS OF
3 P.M. AND 4 P.M.
PACIFIC STANDARD TIME

• •

3:01 P.M. PST
Farrah's Loft

Farrah pushed the Kimber into Jack's hand. "The head or the chest, I don't care. But try to keep the blood on the plastic."

Jack hesitated for a fraction of a second. This was a test, of course. No law enforcement agent would commit murder to maintain his cover. Jack Bauer, however, was not a police officer.

He raised the gun and fired. The round blew off the victim's pinky finger before lodging itself in the desk. The victim screamed and crumpled to his knees, grabbing his mutilated hand.

"Hey!" Farrah shouted angrily. "That desk cost money!"

Jack handed the gun back to him. "If you want me to do more than that, you have to pay for it. I'm a businessman, just like you."

Farrah grabbed the gun away, but his anger was already turning into amusement. "Okay, okay, my friend, I understand your point. You're a good man, I'm liking you already. Come with me on a little errand I have to run. You two, let's go."

The two Armenian giants followed Jack and Farrah to the door, leaving the mutilated victim behind. Farrah pressed a button and the elevator doors opened with a whoosh. "Oh, wait," Farrah said. He raised the Kimber and fired twice, both rounds puncturing the victim's chest. He fell over onto the plastic. "Okay," Farrah said. The elevator doors closed.

3:10 P.M. PST
CTU Headquarters, Los Angeles

"Where the hell is Jack Bauer!" Ryan Chappelle demanded. "He's got a prisoner gathering dust in a holding cell and he's nowhere to be found. And where's Kelly Sharpton!"

He zeroed in on Jessi Bandison, who was the only analyst not cowering under his tirade.

"Jack Bauer is following leads from the terrorist threat," she stated. "He tracked down a man who may have smuggled the terrorists into the country, and he is now checking into the man they were dropped off with. Kelly Sharpton went to investigate an address for a militia member who has not been accounted for. He discovered a bomb there. He managed to defuse it, but nearly got his hands burned off. He's being checked out at the UCLA emergency room before being okayed to return here."

Chappelle was caught mid-rant. The analysts in the room, and Chappelle himself, experienced a shared vision of Bauer and Sharpton, two rugged field agents, out in the world doing their jobs, while Chappelle, pale-faced and blue-blooded, raged inside the sunless CTU office. As his ears turned red, Chappelle merely grunted and turned away.

3:36 P.M. PST
CTU Headquarters, Los Angeles

Kelly walked back into CTU under his own steam, with both hands still wrapped in bandages. The prognosis was good. He'd have scars, but no permanent damage.

Jessi met him halfway through the door, resisting the urge to hug him. "Chappelle wants to see you."

Kelly nodded. A meeting with Ryan Chappelle was the perfect homecoming after a date being sprayed with napalm.

Chappelle had camped out in Kelly's office anyway, so Kelly went up there and sat down in the guest chair.

"Do you want—?" Chappelle offered him the desk chair.

Kelly held him off. "No, I'm fine here. You wanted to see me."

"Yes." Chappelle took a deep breath, trying to excise the pedantry from his voice. "I'd like it if you could tell me what's going on. What's really going on."

"Why do you ask like that?"

Chappelle chuckled. "Look, I may not be a field agent like you and mighty Jack Bauer, but I'm not an idiot. You're caught hacking the Attorney General's computer and the next thing I know the AG himself is calling to exonerate you. Jack Bauer's running all over Los Angeles looking for terrorists no one else believes exists. You try to blow yourself up. Tell me everything." He made his voice as gentle as possible. "Maybe I can help."

Kelly was impressed by the monumental effort it must have taken for Chappelle to sound like a human being. He proceeded to summarize every piece of information that he and Jack had gathered. He even— against his better judgment—included the Attorney General's attempt to blackmail Senator Drexler.

He expected Chappelle to reject his story about blackmail. Instead the District Director touched his fingers to his thin lips, then said, "But you don't have any proof of this blackmail?"

"I erased everything from Quincy's computer. Drexler is a witness, of course, but she won't testify. If she does, she'll drag her staff in and it will hurt them. She's also got some contact with the CIA that she's protecting."

Chappelle nodded. "It'd be impossible to prove anyway. A politician that high up doesn't make a play of that nature without having an out." He switched gears mentally. "So Bauer's sure these terrorists exist? He's got eight of them being smuggled into the country?"

"The only piece that doesn't fit," Kelly said, repeating information Jessi had gathered from Jack, "is that his informant told him they were brought in a couple of months ago. If these guys are attached to the same rumor Jack first heard, they'd have to have been here for at least six months."

"A lot of loose ends," Chappelle said. For once, he was not being critical, he was simply analyzing the situation. "How does this damned militia fit in. Do they?"

"Well, I don't think the Greater Nation does," Kelly suggested. "I think their part of the story ends once they learn about terrorists and we stop them. All the rest has been Jack. The only part of the Nation that doesn't figure is Frank Newhouse. If he's under cover for the AG why not identify himself? If his job was to spy on the Greater Nation, then it's over. If his job was to track down the terrorists, why not join forces with us?"

"And why blow up an entire building?" Chappelle added. "It was him, wasn't it?"

Kelly held up his damaged hands. "I would so love to ask him that question in person." Chappelle nodded in understanding. The two men shared a moment of silence, awkward and self-conscious. Kelly, not ready or willing to share an extended human moment with Chappelle, looked away. He was relieved when the intercom buzzed.

"Kelly, I know you're meeting, but can I come up?" Jessi Bandison asked.

"Come," he said.

She was there in a few minutes. "We got our initial analysis of the wiring they found in the apartment. The data is available off the server, but I can give you the rundown. The wire bits we brought back were heavily insulated. The connectors that we found were also insulated. They were specifically designed to protect wiring at points of contact with machines or other wires. It's almost like some kind of shield."

"Do we have any idea what that means?" Kelly asked.

"Not yet, but we think we'll have a working theory by the end of the day."

3:44 P.M. PST
Peppermint Club

Farrah's car pulled up to the Peppermint, a strip club southeast of downtown in an industrial area nestled between the downtown businesses and the beach communities. The place had just opened for business and the parking lot was nearly deserted. There were plenty of spaces in front, but one of the Armenian giants, acting as the driver of Farrah's limousine, pulled around to the back anyway.

The sun was bright in the parking lot as they got out. Jack looked around. There was nothing like going to a strip club on a sunny afternoon, he thought, to make you feel like a total loser.

One of the giants opened the back door to the club and Farrah walked in, followed by Jack. The two giants brought up the rear.

Farrah walked through the club's little kitchen, saying hello to the two men working there. He passed into the main room, which was as dark as midnight. No effort had been spared to shield the Peppermint's clientele from the world outside. Darkness ruled here, despite the fact that two stages were awash in multi-colored stage lights. Music blasted enthusiastically, and a silky-voiced DJ introduced the next dancer as though the club was totally packed instead of almost completely empty, which it was.

A dancer was on stage, going through the motions. A man in a Von Dutch T-shirt sat at the edge of the stage drinking an O'Doul's nonalcoholic beer. Jack saw one or two other men sitting at tables in the shadows. There were clearly not enough prospects here to give the dancer much enthusiasm. She was naked; she had the body and the moves, but there was no oomph in her performance. She'd gotten stuck with the early shift, and there was nothing to do but get through it as painlessly as possible.

Farrah walked through the Peppermint like he owned the place, clapping for the girl on the stage and whistling. Jack noticed that the twin giants had disappeared. "Ah, Tina, you can shake your ass better than that, I know this from personal experience! Hey, Mikey!" He turned to the DJ tucked away in a corner. "Get one of the other girls on the stage, I've got a guest here and Tina is my treat for him!"

The DJ shooed Tina off the stage in his radio voice, and another dancer appeared to take her place.

"Sit, sit, Jack Knudson who needs to get paid to kill." Farrah laughed. "You are in for a treat, my friend."

The girl, Tina, came over. She had put her clothes back on, such as they were. Her dark hair was in pigtails. Her blouse was rolled up and tied in a knot under her breasts. She wore a schoolgirl skirt specifically engineered not to cover her ass, and thigh high stockings.

"Hey, big tipper," she said to Farrah. "I'd ask what brings you in here so early, but I know it's me."

"Oh, it's you, it's you," Farrah said. He was like a kid in a candy store. "But it's also a little business. I want you to keep my friend entertained while I go talk to someone. The dance is on me, okay, okay?"

She smiled at Jack. "Well, as a matter of fact, the dance is on *you*, but he's paying for it." To make her point, she fell onto him and slid her body down his until she was kneeling in front of him.

Jack tried to look as though his attention was on the girl while at the same time trying to track Farrah and his bodyguards through the darkened nightclub. Unfortunately, the table Farrah had chosen left half the club behind Jack, and turning his back on the girl would have been way too obvious. The girl lowered her head and brushed her thick black hair between his legs, then lifted her chin up to look at him and smiled as she pressed her body against him. "You're awfully good-looking to be one of his friends," she said with a well-practiced squeak.

"And you're way too good to be working the dead times," he said. "You new?"

She shook her head. "Part of the deal. Every girl's gotta work one afternoon a month. Otherwise, no one would do it." She jumped to her feet and turned around, arching her back and shifting her hips in a way that reached past all of Jack's training and grabbed him in that deep place where all his primal urges lay.

A fast movement to his right caught Jack's eye. A man ran by, followed by a big shadow. The smaller figure headed for the front exit and looked like he'd get there, but a second shadow detached itself from the wall and swallowed the little man. Jack heard a squeal. Then he heard Farrah's voice say, "Come on,

Farid, okay, okay. Come outside and talk with us. That's all."

The two giants turned around and started toward the back. In a flash of light from the dance floor, Jack saw a smaller man, looking like he'd just been sentenced to death, walk between them. He looked Middle Eastern.

"What's all that?" he asked.

Tina looked over her shoulder seductively and shrugged. "Shit goes on here sometimes" was all she said.

"You know that guy with them?"

She looked, as though paying attention for the first time. "The little one. No. I mean, he's come in once or twice but he doesn't go for me. He's an Arab, and they all go for the blonds."

"An Arab," Jack wondered, taking a long shot. "First time you saw him was maybe a few months ago? With Farrah?"

The girl shrugged. "I guess, maybe."

"Excuse me," he said, standing up. If Farrah's actions in the loft were any indication, they were going to kill this man, and it occurred to Jack that this victim might be one that he needed alive.

```
 1  2  3  4  5  6  7  8  9
10 11 12 13 14 15 16 17
18 19 20 21 22 23 24
```

4:00 P.M. PST
Peppermint Club

Jack walked across the dark club, leaving the hot-bodied girl in the schoolgirl outfit behind and chasing after the Armenian thugs and their prisoner, thinking, not for the last time, that the twists and turns of his job were sometimes ridiculous.

He reached the back door as it swung closed, and caught the handle with a sliver of light still visible. Farrah was close enough to the door that he could hear the man talking. Not wanting to reveal himself, Jack kept the door ajar and listened.

"Farrah, please, please," the other man was pleading. "I didn't know Rasheed would steal from you. He never stole from me."

"Okay, okay," Farrah said angrily. "I believe that. I believe he was stealing with you, how's that!"

"No, please—"

"No, please," Farrah mocked. "What I know is that you recommended that cocksucker and he stole from me. That makes me think he stole from me and maybe moved some of the merchandise through you, eh?"

"No, I swear!" the other man, Farid, pleaded.

Farrah laughed. "And do you know what else he did? What you did? You used my place as a dropoff. My place. I'm not the bus station, Farid, okay? You drop off people like that, it brings attention that I don't want, okay?"

"Don't kill me!"

"Why not? I thought your type was always ready to die for your cause. Isn't that what you do, give your lives to Allah?"

"I'm not one of those!" the other man said.

"No? Your friends were, weren't they? The ones you and Rasheed brought in. They were supposed to work for me, weren't they, but they went off with my guns and some of my money and now where are they? Where is my money?"

"I-I don't know. I swear I don't know!" Just as he had with Ramin, Jack could tell that this Farid was telling the truth. He could also tell that Farrah didn't particularly care and planned to kill him anyway. He couldn't let that happen.

Jack pulled the door wide open and sauntered out into the bright sunlight. He blinked a little till his eyes adjusted, making all his movements big and careless.

"What the fuck—" he said casually, seeing the two big Armenians and Farrah looming over Farid, who was on his knees. Farrah, with his back to Jack, held a gun, his hand hanging low along his side.

"Just a little more business," Farrah said.

Jack walked up to them, eyeing Farid. He was Persian, not Arab, which fit the profile Jack was looking for. He was also clearly terrified.

"Like I said, I'm looking for business," Jack said. "You want to pay me a little something, I'll kill him for you."

Farrah laughed. "What, you think I catch the fish and then I need someone to carry him for me?"

"Suit yourself," Jack said. He stepped back.

Farrah raised his gun. When he did, Jack lunged forward, covering the distance between them in a single burst, his arms extending as far as possible. One hand caught the gun and the other hand clutched Farrah's wrist. Jack twisted his body and snapped the gun from Farrah's hand. In nearly the same motion he smashed the muzzle into Farrah's face and shoved him backward. He jumped away from the clutches of the two startled giants and turned the weapon on them.

Farrah spat blood out of his chubby mouth. "Okay, okay, I got to kill some people for this."

"I've had one of those days, too," Jack said. "You, Farid, I need you to stand up and come over here. You two, Dumb and Dumber, you stay where you are."

The Peppermint's back door flew open and Tina walked out. "Hey, someone's got to pay me!"

The sound of the door flying open seemed to break a spell that bound them all. The two giants lumbered into action. Farid bolted like a frightened rabbit. Farrah reached down to his ankle for what was undoubtedly a backup weapon.

Jack fired, but Farrah's gun jammed. The first giant put a huge hand on him and Jack, still holding the weapon by its grip, punched the muzzle into his teeth. He snatched his own weapon from the Armenian's belt and, at the same time, kicked the other one in the groin. Both giants sagged down to their knees. Jack took off after Farid, who had nearly reached the corner of the building.

4:31 P.M. PST
CTU Headquarters, Los Angeles

Jessi Bandison buzzed Kelly Sharpton in his office. "Kelly, we have results."

"I'll come down. Call Chappelle."

Kelly descended the stairs and headed for the conference room. Chappelle was there before him, along with Nina Myers and half of CTU. Nina Myers said specifically to Kelly and Chappelle, "Let me introduce Amy Brant. She's on loan to us from the NSA, because we didn't have anyone who recognized the wiring we found. Ms. Brant."

A heavyset woman with the face of a farmer's daughter stood up. She held a tiny piece of blue rubber in her hand. When she pressed a button on the conference display, an image of the same piece of blue rubber appeared on the screen, greatly magnified.

"This is a sample of what your forensics team found in the condo," Ms. Brant said in a Minnesota accent. "This, plus some interesting plastic connectors, like this." She clicked a mouse, and a new image popped up. This piece looked like an orange plastic cap. "This is a connector, the kind you use when you have two wires you want to put together."

"Like if you're installing a lamp in the ceiling," Kelly offered.

"Right there," Brant said. "So the functions the wire and the connector serve aren't anything special. But the rubber coating on the wire, and the shape and content of the plastic connector, these were things we hadn't seen before."

"Do you know where they come from?" Chappelle asked.

"We do now," Brant said. "They come from us. We make them."

"What do they do?"

Brant said. "This rubber coating and these connectors are designed to insulate electronic devices against attacks from electromagnetic pulse weapons. EMPs."

The room filled with the low buzz of questions. Chappelle leaned over to Kelly. "Another loose end," he whispered.

Kelly tapped his knuckles on the table for attention. "Wait, wait. I understand what electromagnetic pulses are. Those are the things that knock out electronic devices, right?"

"A nuclear blast might cause one," Nina Myers said.

"A number of people have been working on devices that cause EMP bursts without wiping out the territory with a nuclear blast," Amy Brant said. "EMP burst weapons would neutralize unshielded enemy electronics, everything from night vision goggles to fighter bombers. Some of the research is going on at Cal Tech over in Pasadena."

"Working on," Chappelle repeated. "Do functioning devices like these actually exist."

"Oh, yes," Brant said. "But only as prototypes. That is, the functionality is certain. Field application such as proper transportation, field repair and diagnostics, all of that is in its infancy."

Nina Myers gave voice to a concern they all felt. "We spend a lot of time worrying about nuclear, chemical, and bio threats. Why not this? What would happen if someone set one of these things off in a city like Los Angeles?"

"Of course, it depends on the size of the pulse. There are other factors, too. The ground acts as a natural, well, ground, so the closer the device is to the Earth, the less effect it has. But if it were big enough and high enough, it would knock out everything.

"There's another kind of EMP device being developed. It's called HERF gun. That's high energy radio frequency gun to you laymen. It's exactly what it sounds like—a directed weapon that can be aimed at a specific vehicle or machine. It's obviously much less dangerous to the population at large, but it can totally shut down whatever it's aimed at."

"The military applications must be staggering," Kelly said.

Ms. Brant nodded. "Yes, I think so, but I'm not sure. The downside to an EMP device is that you can shield against it. That brings us back to these wires. You can shield a device in two ways: by putting it in a Farraday Cage, or by wiring it with insulation like this."

"Farraday Cage?" Nina asked.

"Basically it's a big metal tube that deflects electromagnetic pulses. It works really well, but you have to have one big enough to cover whatever you want to protect. So the wiring option is usually better. You could wire an entire airplane if you had to, but it would be a huge project."

Chappelle groaned. "Okay, so now we know what an EMP device does. And we know that someone in that condo had wiring specially designed to resist one. Do we know who was in the condo?"

Kelly answered. "Best guess is Frank Newhouse, undercover for the Department of Justice, pretending to work with the Greater Nation militia. But why he continues to go undercover, I don't know. And I don't know why he'd plant a bomb in his condo."

"Maybe the militia got him," Nina suggested. "Maybe they planted the bomb."

"Forensics?" Chappelle inquired.

Another CTU agent, Janet Takuyama from the forensics department, spoke up. "We pulled up thirteen separate sets of fingerprints, including Frank Newhouse, a set we matched to a maid, and two sets we matched to maintenance workers. The others don't show up in our database, which could just mean they don't have records yet."

"It also means they're not military or law enforcement," Chappelle noted.

Takuyama continued, "We also pulled a bad partial off of one of the buckets. We're running it against possible matches, but that list is going to be long. We'll try to whittle it down."

4:39 P.M. PST
Peppermint Club

Farid rounded the front of the Peppermint Club and ran back into the building. This was either a brilliant strategy because it was unexpected, or it would deliver him right back into the hands of his enemies if they cut through the building.

Jack burst inside, shoving his way past the startled doorman who clearly had already been knocked off his stool by Farid. The man grabbed Jack's shoulder. Jack spun and punched him in the throat and the man dropped with a gasp. Jack pushed through the thick velvet curtains into the club again.

"Ah!"

His eyes hadn't adjusted to the dark, but he heard the sound and he could just make out Farid struggling with one of the Armenians.

"Freeze!" Jack yelled. He put a warning shot into the ceiling. The girls in the room screamed and a few male voices shouted in alarm. Shadowy figures scattered in several directions. Jack leveled his Sig, but in the dark, with two struggling figures, he had no shot. He raced forward and threw himself at the bigger of the two figures. It was like hitting a tree. He bounced off, but managed to keep his feet. The giant shoved Farid aside and punched Jack in the face. The room spun. Jack felt the giant grab his hair and punch him again. Jack shoved his gun into the Armenian's stomach and fired three times. The giant crashed to the floor.

Jack staggered backward, his head swimming. He shook the cobwebs out and spun in time to see Farrah and the other bodyguard burst into the room. He raised his weapon and fired, but his vision was blurred, ruining his aim. Dazed though he was, he had the sense to duck as four or five gunshots answered his own. He rolled to his left, bumping into a chair. He crawled along the floor. He felt blood pour down his nose, but he didn't care about the bleeding. He needed time for his head to clear.

He nearly forgot about Farid. He caught a glimpse of the man running for the back door again. Jack rolled to his back and aimed for the exit, squeezing off a few more rounds. Farid yelped and hit the deck again. "Don't move again!" Jack ordered.

A bullet punctured the lounge chair next to him. Jack rolled back to his stomach, searching for targets. Somewhere in the room a girl kept screaming. A shadow moved across his field of vision. Jack aimed low, firing four times. He was rewarded with an angry bellow and the other Armenian collapsed, his ankles blown away. Jack felt his head clearing at last and he rose to a crouched position, keeping his head below the level of the tables.

Someone somewhere turned on the lights. Jack spotted Farrah in the corner at the same time Farrah spotted him. He was holding the dancer, Tina, by the neck. When he saw Jack he spun in that direction, putting the girl between himself and Jack's line of fire.

"I don't know what you want, okay!" Farrah yelled. "But I want Farid. You get him for me or I will kill this girl."

....

**THE FOLLOWING TAKES PLACE
BETWEEN THE HOURS OF
5 P.M. AND 6 P.M.
PACIFIC STANDARD TIME**

....

5:00 P.M. PST
Peppermint Club

Jack's ears were still ringing from the big Armenian's
punches. He took a deep breath and focused. He
wasn't giving up Farid. That was his primary goal. He
was tempted to just back away, taking Farid out the
back door. But Farrah was a cold-blooded killer and
in the one hour he'd known the man Jack had developed an intense dislike for him.

He aimed his weapon.

"Get away!" Farrah yelled, seeing him. "I'll kill her!"

That was everyone's mistake, Jack thought. Thinking of him as a police officer. Thinking of him as
someone who had to play by the rules all the time.

He fired.

The bullet whistled past the stripper's cheek and entered Farrah's face, exiting the back of his skull and lodging itself in the plasterboard and taking a significant amount of Farrah's brain with it. The dancer fainted.

Jack glanced behind him, seeing Farid cowering on the floor. "Don't go anywhere," he warned.

Jack hurried to each of the two Armenians. One was dead, but Jack took his weapon anyway. The other was in shock, both his feet dangling from strips of flesh where his ankles had been. Jack kicked his gun away.

From somewhere in the depths of the building, someone yelled. "Get out of here. I called the police!"

"Good," Jack said, suddenly feeling exhausted. "That's very good."

He checked Farrah, too, although there wasn't much left of him. He tossed the gun aside. The girl, Tina, was out cold, but her breathing was regular and her heart beat was strong.

Jack staggered back over to Farid, who was looking up from the floor in astonishment. "Who the hell are you?"

Jack sat down in a lounge chair next to him. "I'm the guy asking you the questions," he said. "And before I start asking I'm going to tell you this one time. I have no patience left, so unless you want to end up looking like Farrah over there, you answer me right away. Understand?"

Farid nodded.

Jack asked questions, and this was the story he heard:

Farid Koshbin had been a runner for a few Iranian fences, front men who took stolen and knockoff merchandise and put it into their stores as the real deal. About a year ago he had discovered that he knew enough people to be a valuable contact himself, especially for Persians and Arabs coming over to the United States. He had worked for Farrah several times. Babak Farrah liked to bring over Iranians to work for him, because they relied on him and he could pay them low wages for a year or two before they got wise and quit. Since 9/11, of course, that was harder to do. Farid Koshbin made a little money on the side finding employees for Farrah. He'd learned about eight Persians coming into the country illegally who would need work, so he arranged to help them.

"How'd you hear about them in the first place?" Jack asked.

"Phone call. A guy said he had friends coming over the border who could use some help."

"Was there a name?" Jack demanded.

"No. The guy told me how to reach the coyote who was smuggling them in, so I called him. I got them jobs working for Farrah, but I guess they fucked up. They took off or something and they caused all this."

"When did they arrive?"

"A month ago. Maybe six weeks."

That stumped Jack for a minute. "Weeks ago? Not months? Not six months?"

Farid looked at Jack's gun. "I'll say six months if you want me to, but it was a month."

Something didn't add up, but Jack let Farid finish his story: when the eight Iranians went missing, some guns and money went missing, too. Farrah was mad enough that his hired help was gone, but never let a theft go unpunished. Since he couldn't find the Iranians, he tracked down Farid and was going to punish him.

"So there are eight Iranians in the country. You've seen them with your own eyes," Jack confirmed.

"Yeah, sure."

Weird as it was, this was a relief to Jack. Finally, confirmation of what he'd been saying all along.

There were sirens outside, loud enough and close enough to penetrate the Peppermint's thick walls. Police poured into the room, shouting. Jack held up his badge.

5:37 P.M. PST
Santa Monica, California

Frank Newhouse woke up, instantly alert. This was more out of habit than necessity. The apartment was quiet, as he expected. This address was so far removed from the life and name of Frank Newhouse that no one, not CTU and not even the Attorney General, would connect it with his current activities. His girl, lying next to him, was still asleep. His eyes followed the shape of her body, outlined by the sheets. He appreciated the fact that she stayed in good shape for him. She was a good woman, patient with him during his long stays away from home, and welcoming (very welcoming, he thought, remembering the sex they'd had a short time ago) when he returned.

Newhouse stood up and stretched his body, still lean and muscled after forty-eight years of use. Slipping on jeans and a t-shirt, he walked around the apartment to limber up, then sat down at the kitchen table, where two separate cell phones sat charging. He spent a few minutes running over the plan in his mind. It hadn't all worked out entirely as he'd hoped. He'd never expected his deep cover file to get out of

Langley. Jack Bauer never would have requested it, and if he had, well, Bauer had dropped so low on the food chain, the request probably would have been ignored. Newhouse hadn't expected the information to slip out from a different source. He'd underestimated the Senator and her resources. He made a mental note to find whoever had slipped the files out of the CIA and deal with them personally.

That had been the one slip. The files had led to the condo, which he had had to abandon, because unlike this apartment, the condo was connected to Frank Newhouse.

Still, it would be nearly impossible for CTU to put two and two together, and if they did, by that time it would be too late. The CTU agent had dismantled his bomb and that worried him a little, although he didn't see how it could affect his plans. It didn't really matter if CTU knew about the EMP device. In fact, in some ways it was better if they did. But if Jack Bauer and his team focused on that building, they might learn more than he wanted them to, and that would lead them to places where Frank didn't want them poking their noses. He'd have to tie up a few loose ends.

It also worried Frank that Farrah was taking so long to kill Farid. Farrah should have called in by now. Frank checked one cell phone, but no one had called. Where was Farrah? He had a perfect excuse to get rid of Farid, and plenty of muscle to do it. Newhouse knew how persistent Jack Bauer was, and how vital it was to seal off certain avenues of investigation.

Two cell phones sat in their cradles on the bar near the kitchen. Frank picked one up, dialed a number and waited while it rang.

"It's about time," said Attorney General James Quincy. "What the hell is going on?"

Frank said, "You sound unhappy, sir. Isn't it all happening the way you wanted? You did great on CNN."

"Yes, I got my forum," Quincy said. "But I need the end game now. I'm catching a lot of heat here, Frank." The Attorney General paused. Frank could hear the anxiety in his voice, and he relished it. "You're sure you've got these guys under control. There's no real threat, right?"

Frank did a convincing job of inserting surprise into his voice. "You didn't want a real threat, Mr. Attorney General. You wanted the threat of a terrorist cell to boost your chances for your bill to pass. And you've got it."

"I heard a CTU agent nearly got killed trying to dismantle some kind of bomb. If it had gone off, people would have died."

"The bomb wouldn't have gone off," Frank assured him. He leaned back in his seat and closed his eyes. Politicians were all alike. They talked a tough game, but when it came to doing the heavy lifting, they turned into girls. "As for him getting hurt, I had to do something to make it look dangerous."

"I didn't know anything like that was part of the plan."

"It's better if you don't know some of it," Frank said.

"Just tell me that it will all be over tonight."

"I guarantee it," Frank said. He hung up.

He would have felt sorry for Quincy if he'd had even an ounce of respect for him.

"Hey, baby." His woman stood in the doorway, stretching her lean body and smiling at him. "Mmmm, there's nothing like afternoon sex."

"Nothing like sex with you," he said. She walked forward, sleepy-faced, and he pulled her into his lap. "So I'm going to be busy tonight, but tomorrow I should have plenty of time. We should go up to Santa Barbara."

"Okay, I'll finish my painting." She yawned. "Oh, hey, that reminds me, do you still have those white buckets?"

Frank cocked his head. "White buckets?"

"Yeah, you had a bunch here the other day. I used one as a rinse bucket for my brushes. Mind if I use it again?"

"Sorry, they're gone," he said with a smile. But inside, his heart was breaking. One more loose end to clean up.

5:51 P.M. PST
CTU Headquarters, Los Angeles

Jack pulled in to CTU headquarters. There would be a truckload of paperwork to fill out in the Peppermint shooting, but for the moment he ignored it. He had his phone to his ear, talking with Kelly and the other CTU staff on the crisis even as he entered the building. He was on speakerphone in the conference room, so he kept talking as he entered the building.

". . . so someone hires Farid to organize their transition into Los Angeles, and also hires the smuggler that gets them over the border," Jack was saying. He reached the conference room and saw Sharpton, Chappelle, Nina Myers, CTU chief analyst Jamey Farrell, and Jessi Bandison. He heard his voice coming out of the squawk box on the conference table and hung up his phone. "They get into the country. But it wasn't six months ago, it was just a few weeks ago. That doesn't jibe with our warnings about Ramin Rafizadeh. It also gets him off the hook officially." He took a seat. "It doesn't make sense that the rumors come first, and then the terrorist cell appears. That's bugging me." He had a list of items that bothered him, including the coyote's connection with MS-13 and Farrah's obsession with killing Farid. Farrah could just as easily have escaped the building. Instead he'd taken a hostage.

Kelly added, "There's more that doesn't make sense. Why did these guys have a cheap apartment in Westwood and an expensive condominium a mile away? Why did they try to blow up the fancy condo but leave the apartment intact, when the apartment had the clues to their plans?"

They looked at one another, searching for answers but finding only bewildered looks, until Nina bobbed her head in the direction of an idea. "It's a head fake."

The entire group looked her way. "Go on," Chappelle encouraged.

"They want the apartment found. They don't want the condo found, because the condo has real evidence. So they rig the condo to get rid of the evidence."

"But the condo is connected to Frank Newhouse, not the Iranians," Jessi Bandison observed. "Frank Newhouse is connected to the Greater Nation and the Attorney General."

"Frank Newhouse is the key to all this," said Ryan Chappelle. He spoke definitively, using that voice that Bauer hated. However, Jack had to admit that the director was right. "The unanswered questions all revolve around him."

"Agreed," Jack said. "Jessi, are you up for staying on?"

"She's way overtime," Chappelle said, falling back into character.

"I'm good to go," she said. "I'm getting kind of annoyed with that guy. I've got records I can check."

Jack nodded. "Good. Go. Nina, I think we need to go with your head fake idea. Until we know more about Newhouse, let's assume this EMP lead is the real one and the Islamic poetry clues are a false lead. Get on the phone. Call UCLA and Cal Tech. Tell them to check on everything they have related to EMPs. Do that now."

Nina understood that "now" meant "right now" and she left the table while Jack was still talking.

"Then get going. Kelly, Jamey," Jack said. "We need to learn more about this Babak Farrah, may he rest in peace. You should . . ." He paused. Kelly was grinning at him so brightly that Jack almost blushed. The two of them were left at the table with Ryan Chappelle. "Damn, Kelly, I'm sorry. I'm not the SAC here anymore. You should be divvying these assignments."

"No problem, sir!" Kelly said, but he was laughing. "You can't help yourself, Jack. I'd be the same in your shoes. This is your ship. You ought to be running it. No offense," he added for Chappelle's benefit.

The Director wasn't quite as amused. "I'm surprised you'd let Bauer undermine your authority, Kelly," he said critically.

Kelly patted his two bandaged hands together. "You serve in the military and you see some interesting things," he said. "Everyone salutes the officers, but when the excrement hits the fan, everyone turns to the real leaders. Usually it's some NCO from Bumfuck, Alabama. Doesn't matter. He's the guy in the foxhole that everybody listens to."

Chappelle couldn't help the disdain that crept into his voice. "Are you saying you're not that man?"

"Oh, I am," Kelly said, with a wink to Jack. "This just isn't my foxhole."

Jack and Kelly stood up from the table as Nina Myers entered the room. Her face was grave. "We've got a problem," she said. "I talked to Cal Tech. Someone stole their EMP devices. Yesterday."

....

THE FOLLOWING TAKES PLACE
BETWEEN THE HOURS OF
6 P.M. AND 7 P.M.
PACIFIC STANDARD TIME

....

6:00 P.M. PST
CTU Headquarters, Los Angeles

The power that CTU brought to bear in the next
quarter of an hour was, to say the least, awesome.
Within minutes, every computer terminal of every analyst and programmer inside CTU was turned loose
on the subject of Cal Tech in Pasadena. Data flowed
into the clandestine unit's Los Angeles headquarters
like water flowing into a reservoir. Employee records
were checked. Student names and I.D.s were cross-
checked against the names of known terrorist suspects. E-mail accounts were run (without the owners'
knowledge) and phrases were matched against key
words related to EMPs, Iran, Allah, Persia, and a

thousand other phrases that might offer a connection. Two thousand gigabytes of security footage were dumped into CTU's computers and scanned by Jamey Farrell and a team of analysts. Students and teachers at Cal Tech who never knew they were on camera had their images analyzed by CTU's facial recognition software. On one single screen, cars running in and out of the Cal Tech parking lot closest to the building that had housed the EMP devices were analyzed, looking for any car that was out of the ordinary.

Meanwhile, Jack and Kelly received more information from Nina. "Two devices are missing. The first is a bomb. Not a bomb like we think of," she added, "a pulse weapon. Set it off, it emits an electromagnetic pulse that wipes out all electronic devices in its range. The second one is, as far as I can tell, the rocket-propelled grenade of the sci-fi world. Aim it, fire, it zaps its target with an electromagnetic beam that fries all its circuits. The Cal Tech people called it a HERF Rifle—HERF for high energy radio frequency."

"What's the range?" Kelly asked.

"Unknown. They were testing. The bomb's potential depends on how it's delivered. The rifle is more directed. You can build a little one for a few hundred bucks, but it doesn't reach more than a hundred feet. This one is supposed to be the surface-to-air missile of radio waves.'

"Why did Cal Tech have these things?" Kelly asked. "They don't build weapons there, do they?"

"That's what I asked," Nina replied. "I got two answers. The Director of Research for the Advanced Physics Department told me they had a contract with DOD and I should mind my own friggin' business."

Jack considered this. "I know Cal Tech is the research branch of Jet Propulsion Laboratories."

Nina nodded. "Then some public relations person with a little more tact got on the phone and said they'd been loaned the devices to test some shielding mechanism. Either way, they're both gone."

"We should have known this earlier," Jack said. "Why didn't they report it?"

"They didn't know. The devices had been stored and weren't scheduled for use again for two more days."

Jack had the distinct sense that they were fighting on too many fronts. In combat, a classic strategy was to engage the enemy in one location, causing him to move resources to that front, then attack him elsewhere. He had the vague sense that he was falling victim to that strategy, but he couldn't tell where the real attack might happen.

His intercom buzzed. It was Jamey Farrell, CTU's head programmer. "We've got something."

6:09 P.M. PST
CTU Headquarters, Los Angeles

Jack watched the video screen as Jamey Farrell fast-forwarded through video from a security camera at the edge of the parking lot. It showed a walkway from the lot toward the buildings near the Physics Labs at Cal Tech. "They did a really good job," she said in grudging admiration. "If there hadn't been about eight of us working on this, we'd have missed it. There." She froze the video. Jack saw two men walking together. They were dressed like grad students;

that is to say, they wore sloppy jeans and sloppy T-shirts, and they looked like they didn't eat well enough. Both were dark-skinned, but that meant nothing. Half the student body of Cal Tech was Pakistani or Indian. There were other people in the shot, but Jamey used computer enhancement software to zoom in on the two men.

"Do you see anything unusual about them?" Jamey asked.

Jack pressed the keyboard, zooming out so he could see other students. "No."

"You will," Jamey promised.

She fast-forwarded and froze. "There. This is ten minutes later."

Two more men, both dark-skinned, both dressed like graduate students. "I don't see it yet."

Jamey fast-forwarded again. On the third set of two dark-skinned men, Jack understood. "No backpacks."

"Right. There's a fourth set, too. Yesterday afternoon we had four sets of two males, probably of Middle Eastern descent, walk on to campus with no backpacks within a five- to ten-minute span of each other."

Kelly nodded. "Are you working to ID them?"

Jamey looked mildly insulted. "Of course. So far, they aren't in the records."

"That's them, then," Jack said. "Transportation?"

Jamey nodded and clicked her keyboard, minimizing video of the walkway and calling up a camera shot of the driveway into the lot. "We studied the parking lot for a half-hour window prior to the appearance of the first two." The video ran until she froze it on the image of a blue van. "This van pulls in. It doesn't leave until nearly midnight that night. The eight guys never appear on camera again. When they left, they definitely avoided any areas that had cameras."

"License plate?"

"Obscured." Jamey zoomed in and digitally enhanced the video. The front license plate was missing. She jumped to another screen, late night footage that showed the van leaving. The back plate was half covered with mud, and only the digits 42[][]G[] were visible. "We're running all permutations of those letters to see what comes up."

Jack nodded. "It'll be stolen or false. That's our target."

"There's one more vehicle we can't account for," Jamey said. She rewound the tape and froze on a second van. This one was white with the name "Ready-Rooter" on the side panel. "This van comes in a little after nine in the morning. We have no record of it leaving."

"You checked with Cal Tech, I assume."

Jamey nodded. "Oh, yeah. They definitely called for plumbing service, and Ready-Rooter checks out, too. But it bugs me. Here." She sped ahead to a shot of the van leaving.

"I thought you said it didn't leave," Jack said.

"That's the thing. You saw it arrive. Now you see it leave. Now," she zipped forward for the last time. "Now it arrives again. But I've got no final departure. Far as this video's concerned, that van is still in the parking lot."

"Did we send someone over?"

"Tony Almeida offered to go. We're expecting a call."

"Stay on the blue van," Jack suggested.

"My team is tracking it," Jamey said. "Give us a few more minutes."

"Okay," Jack said. "I'll be right back."

"What are you going to do?" Kelly asked.

"I'm going to talk to the guy that started this whole thing."

6:14 P.M. PST
CTU Headquarters, Los Angeles, Holding Room 2

"And here I thought you'd forgotten about me," Brett Marks said.

Jack closed the door behind him and sat down. Marks was, finally, starting to look tired. He'd been kept in that room all day with only one toilet break. There was nowhere to lie down, and the chairs were anything but comfortable.

"You were right about the terrorist cell," Jack said. "They're in the city."

"We knew that this morning," Brett said.

"We've learned a little more," Jack said. "But the puzzle piece that doesn't fit is your friend Frank Newhouse."

Marks's face wrinkled as though he'd been presented with a foul-smelling food. "If he's who you say he is, he's no friend of mine. Apparently I'm a lot less perceptive than I thought. I thought it was bad enough that I got fooled by you, but Newhouse seems to have played me for a lot longer."

"How long have you known him?"

"For years. Ever since—" Brett Marks stopped.

"Go on," Jack said.

Marks sat up straight and stretched. "You know, it occurs to me. I'll tell you everything I know about Frank Newhouse," he offered, "if you let me go."

Behind the one-way glass that looked onto holding room two, Kelly Sharpton and Ryan Chappelle both groaned. "Oh, shit," Kelly muttered.

6:17 P.M. PST
CTU Headquarters, Los Angeles

"No!" Jack fumed. "No way!"

Ryan Chappelle held up both his hands to appease Bauer. "Jack, it's not a bad deal. Marks is low-level. We don't even know if he could have pulled off the sodium cyanide bomb."

"He has a fortress up in Palmdale!" Jack protested. "Two days ago they were ready to kill that foreman and steal ten gallons of poison. He's as much a nutcase as Frank Newhouse or these Iranians. He's got his own army!"

"He's a political radical, but he's not very capable," Chappelle said. "His guys proved willing to do damage, but mostly inept, right? I talked to the prosecutors. They think the best they'll get is a number of weapons charges."

Jack got right up in Chappelle's face. "And conspiracy to commit murder, and conspiracy to commit a terrorist act—"

Chappelle, though much shorter than Jack, didn't back down. "Most of his men won't testify. All we've got is Heinrich Gelb's testimony, and Martin Padilla thinks Marks's defense team will chop him into pieces."

Chappelle and Bauer locked eyes so fiercely that Kelly Sharpton imagined he could see a line of fire blazing between them. Kelly spoke very calmly, "Jack, I hate to say, but it might be worth it."

Bauer broke eye contact with Chappelle to look at Kelly in surprise. "What?"

"Think about it," Kelly said. "You've already broken up the Greater Nation. Marks by himself can't do anything, and we can make it part of his agreement that he never engages in militia activities again."

Jack didn't like it. He wanted to keep his eye on the Iranians, too, but that didn't mean completely abandoning Marks. "He won't respect any agreement he makes with us. He believes the entire Federal government is illegal."

Kelly shrugged. "Then if he starts up, we bring him back in, and it's all over."

"I spent six months listening to that madman talk. I can't stand to see him walk." Jack didn't even try to hide his disgust.

"But at the same time, you get what you were after originally. You get a chance to stop the terrorists you said were here all along. It's worth the risk."

6:22 P.M. PST
CTU Headquarters, Los Angeles, Holding Room 2

"The time is six twenty-two, Pacific Standard Time. This interview is taking place inside the Los Angeles headquarters of the Counter Terrorist Unit, holding room two. Special Agent Jack Bauer interviewing. State your name for the record," Jack said sourly.

Everything in holding room two was the same as before, except now there was a video camera set up in the room, recording his conversation with Marks.

"Brett Ellis Marks."

"Mr. Marks, are you prepared to make an official statement in relation to information on a man known as Frank Newhouse?"

"Yes, in exchange for my immediate release from custody and *your* government's agreement to waive any and all charges it is considering for my prosecution."

"You mean *the* government's agreement."

"No, I don't."

Jack rolled his eyes toward the one-way mirror and shook his head. "Okay. Tell us everything you know about Frank Newhouse."

The story Marks told started out familiar to everyone who had seen the CIA file. Newhouse had been born in Glendale, Arizona, when that part of the country was sand and sage brush. He'd joined the army at eighteen and re-upped three times, finding a home in Special Forces. He'd seen action in Grenada and Panama. He was in the middle of the ugliest part of Somalia.

"So far you're not telling me anything I can't read in the newspapers," Jack said acidly.

"Then you must know about the friends he made in Iraq," Brett said.

Everyone perked up at this. Brett Marks was a good storyteller, and they listened breathlessly as he described Newhouse's experience during Operation Desert Storm. "Frank was one of the first in. He dropped behind enemy lines as a forward observer, calling in coordinates for the Air Force. He was nearly caught by the Republican Guard. In fact, they did capture him. They were torturing him, but he was rescued."

"That's not in the file," Jack said.

"Because he wasn't rescued by our guys. He was rescued by Iranian agents working inside Iraq."

"Bullshit," Jack said.

"Is it? You know Iran wanted Iraq destroyed. They made a lot of noise in public about U.S. aggression, but Iraq was also their mortal enemy. They were happy to see us blow up Saddam Hussein. They'd been sneaking in agents from the beginning. Most of them got caught by Saddam's police, but a few made it through. One of the Iranian agents rescued Frank and helped him finish his mission."

"Did this Iranian agent have a name?"

"Babak Farrah."

Jack slammed his reaction down, keeping Marks from reading him. "Why didn't Frank tell anyone about this?"

"As far as I know, he did," Marks said. "But if he didn't, I can't blame him. Desert Storm seemed to have made Frank lose his taste for government work. He was pissed about everything: soldiers who came back with Persian Gulf Syndrome and weren't treated for it, lies the government seemed to tell about why we went. He had already left the Army. He kept working for the government, but in his heart he'd already joined the Greater Nation by the time the second Iraq War happened. You can imagine how that put him over the edge. He was doing consulting work for Homeland Security. With his record, he easily passed all the security checks. He and I were careful not to expose his connection to the Greater Nation. Eventually he was put on a task force to investigate us, which was perfect. For us, I mean."

"Something's not making sense to me," Jack probed. "You say Frank Newhouse had Iranian friends. But you also say that he was part of the Greater Nation plan to stop the Iranians. Those two things don't add up."

"Our information about the terrorists didn't come from Frank," Marks said. "We have other friends that let us know what's going on."

"Names," Jack demanded.

"That's not part of this deal."

Jack glowered, but said nothing. Marks continued.

"I assumed that Frank didn't want to see the terrorists succeed. Frank joined us because he's anti-Federalist, not anti-American. To be an anti-Federalist is a noble cause, Agent Bauer. We are fighting for the freedom of the states and the freedom of the individual. We are not un-American. When we heard that there might be some Iranian terrorists entering the U.S., I assumed he had heard something from old friends and wanted to stop it."

"Maybe he's still doing that," Jack suggested.

"Then he's doing a lousy job, especially considering that he seemed to know the guys that are behind it."

6:31 P.M. PST
CTU Headquarters, Los Angeles

"He's a good storyteller," Jack growled, walking into the conference room behind Chappelle and Sharpton.

"You don't believe him?" Chappelle said. "It makes sense to me."

"We need to get background on Babak Farrah," Jack said.

"Already on it." Kelly tossed a file to Jack. The manila folder was thicker than the sparse paperwork inside. Jack thumbed through it as Kelly spoke. "We don't get much out of Iran. What we have is innocuous enough—the CIA says he was a sergeant in the Iranian army, owned a small computer store, that's pretty much it. He might have been the President of Iran before coming here, for all we know."

Jack rubbed his eyes. He hadn't slept in a very long time. "So Frank Newhouse plays the Federal government but secretly works for Greater Nation. Then he plays Greater Nation but secretly works for Iranian terrorists. That's our theory?"

"I'll listen to a better one," Chappelle said.

Jack didn't have a better one. He tried to isolate his own concern, and that came down to only one thing: Brett Marks. He didn't like him, he didn't trust him, and he didn't want to listen to him anymore. The idea that some of the evidence was coming from Marks—not to mention the fact that the nutcase would walk because of it—made him furious.

"I still have a problem," he said at last. "Marks didn't give us anything. We're not any closer to finding the terrorists. We're not any closer to finding Newhouse."

Jamey Farrell walked in on the middle of his sentence. She had a huge grin on her face. "Who says we're not any closer to finding the bad guys?"

Without a word, they followed her back to the conference room where she'd set up yet another display.

"I expect a raise after all this," she said. "Just follow the pictures." She pressed a button and a slideshow played for them. The pictures were all different angles—sometimes straight on, sometimes downward angles. Sometimes the objects seemed very close, more often they were far off, and always they were blurred and black and white. But one thing was obvious in all of them: the blue van. The slideshow was a pictographic recreation of the van's journey, and it ended at a private hangar at John Wayne Airport in Santa Ana.

Kelly Sharpton whistled. "Now that is good detective work."

"We checked the logs at John Wayne," she went on casually, as though it was all in a day's work. "Only two flights left from that hangar or the one next to it that evening. One was a hobby flier who flew to Santa Barbara. She checks out. The other logged a flight plan for San Diego, but didn't go there."

"How do we know?" Chappelle asked.

Jamey said, "According to FAA records, it never landed there. We just got off the phone with the traffic controller who was on duty yesterday. He recalls tracking that plane and asking why it had veered off its course. They didn't answer. He didn't think much of it because hobby fliers take joyrides all the time."

Jack asked, "Did he have any idea where it was going?"

"East."

"Nice of you to come back," Brett said. "Are we finished here? Can I go?"

"I'm not sure," Jack said. He hadn't turned the camera back on. "You haven't really given us anything. I mean, you told us a great story about Frank Newhouse. You gave us an explanation for the terrorists. But we didn't get us any closer to finding anyone. If you want to walk, you better do more than just tell a good story."

He turned the cameras back on. "You said that Frank Newhouse didn't give you information on the terrorists, but you won't tell us who tipped you."

"No."

"What did Frank do when you learned the information?"

"First, we called the FBI and Homeland Security. They didn't seem to believe us. Frank, who was our inside man, said that it was because some government agency had already botched some Iranian investigation." Marks let that sink in. Jack could tell by the grin on his face that he knew of Jack's involvement there. "Anyway, you may not agree, but we know that we have the right as citizens to act in defense of our country, so we took it into our own hands. Frank led our investigation."

"You let him do that even though you knew he had Iranian friends?"

Marks shrugged. "He fooled you guys a lot worse than he fooled us."

"Did Frank mention what he thought the terrorist plan might be?"

"That's what we were trying to find out. We had a lead on someone who knew the terrorists. Ramin Rafizadeh. We were looking for him when you got in the way. Other than that, all Frank knew was that they were going to attack the President sometime when he came to Los Angeles. It was going to be soon, I think."

That's the head fake, Jack thought. *So we fell for the same fake Marks did.*

Jack wasn't sure where to go next. It was time to start fishing.

"Tell me what you know about EMPs."

Brett Marks blinked. Jack had seen him do it before, but not very often. The militia leader was cool and composed and rarely caught off-guard. This had surprised him. "You mean electromagnetic weapons?" Brett asked.

"You know what I mean," Jack said, pressing his small advantage.

"I know the government is developing weapons that short-circuit electronic equipment. I know that nuclear blasts can do the same thing, but cause a lot of other damage. My theory is that the powers that be would use weapons like that to shut down the entire infrastructure of the country if the people ever rise up and overthrow the illegal government. That's just my opinion, of course."

"My opinion," Jack said, losing patience, "is that you're insane. You couldn't shut down the whole country."

Marks gave him that professorial smile, the one he reserved for naïve students who had not read their Constitution. "You really don't know anything, do you, Jack. A decent-sized EMP blast, either from a nuclear weapon or an EMP weapon, could black out the entire country. All you have to do is set it off high enough and in the right spot. Nineteen miles over Kansas would do the trick."

6:59 P.M. PST
CTU Headquarters, Los Angeles

Kelly Sharpton was already on the phone by the time Jack left the holding cell and burst into the observation room.

"I'd say he's given us something now, wouldn't you, Jack?" Chappelle said.

"We'll see," Jack growled.

Sharpton hung up the phone. "Jesus, he's right. I just got off the phone with DOD. Nineteen miles up you lose all grounding effects and the blast range extends far enough to reach the whole goddamned country."

• •

THE FOLLOWING TAKES PLACE
BETWEEN THE HOURS OF
7 P.M. AND 8 P.M.
PACIFIC STANDARD TIME

• •

7:00 P.M. PST
CTU Headquarters, Los Angeles

"Jamey!" Jack roared, leaving the observation room
and steaming into the main computer room, pulling
Sharpton and Chappelle in his wake. "How far can
they get?"

"I'm on it!" Farrell called from her workstation.
"Come see."

Jack was hovering at her shoulder in seconds.

"All we have is a process of elimination," she explained. "Assuming our terrorists aren't just joyriding
up to Santa Barbara to visit their boyfriends, then the
plane that took off from that hangar is a Cessna Cita-
tion Encore."

Her computer screen filled with specs on the aircraft, a sleek twin-engine jet with a certain executive-level appeal.

"Once they deviated from their flight plan, they could go anywhere. There's enough traffic up there that they'd be hard to track. But . . ." she added, before Jack could interrupt her with a question, "this Cessna's maximum distance is right around two thousand miles, so either they have to refuel somewhere, or their destination is less than that."

Sharpton said, "Kansas City. Seventeen hundred miles."

Jack nodded. "We need to pull the trigger on this." He looked at Chappelle. The District Director nodded.

7:05 P.M. PST
Westin St. Francis Hotel, San Francisco

President Barnes was on his third attempt to tie his bow tie. He grimaced at himself in the mirror as the wings came out lopsided yet again.

"Hal, I keep telling you Chris will do that for you," his wife said. Juliette Barnes was already dressed—her ability to be ready on time for all social functions was one of the reasons he'd fallen in love with her—and watching him in the mirror from the sitting room attached to their suite.

Barnes's frown deepened. "It just seems ridiculous to be the leader of the free world and not be able to tie your own goddamned bow tie."

"Well, Mr. President, we're running out of time.

You'd better either do the job yourself or get the stew-
ard to do it."

He snorted. "Let's hope you're only referring to my
bow tie when you say that."

Her laugh was interrupted by a knock on the door.
She turned to answer it, but by that time there were
seven Secret Service agents in the room, two for her
and five for him. The head of the detail, Avery Taylor,
was a handsome man with a square jaw and jet-black
skin. "Mr. President, sorry for the intrusion."

"What is it?" he asked. The Secret Service worked
incredibly hard to stay hands off, even in a public en-
vironment like the Westin Hotel. If they had walked
into his private room like this, something was wrong.

"Just a minute, sir," Avery said. He put a hand up
to his ear bud and listened. "Affirmative. Patriot is en
route." Avery focused on Barnes. "Sir, we need to
move you immediately. We're taking you to a secure
area of the Presidio on the east side of the city."

"Why?" Barnes asked, "What about the dinner?"

"It's being canceled, sir. This is blue."

"Hal?" his wife asked anxiously.

"Blue" was Secret Service shorthand for an extreme
emergency—one in which their commands overrode
even his own. Their job was to protect him, and if
they felt the danger was extreme enough, they would
countermand his orders with their own.

"Go with them, Julie."

With enough manpower and control, a man can
exit any building quickly. Whisked out the door to a
waiting elevator, its call button overridden, and down
to a waiting car, President Barnes departed the
Westin in less than three minutes, while his wife was

escorted by Secret Service agents out a separate exit. By that time, Barnes was already on the phone with Admiral Toby Scarsdale (Ret.) his Homeland Security secretary, Mort Jacobs of the NSA, and Jim Quincy of Justice.

"Electromagnetic?" he was saying. "We spend sixty million a year trying to gather up nukes in Eastern Europe, and someone steals a fucking giant magnet in our own backyard?"

Scarsdale spoke up. "We're still waiting for Rudy at the CIA to join the call, but I was told that these terrorists may have been in the country for over a year."

"Six months," Quincy corrected. "But it's still a goddamned long time."

"What are all our intelligence people doing!" Barnes roared. "Forget Rudy. Get me the guys on the ground that are in charge of this operation. Now!"

7:09 P.M. PST
CTU Headquarters, Los Angeles

Jack was on the phone with air traffic controllers in Kansas City, Kansas, when Jessi Bandison, her coffee-colored face suddenly pale, handed him the phone.

"Hang on," Jack said.

Jessi shook her head so vigorously it could have popped off. "Uh-uh. It's the President. For you."

Jack hung up one phone and took the other. "This is Jack Bauer."

"Bauer, this is Harry Barnes."

"Yes, sir, Mr. President." He straightened automatically.

"I'm told you're the guy on the ground causing this crisis."

"After the guys who are causing it, yes, sir."

"Bauer, you understand the shit storm you are about to unleash with this? The kind of disruption this is about to cause. You're clear on this, right?"

Jack swallowed. "Yes, sir."

"You're sure what you're doing?"

"Sir, we know that the EMP was stolen, we know that eight—"

"Shut up, Bauer!" Barnes snapped. "Don't play that bureaucratic shell game with me. I'm not asking you to give me evidence so I can decide. You look at the evidence and you decide. That's what you get paid for. Is the risk worth the damage?" Barnes asked the last question slowly and clearly.

Jack didn't hesitate. "Yes."

"Then do it." Barnes hung up the phone.

7:15 P.M. PST
Lackland Air Force Base, San Antonio, Texas

Bob Lundquist swung his flight helmet jauntily in his right hand. One more day, he thought. Then two weeks of leave, and a new baby.

The F-16C loomed large in front of him, a fierce silhouette against the landing strip's night lights. She was his second love, the F-16, though soon she would get bumped to third. His wife came first, and when his baby arrived . . . well, he knew the jet would forgive him. A lot of his colleagues had fallen under the spell of the sleek F-117 Stealth fighter, or gone for the newness of the F-22, but Lundquist could see that the grass wasn't always greener. His F-16 had kept him in the sky over Iraq when the enemy's planes went down in flames. As far as he was concerned, they were mates for life.

Lundquist's wife was scheduled to have her labor induced in three days. They had timed it perfectly. He had plenty of leave saved up, and he had just come back from a six-month tour overseas, which meant that, barring a new war, he'd remain stateside for a full year. One whole year to watch his new baby grow.

Lundquist reached the F-16 just as one of the flight crew ran up to him. "Get in there. Hurry!" the man yelled.

Lundquist checked his watch. He wasn't late. What was the guy's problem? Still, the airman wouldn't leave him alone, so he hustled up the ladder and dropped himself into the pilot's seat. He slid his helmet into place, sealed the canopy, and plugged into the Thunderbird's communication system. Immediately, the box started squawking at him.

"Mustang 1-9, Mustang 1-9, emergency flight check and you are go for takeoff," the control tower shouted at him.

"Tower, this is Mustang 1-9. Did I miss a flight change? I'm scheduled for practice nighttime takeoffs and landings. What's the hurry?"

"Mustang 1-9, you are being scrambled for immediate takeoff against hostile targets. This is not a drill."

"Holy shit!" Lundquist yelled. He threw the starter switch to warm his engines.

7:18 P.M. PST
CTU Headquarters, Los Angeles

Jamey Farrell and her team worked frantically, routing every erg of power their network had to draw information into CTU. Miles above their heads, satellites hanging in the vacuum of space shifted ever so slightly in their orbits, and onboard telescopic cameras rotated their lenses to scan the middle portion of continent far below. From Lubbock, Texas, to Lansing, Michigan, every civilian and military radar station went on high alert.

Ryan Chappelle hung up the phone. He licked his thin lips nervously. "Well, this is no longer a clandestine little operation. We just got Homeland Security to ground every airplane in Kansas, and every plane flying over Kansas just got rerouted."

Kelly pulled the phone away from his ear to say, "Lackland Air Force base just scrambled fighters. They'll be over Kansas in half an hour."

"Lackland?" Jack asked. "Isn't that in Texas? Don't we have any Air Force bases in Kansas?"

Kelly shook his head. "Not unless you count the 137th Air Refueling Wing, but I don't think they'll be shooting anyone down."

7:24 P.M. PST
40,000 Feet Above Oklahoma

Lundquist raced across the night sky, with the wide flat expanse of Texas and then Oklahoma sliding away beneath him. Patches of glowing light looked like pools reflecting the stars above. To his left and slightly behind, he saw the silhouette and wing lights of his wingman, Sam Amato.

God, he loved this. He was jockeying one of the most powerful machines ever designed by man, flying at the speed of sound.

"Tower, this is Mustang 1-9, leveling off at forty-five thousand feet, speed mach 1.1. Heading zero-one-zero. Over."

"Roger, Mustang. Continue on your present course. ETA to Kansas City approximately twenty-three minutes. Over."

"Roger, Tower," Lundquist said. He checked his guns and missiles. He'd fired on enemy combatants before. But his combat had taken place eight thousand miles away over the desert. This was Kansas! He gritted his teeth. "Just tell me what to shoot."

7:26 P.M. PST
Kansas International Airport (MCI),
Kansas City, Missouri

Barry Wynn dragged his ass back toward the news van. His feet hurt and his back ached, but mostly his ego had been hurt. He'd been on his feet all day, doing a live report on a police chase at 5 P.M., then following his camera crew out to the airport to film a segment on airport security. Barry had done so many of these scare-based stories that he had begun to narrate his own life using the larger-than-life, be-very-afraid promo lines that his station used; things like: "Airport Security: Is It Making You Safer?" He reached the news van and started to climb in. It was almost seven-thirty. Too late to kiss the kids good night, but just on time for one of Angie's patented chewing-out sessions. "Barry's Home Life: The Show You Don't Want to Miss!"

His cell phone rang. He checked the screen and saw that it was Wendy, the executive producer. He was tempted not to answer it. He'd just learned that morning that he'd been passed over for the anchor job ("Is Your Boss Planning to Fire You?") and was in no mood to kowtow. He nearly dropped the phone back into his pocket. At the last minute, he chickened out ("The Inside Story on Human Doormats, Next Time On Barry's Life").

"Barry," he said wearily.

"Bare, it's Wendy. Are you still at the airport?" she asked breathlessly. "Please tell me you're still at the damned airport!"

"I'm at the damned airport," he said, dragging himself into the van.

"Good. Stay there. There's something big going on."

"What?" he said, resisting the urge to get excited. ("Falling for the Same Old Song and Dance? Watch 'You'll Never Learn' Tonight at Eleven!")

"That's what I want you to find out. You're a reporter, remember? All we know is they just grounded every airplane over in Kansas!"

7:31 P.M. PST
CTU Headquarters, Los Angeles

Half the computer screens at CTU headquarters were now proxies for radar screens across the Midwest.

Radar over Kansas showed a few remaining blips, but each of them had been identified by the FAA, and all of them had been contacted and ordered to ground. They were dropping from sight one by one. Soon the sky would be clear.

Jack kept one eye on the screens and both ears on the speaker box. He and Kelly were on the phone with Major Scott Wilcox, United States Air Force, who worked as a military liaison between the DOD and the CIA. The word had come down quickly from higher up that they should contact him and keep him informed. The Department of Defense didn't like being ordered around by the CIA, or its bastard child CTU.

"Listen," Wilcox said. "We've got fighters scrambled. They'll be flying air cover over Kansas City in a couple of minutes. But I've got a problem with your theory." Wilcox had been briefed on the EMP device and the terrorists.

"It's more than a theory, Major," Jack replied.

"Whatever it is, it's got a big hole in it," the Air Force officer shot back. "Do you guys have any idea how high nineteen miles is? Your terrorists don't have any way of getting a plane that high. We don't even have any planes that go that high!"

Wilcox couldn't have stopped Jack Bauer in his tracks more suddenly if he'd slapped him across the face. "Nineteen miles, well, they . . . I mean, they stole the fucking thing, they've got to have a plan . . ." He trailed off, furious with himself. He must be getting tired. He hadn't even thought of that.

Sharpton filled the silence. "Something must go that high."

"Sure," Wilcox answered sarcastically. "The Space Shuttle. Rockets. ICBMs go that high. The theory you're referring to, this whole Kansas idea, originally comes from the idea of bursting a nuclear missile over Kansas. Nuclear missiles go a lot higher than airplanes."

"A rocket, then," Sharpton said.

"Okay," Wilcox said condescendingly. "So your guys who just stole an EMP device now plan to fly to Kansas and steal a rocket?"

It sounded unbelievable, of course. Only the military had access to high-altitude rockets, and breaking into a military base would be a major terrorist activity in itself.

"It doesn't have to be a rocket."

Jack practically leaped at Brett Marks, who was standing in the door way. "What are you doing here. Get out!"

"They released me, Jack," Marks said. He was dressed in a pair of gray sweats and sweat shirt with the generic "FLETC" across the front. "That was the deal."

"Letting you eavesdrop on our conversations sure as hell wasn't!" Jack glared at the uniformed guard behind Marks. "Get him out of here!"

Brett stepped back toward the guard, offering no resistance. "I'm gone, Jack. But it doesn't have to be a rocket. You ever heard of the X Prize?!" The security guard led him away.

"What's the X Prize?" Sharpton said. "I think I've heard of that."

"Oh." It was Major Wilcox, his disembodied voice suddenly hesitant and thoughtful in the speaker box. "Hey, that's possible."

"What is?" Jack asked impatiently.

"The X Prize. It's a prize being offered to any private company that can build a reusable spacecraft. It's five or ten million dollars to the winner. A lot of private sector scientists are taking it seriously. There are some designs on the board that might work."

"Could these guys build one?"

On his end of the phone, Wilcox hesitated. Jack stared at the speaker box, growing more frustrated by the moment. He felt like a dog chasing its tail. He was in charge of this operation, but he didn't feel confident in it.

"It's next to impossible," Wilcox finally said. But the self-assured, acidic tone had disappeared from his voice.

7:40 P.M. PST
CTU Headquarters, Los Angeles

The computer room at CTU was full of people, but it was silent as a graveyard. Programmers sat at every terminal, analyzing data. Field operatives watched and waited anxiously. Jack paced back and forth behind the lines of analysts studying their screens. He was missing something. There had to be something.

Chappelle was nearby, leaning over Jessi Bandison's shoulder. "Why are there still blips on the radar screens?" he asked. "Isn't all air traffic grounded?"

Jessi nodded. "We're getting relays from Strategic Air Command, ground-based radar in Kansas, and AWAC radar planes over Kansas. Those two blips there are fighters out of Lackland. Those and those, the slow-moving ones, are high-flying flocks of birds. It's spring. They're all heading back north for the summer."

7:45 P.M. PST
40,000 Feet Above Kansas

"Mustang 1-9, maintain your current pattern and wait for further instructions," Lundquist heard in his earpiece. He was no longer talking to the controllers back at Lackland.

"Roger, Command," he replied.

Lundquist made his second pass over Kansas City, so high that the entire metropolis was no bigger than the tip of a glowing cigar. His radar screen was empty. He hadn't been briefed on the nature of his target, or its purpose. He didn't need to know. He read everything necessary in the tense voices of his commanders back home. Something was amiss. There was some danger present in the prairie skies. Well, he knew his duty. No one was messing with his country, not before, and certainly not now that he had a baby on the way. Lundquist banked right and angled for his third pass.

7:58 P.M. PST
CTU Headquarters, Los Angeles

"Maybe they're not planning it yet," Sharpton wondered aloud, back in the computer room with all the other watchers. "Maybe they need time to prepare."

"Fine by me," Jack said. He was wondering if they'd gotten lucky. If Kelly was right, the terrorists had lost the initiative. CTU could keep planes flying over the Midwest indefinitely, while ground teams tracked down their airplane and, eventually, the terrorists.

"Chappelle, do you think we should—" He looked

around for Chappelle. The Director hadn't left the computer screen. He watched it, his eyes barely blinking, while he chewed his thumbnail absentmindedly. When he heard Jack call his name, he glanced up and motioned Jack to come over.

"Look at that image," the Director said. "It's about the only one left in all of Kansas."

The image was just a dot, moving with incredible slowness across the radar screen.

"Yeah?" Jack asked.

"It's moving really slow," Chappelle explained. "In fact, I'd say it's not really moving at all. At least not left to right. But it is going—"

"Up," Jack said in a horrified whisper.

Up. It was going straight up. Jack's face turned as white as a sheet. "A balloon. A weather balloon. They put the bomb on a weather balloon."

"What?" Kelly drawled, not yet comprehending.

"Patch Wilcox in here! Everybody be quiet!" Jack yelled. The crowd of analysts, so silent a moment before, now responded to his reaction with murmurs of confusion.

"He's on," Jamey Farrell said, tapping the speaker button on a nearby phone.

"Major, how high can a weather balloon fly?" Jack asked.

"Stand by," the Air Force officer said.

Jack watched the tiny dot. "Not much time, Major."

"I've got it here. Most weather balloons reach heights of about ninety thousand feet. Some can reach heights of 120,000 feet."

Jack did the math in his head. Twenty-three miles. It was high enough. "Goddamm it," he growled. "We've been talking about rockets and experimental airplanes and they chose a fucking weather balloon. That's it, that's our target!"

Most of the room had caught up with him. Jack heard someone on the phone with Strategic Air Command, relaying target coordinates that would then be sent on to the pilots over Kansas. "How high is it?" he asked.

Jamey Farrell checked the radar screen. "It's at forty-nine thousand feet, rising at a speed of . . . five hundred feet per minute. ETA for the fighters is 8 minutes."

Jack heaved a sigh. "Good. It's only halfway to its detonation height. We've got time."

"No we don't!" Major Wilcox's disembodied voice screeched in his ear like a scolding conscience. "Tell those fighters to haul ass!"

"What is it?" Jack asked.

"The max altitude for those F-16s is fifty thousand feet. That target is going to be out of range."

1 2 3 4 5 6 7 8 9
10 11 12 13 14 15 16 17
18 19 20 21 22 23 24

••

THE FOLLOWING TAKES PLACE
BETWEEN THE HOURS OF
8 P.M. AND 9 P.M.
PACIFIC STANDARD TIME

••

8:00 P.M. PST
Kansas International Airport (MCI),
Kansas City, Missouri

". . . and the skies over Kansas are quiet tonight, but it's an ominous kind of silence, like the calm before the storm, interrupted only by the distant roar of jet fighters guarding against an unknown threat. This is Barry Wynn, FOX News, Kansas City." Barry finished in round basso tones. He was posed with his left foot slightly forward, his hips turned slightly sideways and narrowed to the camera, but his chest rotated forward. It made him look trimmer. His face looked grave but competent, and he kept his eyes focused on the camera lens.

"We're out," the cameraman said, relaxing and lowering his camera. "Nice work, Bare."

Barry heaved a sigh of relief. "Thanks. I can't believe it. I just did my first network piece. Screw that anchor position. This could take me national!"

8:02 P.M. PST
45,000 Feet Above Kansas

"Mustang 1-9 to Command, requesting bogey dope."

"Mustang 1-9, alter course to zero-three-two, throttle to full. Relaying the target to your computer now."

Lundquist turned his joystick, the F-16's fly-by-wire controls responding like a dream. His radar screen shivered and reset, and he saw the tiny blip his system hadn't picked up before. That was it? He wasn't picking up any heat signals, no electronics . . .

"Command, can you tell me—"

"It's a weather balloon, Mustang. Shoot it down. Over."

Lundquist read the target's altitude and rate of ascent and didn't need to be told the obvious. "Roger. Mustang 1-9 going supersonic."

8:05 P.M. PST
San Francisco Airport

Debrah Drexler walked away from the desk of her charter airline in frustration, reaching for her cell phone to make a call when it started ringing. The display flashed the number for her Washington, D.C., office.

"Drexler," she said. "Did you guys know that flights were grounded?"

Juwan Burke said, "It just happened a few minutes ago, Senator. Do you have a television there?"

Drexler looked around. The charter service terminal wasn't as large as the main terminals and gates at SFO, but was posh. There was a plasma screen set into the wall, currently broadcasting CNN. "Yes."

"You should watch FOX right now."

Drexler hung up. "Excuse me," she said, walking back to the clerk at the counter. "Can you change that to FOX?"

The girl behind the counter made a face. "If you really want me to . . ."

She aimed a remote at the screen. The picture flashed and changed to FOX, and the sober image of Attorney General James Quincy appeared.

". . . questions should be directed to Homeland Security more than Justice. But I can tell you this. My understanding is that the terrorists who've caused this crisis, if the threat is indeed real, have been in this country for months. In fact, the agents assigned to the case originally pursued them six months ago, but their investigation was hamstrung by legalities. I feel like I'm shouting at the ocean now, but if Congress can't see why we need to pass the NAP Act now, I don't know what they're thinking."

Debrah felt something inside her wither.

Nina Myers decided it would have been easier to track down a ghost.

While the boys were playing with their toys back at CTU, she and Jessi Bandison had taken on the grunt work, pursuing the mysterious Frank Newhouse. Jessi had been poring over Newhouse's CIA file, checking it for any loose ends. For the last hour, Nina had kept in touch with her by telephone while she tracked down leads pulled off the fingerprints. She'd gone back to the condominium and interviewed the maid and the maintenance workers. All three recognized a picture of Frank from his CIA file, all three knew him only as Pat Henry, owner of the condominium, and said he was rarely there. That was it. Almost all the other sets of fingerprints were dead ends. That was the frustrating aspect about having fingerprint or DNA evidence. To catch someone with biometrics, the person had to be in the system.

Meanwhile, her quarry's life as Frank Newhouse was full of information, but none of it was helpful.

"I can't find anything on him that doesn't check out," Jessi had confessed a half hour earlier. "The CIA record is pretty much what you'd expect. We had the FBI investigate all his points of contact, but he's not there."

"Has the CIA run down any more information on this Babak Farrah? The one who was supposedly his Iranian contact?"

"Nothing more than we've got already."

Nina tapped her knuckles on the steering wheel. She didn't believe this; it wasn't logical. Frank Newhouse might have fooled the Greater Nation idiots easily enough, but no one could make this big a play with the United States government without making at least some mistakes. There was a loose end some-where, and Nina was determined to find it.

"What about the guy Jack brought in, Farid some-thing. Has he been interrogated?"

At her desk at CTU, Jessi looked around. Every eye-ball she sought was glued to a computer screen. "I don't think so."

"Get someone on it. He knew this Farrah, maybe he's a lead." Nina pulled up in front of an apartment building off of Lincoln Boulevard in Santa Monica. "I'm at my next stop, Jess, one of the possibles on that partial print. Call me if Farid gives up anything."

Nina hurried out of the car, wanting to get this over with. She had already burned through the likely leads and was now working on the unlikely. Forensics had pulled a partial print off a white tub Newhouse (or whoever he was) had used to make a bomb. The prob-lem with a smudged print was that, even if the subject was in the database, it might not match. Jamey Farrell had run a program that brought up possible matches, but there were more than two hundred names in Los Angeles alone. On a hunch, Nina had broken the list down into names on L.A.'s West Side. She had no real reason for doing this other than her gut. The Frank Newhouse who worked with the terrorists seemed to prefer downtown and East Los Angeles, since that Newhouse had worked with Farrah, Farid, and Julio Juarez, and had rented an apartment for the terrorists near USC. But the other Frank Newhouse owned a condo (under the name Pat Henry) on the West Side.

One of the names on her possibles list was for

Matilda Swenson. Nina reviewed her rap sheet, such as it was. Matilda was a pretty blond, younger in the mug shot but she'd be thirty-six now. In fact, Nina noticed, today was Matilda's birthday. She was an artist who'd been busted twice. The first time was in '94 for marijuana possession. This was hardly an indictment, but it was enough to get her into the system. What intrigued Nina most, aside from her West Side address, was the second arrest. This was for disturbing the peace during the recent World Bank conference in Los Angeles. Apparently, Matilda didn't much appreciate the centralization of power. In that one line, Nina heard the faint echoes of Brett Marks's Greater Nation platform.

Nina climbed the steps to number 204 and knocked.

8:09 P.M. PST
49,500 Feet Above Kansas

"Approaching maximum altitude." Lundquist heard the voice of Sam Amato, his wingman, in his ear. Sam's voice was steady and professional. But behind it, Lundquist sensed the danger Sam was feeling.

"Roger." He looked at his readouts. He was right under the target, then past it. He banked hard left and came around, lifting his nose up. He couldn't see the balloon in the dark, but his radar could. It was more than fifty-one thousand feet and climbing.

With his nose still pointed up, Lundquist selected AIM-9N Sidewinder missiles and, just like in a video game, guided the small square pointer right over the target. "I can't get good tone," he said. "Switching to guns."

"Forty-nine thousand, eight hundred feet," Sam warned.

"Roger. Pull back to forty thousand, Sam. I got this one."

"Bobby—"

"Don't worry," Lundquist said with a laugh, "you think I'm going to let anything go wrong right before my kid is born?"

Sam Amato didn't laugh. He broke right and tipped his nose to the ground.

8:10 P.M. PST
CTU Headquarters, Los Angeles

No one spoke. Jack watched the screen as the fast-moving blip representing the F-16 pulled right on top of the smaller, slower blip that represented disaster.

8:11 P.M. PST
50,400 Feet Above Kansas

Lundquist felt his engines lurch. They'd been chuffing at him for the last ten seconds. He ignored them. He came up underneath the balloon, and when the crosshairs of his 20mm Gatling guns fell across the blip on his screen, he opened fire.

8:12 P.M. PST
CTU Headquarters, Los Angeles

Jack Bauer held his breath as the two radar blips came together briefly, then broke apart. One of the contacts—the F-16—fell away. The other vanished.

"Target destroyed."

The room erupted in cheers. Hands slapped Jack on the back and shook his arms. Kelly Sharpton, his hands still bandaged, threw his arms around Jack in a friendly hug.

8:12 P.M. PST
50,200 Feet Above Kansas

The F-16 bucked slightly like a startled horse. Then the engines cut out all together. Jets feed on air, which is why the ceiling for most fighter jets is fifty thousand feet. To go higher than that, you need a rocket.

Lundquist had been flying nose up. When the power cut out, the F-16 tipped backward, and he found himself upside down, his plane flat on its back as it fell back toward home. He didn't panic, but he did feel annoyed. He was a captain in the United States Air Force and this was his airplane. He was not about to have it scratched up by something as stupid as a lack of oxygen.

Lundquist initiated his relight procedure. Every display in his cockpit twinkled like Christmas. Then he felt the familiar rumble under his feet and heard the deep-throated roar of the engine behind him, and he grinned.

The grin fell away from his face the next instant when something clanged through the guts of the F-16. Lundquist knew immediately that it was foreign object damage, and he thought ironically that the only foreign object up this high was the goddamned thing he'd been shooting at. His engine groaned at him. "Command, this is Mustang 1-9," he said calmly. "I've got FOD to the engine."

Alarms went off like klaxons all around him. "My compressor is—shit!" He knew what was coming next and he hit the eject button. Small explosive charges popped the canopy off his plane, and a half second later his seat was blown out of the cockpit. At the same time, the F-16 turned into a ball of fire that enveloped him. He blew into the careening canopy and slammed his head, helmet and all, into the Plexiglas.

As the world went dark around him, Bob Lundquist wondered if it was a boy or a girl.

8:15 P.M. PST
CTU Headquarters, Los Angeles

The entire staff of CTU Los Angeles watched in silent horror as the F-16's radar signature plummeted toward the ground.

"Eject, eject," someone whispered.

The radar screen gave no sign that he ever ejected.

"Oh my god," Jamey Farrell whispered. "That pilot . . ."

They listened over the intercom as a control tower in Kansas tried to raise the F-16. The words "Mustang 1-9 . . . Mustang 1-9 . . ." until the words became a lament.

Jack allowed himself a moment of silence, a moment of remorse. Then he steeled himself. He had sent men to die, and had watched them die, before. He reminded himself why that man had died, what he had died for. Then he said hoarsely, "Tell the other pilot to confirm the target is down."

Jamey Farrell looked at him as though he was a monster. "Jack, that pilot . . ."

"Tell him!"

Someone relayed the query, which was relayed to the second F-16 pilot, Sam Amato, who confirmed.

Jack nodded in satisfaction. "Nice job everyone," he said resolutely.

Then he turned away from everyone, down the hall-way toward the holding cells. When he was alone in the dim passageway, he gritted his teeth to bite back tears.

8:20 P.M. PST
Santa Monica

Nina walked around the building, then walked back up the stairs to Matilda's apartment. There was no back door. Nina tried to peek into the window. Through a crack in the drapes, she saw an easel and the back of a canvas. Matilda was a painter.

"Can I help you?"

Nina looked up toward a young man, maybe twenty, in a BareNaked Ladies T-shirt and jeans.

"Maybe," she said. "I'm looking for Matilda Swenson. This is her apartment, right?"

"Yeah," the kid said in that sardonic tone that only the young can master. "I'm sort of the manager. I guess she's not here, which is why the door doesn't open when you knock."

Nina smirked. "Thing is, when the doors don't open, I usually knock them down." She showed him her badge. "Federal Agent Nina Myers. Can you open the door for me, Mr. Manager?"

He did. Nina walked into a sparse but elegant apartment with hardwood floors, Roman shades, and minimalist furniture. There was a two-seat red velvet couch, an ultra-thin flat-panel television mounted on a stand on the floor. There was no dining table, just two stools pushed up against a built-in bar in the kitchen. Almost all the space had been designed to allow room for paintings, and paintings were everywhere. There were small canvases and large ones; some were framed but most just leaned against walls near corners. Oddly, none of them hung on the walls, which had been painted seafoam green.

"She's a painter," said Mr. Manager, hanging out in the doorway behind her.

"How well do you know her?" Nina asked.

"Just sort of hello," he said, waving to show what he meant. "She stays in a lot when she's painting, I guess."

Nina thumbed through a couple of paintings. Matilda favored a Picasso-esque style, but her shadings moved a little more toward pastel. The effect wasn't very pleasing. Horses had become a theme for her. There were galloping horses, horses at rest, and horses with foals. But all the horses were done in that piecemeal, surreal style, with each part of the horses treated as its own unique shape, rather than as part of the whole creature.

"I'm not sure I like it," Nina said.

Mr. Manager laughed. "I don't think her boyfriend does, either."

"Why do you say that?"

"Well, he burned one of the paintings. It was a painting of him, I think. So either he was sacrificing it to the gods, or . . ." He didn't seem to have enough energy to finish the sentence.

"He did? You saw him?"

"Yeah. He burned it in the alley. That's where my apartment looks. I get the crappy one, but it's free."

"Can I see that painting?"

"Why'd you want to see it?" he said, looking at her like *she* was the idiot. "I told you, he burned it. It's a bunch of ashes now."

"Right. Have you seen Matilda this evening? Since he burned the painting?"

"Nope."

Nina nodded. She opened the folder she was carrying and pulled out a picture of Frank Newhouse. "Any chance her boyfriend looks like this?"

8:41 P.M. PST
Santa Monica

"Jessi, it's Nina," she said urgently. "I need your help right away."

"Nina, I'm already searching as fast as I can. There's nothing on Newhouse except his regular service record—"

"Forget that. I need you to get all the information you can on Matilda Swenson. What I want most is a tag on her cell phone. If it's on, I want to know where she is right now."

Before calling, Nina had dug through a small file drawer that held Matilda's bills and found statements for her Verizon wireless account. Nina read off the account number. "Get linked up with them right away. And let's just hope her phone is on."

Nina paced back and forth, tapping her cell phone in her hand as she tried to think. Frank Newhouse had a second life, one that wasn't on the grid, and Matilda was part of it. Find Matilda and you find Frank, or at least a little more about him.

Mr. Manager still stood in the doorway, leaning lazily against the doorjamb and watching her.

"Aren't you going to ask what this is all about?"

The young man blinked at her with heavily lidded eyes. "You're with the government right?"

"Yep."

"Is it possible that what you're looking for might kill me?"

"It's possible."

"Then I don't want to know about it."

Nina's phone rang. "What have you got?"

Jessi spoke quickly. "We pinged Swenson's cell phone. It's on, but the signal is weak. It's coming from somewhere in the Santa Monica Mountains, about eight miles northwest of you, near a fire road off of Mulholland Drive."

Nina knew the area. The entire Santa Monica Mountain Range was a wilderness corridor for Los Angeles. Although the mountaintops were only a mile or two from the city, they were wild and covered in brush. It was a nice place for a picnic, but how many people picnicked at eight o'clock on Wednesday evening? "Call L.A. Sheriff Mountain Rescue. We need to get up there right away."

••

THE FOLLOWING TAKES PLACE
BETWEEN THE HOURS OF
9 P.M. AND 10 P.M.
PACIFIC STANDARD TIME

••

9:00 P.M. PST
Westin St. Francis Hotel, San Francisco

Attorney General James Quincy returned to his hotel room. He wasn't on the Secret Service's short list for VIPs in case of a crisis, but he had been moved to a secure location by the rest of the security staff. Pulling at his tie, he sat down in a chair and turned on the television, flipping through the news stations. The lead story was, of course, the crisis itself, including details of the grounding of air traffic, the loss of the F-16, and theories (all wrong) about the nature of the threat itself. But slowly, over the course of the next few minutes, Quincy heard it start:

". . . why weren't these terrorists stopped at the border . . ."

". . . in the country for months without being uncovered . . ."

". . . current procedures inadequate to deal with the global threat . . ."

Quincy smiled. He couldn't have said it better himself.

9:14 P.M. PST
CTU Headquarters, Los Angeles

Jack received calls from the Secretary of Homeland Security, the Director of the CIA, and the President of the United States.

"Nice work, Agent Bauer," President Barnes said with a laugh. "You have the thanks of a grateful nation."

"Thank you, sir," Jack said.

"But no raise. I'm trying to reduce the debt."

"I understand, Mr. President."

Barnes hung up.

Kelly Sharpton whistled. "Jack Bauer, super spy!"

Jack shook his head. "Do we have a recovery team out there?"

Kelly nodded. "ETA is about five minutes."

Jack sat down in an empty seat and let his shoulders slump a little. "It should never have come to this. We should have found them earlier, we should have stopped them before they ever got a weapon."

Kelly looked up at the ceiling, its recesses hidden in shadows. The overhead lights at CTU hung down on thin bars, illuminating the computer room, but beyond the lights there was darkness. "What can you do? The society we live in, the way we want to be, leaves us open to infiltration. How are you going to stop someone like that coyote?"

Jack curled his lip. "Tougher laws. Better systems."

Kelly sighed. "We'd only wreck what we're trying to save."

"So we let them destroy it?" Jack said skeptically.

"No. Our openness is our weakness. So we just have to be strong in other ways."

9:20 P.M. PST
Pasadena, California

Tony Almeida wished he hadn't volunteered.

Jamey Farrell had noticed two suspicious vans pulling into that particular lot. The first one was the blue van they had tracked to John Wayne Airport. The second was a white Ready-Rooter plumber's van that apparently arrived twice but left only once. The blue van had already been accounted for. It had stood there, silent and waiting, when the CTU team arrived at John Wayne Airport to investigate the hangar from which the Cessna had flown. They were dusting and sweeping, but no one expected them to find much more than they already had.

Tony, on the other hand, had offered to visit Cal Tech and check out the scene there. He had arrived at the parking lot at Cal Tech three hours earlier, just as the sun was setting but before the streetlights came on. There were a few cars parked at this hour, but most of the lot was empty. At the far end of the lot, a group of boys used the empty space to practice curb-jumping and acrobatics on their bicycles. The lot was right next to the physics buildings, which had given the thieves (in either the blue or the white van) perfect access to the EMP devices. First Tony looked for the van itself, but of course it wasn't there. Then he searched for alternative exits that the van might have taken, a route that hadn't been picked up by the security cameras. The parking lot in question had only one driveway—a combination entrance/exit with a white traffic arm that required drivers to stop and take a ticket (on the way in) and pay (on the way out). There was also a kiosk with an attendant. The parking lot was situated on the edge of a low hill that sloped down toward a side street. Tony parked in the lot and walked toward the edge to see if there was another driveway, but he saw only the curb, a sidewalk, and beyond that ice-plant covered slope.

Tony walked over to the kiosk. "Excuse me."

The attendant, a young black woman with a tiny ring in the side of her nose, wearing an orange vest, had leaned out. "Uh-huh?"

"Is there any other entrance or exit to this lot?"

"Other entrances? Naw, this is the only entrance."

Tony heard a soft whirring sound and turned to see the boys on their bicycles flash by. They hopped the curb and then, with whoops of daredevil joy, they launched themselves off the edge of the parking lot and down onto the plant-covered slope below. He went back and looked at the slope again. It wasn't all that steep. A vehicle might just be able to do it.

Tony had phoned in his information: the Ready-Rooter van was gone, and he thought he'd found another way out of the lot. "Which means," he had pointed out, "that someone didn't want that van to be picked up on camera."

Tony walked back to the sidewalk, then turned around. He could just make out the security camera recording the parking entrance. He was sure it didn't reach this part of the parking lot. He stood at the edge of the curb again, staring down the slope. It wouldn't be hard to drive down that slope, especially late at night if no one was around to see. Tony slid down the slope a few feet, crouched down, and began to snoop among the green, water-fat ice plants. It wasn't long before he found what he feared: ice plants crushed by tire tracks. He stood up and looked out on the city of Pasadena, with the lights of Los Angeles glistening in the distance.

The other van had come this way, and they had no idea where the terrorists had gone.

9:29 P.M. PST
CTU Headquarters, Los Angeles

Ryan Chappelle caught Jack's eye from across the room. The Director had just hung up the phone. His face was red, and the muscles in his jaw worked furiously. He pointed at Jack and then at the conference room.

A moment later, Jack and Kelly entered. Chappelle closed the door behind them, then spun around and put his face right up against Jack's. "Do you realize what you've done!"

Startled by Chappelle's aggression, Jack reacted instinctively and bumped his chest against him, knocking the Director off-balance. "What are you talking about?"

Chappelle was livid, ranting nonsensically. "A weather balloon. A goddamned weather balloon! And an EMP device!"

Kelly, as he had done before, stepped in to mediate. "Ryan, you're not being clear. What's wrong?"

Ryan wiped spittle from his mouth. He took a deep breath and spoke in short phrases. "Ground airplanes . . . creating a national panic . . . we lost a man! And all for nothing!"

"What do you mean, nothing!" Jack shot back.

"Nothing!" Chappelle said, raising his voice. "I just got the word from the recovery team. There was no EMP device on that balloon. There was nothing but some kind of meteorological package!"

Jack froze. Everything stopped for him: the clock, his breath, even his heart. He had the sudden and terrifying sense that the floor might simply open up and swallow him, because the natural laws had suddenly been violated. "What?"

"Oh, now you look doubtful! Before, you were pretty damned sure!"

Kelly was just as shocked as Jack. "It's got to be a mistake."

"No, no mistake," Chappelle sneered. "We just got off the phone with the team that launched the damned thing. You know when they launched it? This morning at eight o'clock local time. They've been tracking it all day—right up until the moment it was destroyed." Chappelle closed the distance between them like a terrier ready to fight. "Do you get it, Bauer? You put the whole country into panic mode for nothing!"

1 2 3 4 5 6 7 8 9
10 11 12 13 14 15 16 17
18 19 **20** 21 22 23 24

. . . .

THE FOLLOWING TAKES PLACE
BETWEEN THE HOURS OF
10 P.M. AND 11 P.M.
PACIFIC STANDARD TIME

. . . .

10:00 P.M. PST
Mullholland Drive, Overlooking Santa Monica

East of the 405 Freeway, Mulholland Drive evolved into the curvaceous mountain top road favored by Porsche drivers and other daredevils on their way to parties in the Hollywood Hills. To the west of the freeway, Mulholland transformed into a rural mountain road on the outskirts of the city, quietly fading away from city lights into the rural area between Los Angeles and the beach communities to the north. Here you could still see glimpses of Los Angeles as it had been before the Europeans had come: wild brush growing thick and green during the spring rains, only to bake under the summer sun before dying away before renewing itself the following spring. The Santa Monica Mountains were crisscrossed with trails that had become the salvation of the few nature worshippers who took advantage of them.

Unfortunately, some of those nature worshippers had more love than understanding, and they became lost or injured. A few had even starved to death only ten thousand steps from the second largest city in the United States.

It was hikers like these that kept the L.A. Sheriff Search and Rescue team busy. At a little after ten o'clock that night, the Sheriff's search helicopter dusted down right on Mulholland Drive and Nina Myers hopped out, keeping her head low. A black-and-white search truck, its emergency lights flashing, was parked nearby. She ran to it and shook the hand of a tall, baby-faced man in a green flight suit.

"Deputy Pascal," he said. "I think we've got your missing person."

Nina followed Pascal to the edge of the road. Outside the white lines of the westbound lane, there was a soft shoulder about three feet wide, and then a steep dropoff. Two more sheriff's deputies stood there, one belaying a rope and the other holding steady a standing searchlight that pointed down into the ravine below. Nina saw another sheriff rappelling down toward a red Toyota Acura planted grill down in the brush at the bottom.

"This road is a lot trickier than people realize," the deputy explained. "We pull people out of here once or twice a month."

"I don't think this one went over the side by accident," Nina said.

The rappelling deputy reached the bottom of the

ravine some two hundred feet below them. In the bright glow of the searchlight, they watched him lean into the car for a moment. Then he pulled his upper body out and talked into his microphone.

Nina heard his voice broadcast from the radio on Deputy Pascal's belt. "She's alive," he said, "but not by much. We need a medivac chopper here stat."

10:17 P.M. PST
Westin St. Francis Hotel, San Francisco

When one of his staff told Attorney General Jim Quincy that Senator Alan Wayans was on the phone, Quincy savored the moment. This is it, he thought. Six months of planning had ended in one night of perfect execution. Now came the coup de grace. If there was anything the last year or two in American politics had taught him, it was this: it took war to bring the people together. First you needed to create the need for urgency and the desire for change. Only then would they be willing to accept the gift you had to give them.

The New American Privacy Act was Quincy's gift to his country. Bureaucracy and the worship of individual rights had been a yoke around the neck of justice for too long. Quincy was tired of watching his FBI and his DEA, not to mention other agencies such as the CIA and CTU, paralyzed by laws that protected suspects rather than empowered the law. He despised the liberal left that worshipped the false idol of personal privacy. Who cared if some fringe radical in upstate New York had his library records probed, or if the FBI put wiretaps on him without his knowing? If the person was innocent, it wouldn't matter. If he was guilty, lives would be saved! Jim's legacy would be the enhancement of the Office of the Attorney General, its investment with new powers that could probe the populace with a laser.

He hesitated before picking up the phone, like a wine connoisseur gathering himself for the first taste. He pulled the receiver to his ear and said, "Yes, Senator Wayans. It's late for you, isn't it?"

"I'm up, everyone's up, I think!" Wayans said in a forced voice. "I . . . can you believe this thing? A terrorist attack that would've knocked out the entire power grid?"

"Unfortunately, I can, Senator," Quincy said soberly. "We all know what we're up against."

Wayans sighed. "I guess we do. Is it true that these terrorists have been in the country for months? And that we got wind of them but didn't catch them?"

"That's my understanding," Quincy said carefully. "I'm sure we're going to hear more about that when Congress looks into the matter. And with all respect, Senator, I just want to say that if I'm called before the subcommittee, I'm going to point the finger right at those who have voted to withhold powers of investigation from the Justice Department."

Quincy grinned. He could almost hear Alan Wayans shiver on the other end of the phone. "I-I can't believe our people didn't get these bastards earlier," Wayans sputtered, filling himself with righteous indignation. "I-I think it might be time to consider loosening the reins a little bit more. I'm going to give that privacy act some more thought. Have a good night, Mr. Attorney General."

"Good night, Senator."

Quincy hung up the phone, only to hear his private cell phone ring. He knew who was calling.

"Congratulations," said Frank Newhouse.

"And to you," Quincy said. "Your plan worked."

"I'm happy to play a part, Mr. Attorney General."

"Sometimes you have to make people a little afraid of the illness before they'll take their medicine," Quincy said. "But in the end this thing will be good for them."

"I agree. Will you still be reachable in San Francisco tomorrow?"

"That depends on the President."

"You think he'll veto?"

"I'll know soon enough."

"Well, then, I'm sure we'll be in touch, sir."

10:18 P.M. PST
West Los Angeles

Newhouse disconnected his mobile phone and shook his head in disgust. He was sitting in his car, parked on a side street off Olympic Boulevard in West Los Angeles.

"It always amazes me how a man can be full of shit and right at the same time," Newhouse said to the man in the passenger seat. "He says you need to make people afraid of the illness before they'll take their medicine."

"Well, he's right," said the other man. "That's what we're doing."

Frank Newhouse turned to his companion and grinned. "That's what I always liked about you, Brett. You always know what to say."

10:27 P.M. PST
CTU Headquarters, Los Angeles

Jack Bauer ignored the chaos swirling around him and tried to think. Analysts shouted information at one another, trying desperately to make sense out of their own confusion. Chappelle alternately scolded Bauer and took calls on his telephone from his bosses in Washington, D.C.

He'd been wrong. Somewhere in the process he'd taken a wrong turn. He tried not to think about the panic and tragedy he'd caused. He was useless if he let his mistakes paralyze him; he had to forget the fact that he had put the entire country on high alert and had caused the death of an Air Force pilot.

Jack also had to put aside his fatigue. He hadn't slept in almost forty hours, and he'd been pushing himself hard for over a day without rest. But there was no time to rest—he had to think!

Chappelle returned from another phone call to berate Jack further. "You're being suspended, Jack, pending an investigation into your handling of this disaster!"

Jack shook his head. "We have to assume they're still here in Los Angeles. The flight to Kansas was a mistake. They obviously wanted to send us on a wild goose chase, that's why they parked the van there. Which means they're probably still in Los Angeles planning something."

Chappelle punched a fist into his palm in frustration. "Jesus, Jack, don't you get it. You've blown it, you're off the goddamed case."

"No, no, they're doing something here, in Los Angeles, with the EMP," Jack said. "We've got to figure out what it is." Jack suddenly remembered the code that Professor Rafizadeh had translated. "Wait a minute! The code! The plan that Nina called fake! It said they were planning to kill the President in Los Angeles tomorrow."

"Right, and Barnes isn't even going to be in Los Angeles tomorrow," Chappelle snapped. "Let's not waste time."

Once again, Kelly Sharpton weighed in as mediator, but this time he was on Chappelle's side. "Jack, what can they do? There is no way for them to launch that device nineteen miles into the air. Every flight is grounded—"

"Thanks to you, Bauer," Chappelle added.

Jack ran to the nearest computer and called up a Domestic Security Alert. CTU always got access to any security issues in its area, including the travel schedules of VIPs. The itinerary showed that the President would be finishing a banquet in San Francisco, then heading down to San Diego on Air Force One. "Every flight will be grounded except Air Force One."

Suddenly, finally, a piece fell into place for Jack. He remembered the briefing they'd received on the EMP devices. The plan, like a jigsaw puzzle, suddenly came into focus. He didn't have all the pieces yet, but he understood the design.

"You're right," he said, "he's not going to be in Los Angeles. But he is going to be *over* it." He pointed at the itinerary. "Imagine what would happen to Air Force One if all its power and computers were shut down over the city."

Chappelle's lip curled in disgust. "Jack, you're just reaching now. It's pathetic."

Kelly said, "Jack, I just said, they can't launch it."

"They don't have to launch it," Bauer insisted.

"The EMP still works, its range is just limited. It'll still reach Air Force One if it's flying overhead."

Chappelle backed away. "I've heard enough here. Jack, you're off the case. Officially. You are not to take any action at all. Is that understood?"

"Chappelle, you have to contact the Secret Service. At least reroute Air Force One—"

"Are you insane!" Chappelle yelled so loud that every head in CTU turned toward them. "You just shut down an *entire state!* An Air Force pilot just *died* because of you. No one is going to listen to you. *I'm* not listening to you!"

Chappelle stormed away, leaving the people behind him in awkward silence. Jack looked at them, and few would look him in the eye. Jack felt defeated for one of the few times in his life.

The phone rang, breaking the spell and sending everyone back to busywork. Jessi Bandison handed the phone to Jack. "Tony Almeida."

"Bauer," Jack said.

Tony Almeida said, "You're not going to believe what I found."

10:33 P.M. PST
Hills Above Glendale

Tony Almeida had been working hard. Once he found the unobserved exit out of Cal Tech, he set Jamey Farrell to work her magic. She and her team of analysts had gone back into the records, calling up traffic cameras and security footage anywhere and everywhere in the vicinity of that street. Using scraps of footage,

Jamey had built a very basic scenario for the Ready-Rooter van:

After midnight the night before, the van was spotted heading east away from Cal Tech. A minute later it was on a side road headed north, into the hills above Pasadena. The area had no traffic cameras, so there was a gap of nearly an hour. Then the van showed up on the same security camera heading in the other direction. At that point, CTU lost them. Jamey was widening her search during that time period, trying to reacquire its travel path.

With no other leads, Tony had followed the van's path into the hills. He knew he was on to something: this area was much too desolate for a Ready-Rooter van to have any reason to take this route. He used basic logic to plan his cursory search: the van had been out of pocket for one hour. Driving at a fairly fast clip, Tony drove into the hills for thirty minutes, then he turned around and stopped. He was sitting in the foothills of the San Gabriel Mountains, looking down on Pasadena and the hilly land between the San Gabriels and the Santa Monica ranges. There was nothing but sagebrush and fire roads here, and way too much ground to cover by himself. He'd need a team and daylight.

Tony started his car again and headed back down the road. As he drove he had a thought: he'd gone too far. The driver came up here to do something, and in Tony's experience "something" always took longer than a few minutes. Figuring twenty minutes each way as a maximum, Tony shortened the search area he would recommend to CTU for tomorrow morning.

He was so lost in thought that he barely saw the coyotes. They were scrawny brown and gray phantoms skittering across the edge of his headlights. Their eyes flashed demonlike in the lamp glare. They scattered off to the brush, but they didn't run away. That was odd. Coyotes were scavengers and cowards—the only reason they would resist their flight instinct was if . . .

Tony stopped the car and turned out the lights. It was dark now, but he could still see the coyotes, ghosts in the darkness. They crossed the road again. A few seconds later he heard yapping and snarling.

Almeida grabbed his flashlight and jumped out of his car. Drawing his gun, he ran across the road and into the brush. Most of the coyotes scrambled away from the flashlight beam and the sound of his footsteps, but one big male stood its ground, fur raised up and teeth bared. Tony fired one shot into the air, and the crack of the discharge stole the coyote's courage away. It yelped and ran off with the others.

Tony probed the ground all around with his flashlight beam. The circle of light fell across a large patch of broken ground. The earth had been upturned and then patted down in an area about fifteen feet wide and ten feet long. The coyotes had been digging and scratching at it, and Tony now saw what they'd been fighting over.

A human hand, partially mauled, was sticking up from the earth.

10:40 P.M. PST
CTU Headquarters, Los Angeles

Tony Almeida's news struck Jack like a blow to the stomach. Eight bodies. He'd discovered eight bodies buried in a shallow grave in the hills above Pasadena. In the dark, looking at bodies buried for nearly a day, Almeida couldn't be sure, but he thought they looked Middle Eastern, either Arab or Persian.

Kelly had stood by Jack, even after Chappelle's tirade. Like everyone else in CTU, he knew Bauer had made the wrong call, but Kelly had led men in battle, and led investigations, too. He understood that the only way to get things right was to act, and sometimes the wrong actions were taken. Good leaders learned from their mistakes and overcame their deficiencies.

He was as shocked by the news as Jack was. "Someone killed them. Newhouse?"

"But why?" Jack asked. "Why would he bring them into the country and then not use them? And if there's no terrorist attack, why bring them into the country?"

Kelly shook his head. "We still haven't sweated Farid. He's in a holding cell down there." He jabbed a bandaged thumb down the hall. "I'm probably not very intimidating right now with my Band-Aids on."

"I'll do it," Jack said.

Before he could get up, Jessi called over to him. "Jack, Nina."

Jack picked up the phone. "Nina, what's going on?"

"William Binns."

"Excuse me?"

"William Binns," Nina repeated.

"I'm not in the mood for games, Nina. That name means nothing to me."

"Well, it should. It's an alias for Frank Newhouse. It's an alias he's managed to keep off his record, even from the CIA and Justice. As far as anyone is concerned, William Binns is a nobody. He likes art and doesn't like excitement. Even his girlfriend thought so until he tried to kill her."

"You're sure?"

"Yeah. It looks like killing his girl was the first bad job he's done. He must have been in a hurry. He did take the time to smash her face in and send her car over a cliff but she's a tough cookie for an artist type—"

"Nina!" Jack interrupted. He was too exhausted for her smartass comments. "I need more information. There's no time for a long explanation, but I think this guy is going to try to set off an EMP device here, in Los Angeles, when the President's plane flies over. That's a little after one in the morning."

"The girlfriend doesn't know anything about that, and she's in bad shape. Maybe we can get her healed for a bit and then—"

"To get range for the EMP, he has to get to somewhere up high. Do we have any records on him having a pilot's license, records of owning an airplane—"

"Oh, I've got one thing," Nina said. "William Binns leases an office on the top floor of the Twin Towers in Century City."

1 2 3 4 5 6 7 8 9
10 11 12 13 14 15 16 17
18 19 20 **21** 22 23 24

••

THE FOLLOWING TAKES PLACE
BETWEEN THE HOURS OF
11 P.M. AND 12 A.M.
PACIFIC STANDARD TIME

••

11:00 P.M. PST
CTU Headquarters, Los Angeles

Jack slammed the phone down and relayed the information to Kelly Sharpton as quickly as he could.

"You've got a problem," Kelly said. "There's no
way Chappelle will authorize a strike team for you."

"Yeah," Bauer growled. "Why should tonight be
any different than last night? I'm going to Century
City. You sweat Farid."

"I bet I know what he's going to say," Kelly said,
tearing the bandages off his hands.

"Yeah, but I need to be sure." He took a deep
breath. It had been a long day and he'd already turned
the world upside down once making the wrong call.

He didn't want to do it twice. "What's his game? Frank Newhouse is supposed to be undercover working for Justice to infiltrate the Greater Nation. Then we hear a story that he's got Iranian contacts and he's helping terrorists get into the country. Then we hear that the terrorists have been killed and that Frank Newhouse has an alias called William Binns. Who is this guy really working for? What does he really want?"

"Only one way to find out," Kelly said.

Jack nodded. "I'll go ask him right now. Call me if you get anything from Farid."

11:10 P.M. PST
CTU Headquarters, Los Angeles

Kelly Sharpton walked into the holding cell with a smile on his face. Farid shifted around in his chair like a cat stuck in a small box, his narrow face twitching and his eyes glancing from Kelly to the observation mirror and back to Kelly.

"It's about time someone talked to me," Farid complained.

"We've had a busy day," Kelly said with the air of someone with a burden on his shoulders. "And, let's face it, you're just not that important."

Farid's left eye twitched. "That's right, I'm not important, so I don't know anything, so let me go."

Kelly spun his chair around so the back was facing Farid. He straddled the chair and crossed his arms over the back, then rested his chin on his forearms. "I didn't say you didn't know anything. I do think you know things. Let's start with what you told Jack . . ."

For the next few minutes, Kelly made Farid repeat the information he'd relayed to Bauer: Farid was a finder who helped get jobs for immigrants, especially illegal ones. A man had called him and told him there were eight Iranian men who wanted into the country and who needed work. This man had put Farid in contact with the coyote who was bringing the men over. Farid got them hired by Babak Farrah, but Farrah got angry when the men didn't show up to do any work for him. He blamed Farid and came after him.

"That's all I know," Farid ended. "Next thing, Farrah tries to kill me, and that blond guy comes in shooting everybody, which I appreciate, by the way, and now I'm locked in here."

Kelly smiled, but shook his head. "No, that's not all you know, Farid. For example, I'll bet you know a little about Farrah. Tell me about him from when he lived in Iran."

"Iran? What's there to tell? Farrah was a little nobody, like all of us. Biggest thing about him was that he didn't like to be religious, and he kept getting noticed by the Ministry for the Prevention of Vice, so he came to America. You can make a good living from vice here."

"What about his work for Iranian intelligence?"

Kelly watched Farid's reaction carefully. The reaction would tell him far more than the words. Farid's face was blank for a moment, then it looked confused. In that instant, Kelly learned what he needed to know. If Farid had been pretending, he would have made some kind of reaction—surprised, confused, annoyed, anything—immediately. But his first reaction had been incomprehension—not confusion, but a complete failure to understand Kelly's meaning. After that, the words were almost anticlimactic. "Farrah was never in the intelligence service. He was a little sergeant or something. He got out of the army as soon as he could."

"Why did Farrah want to kill you?" Kelly asked.

"I told you, he was mad because I took his money for the eight workers, but they didn't do any work for him. He was mad because they stole some guns and some money, he said, and he wanted to blame me."

Kelly said nothing. Farid had nothing to give him here. That was the story Farrah had told him, and that's all Farid knew. But Kelly had a theory of his own. From Jack's story, he knew that Farrah had even tried, at the end, to take a dancer as hostage and trade her for Farid. Farrah had been determined to kill Farid at great risk to himself. That didn't jibe with Farrah's reputation as a cold and calculating businessman. Kelly's theory was that someone had wanted Farid dead and told Farrah to do it.

"Tell me about this phone call you received, the one that told you about the eight men in the first place."

Farid shrugged, brushing the question off as unimportant. "I don't know, it was just a guy. I figured he had his reason for calling me, but whatever they were, I didn't care. He had eight guys I could get into the country, and that was good enough for me."

"Name?" Kelly asked.

Farid just laughed.

"His accent. He was Iranian?"

"Not Iranian. American. At least, that's how he sounded over the phone."

"Tell me about the coyote," Kelly demanded.

Farid held up his hands. "Fuck, no. That guy works with MS-13. You know that gang? I want nothing to do with them."

Kelly couldn't blame Farid. MS-13 was the most violent street gang in the country. People who crossed them ended up chopped into little pieces and spread around several states. Lucky for Farid, they already knew who the coyote was, and they already had him.

Kelly stood up and walked out of the holding cell without saying a word. He closed the door on Farid as the man yelled after him. Kelly ran down to Jessi Bandison's station. "Get Tony on the line. Get him to send over a picture of one or two of the bodies. I want faces." She nodded without speaking—there was still tension between them—and he walked down to the next holding room.

They'd sent CTU agents out to get Julio Juarez several hours ago. He'd been arrested without incident—but only because LAPD had gone into his neighborhood in platoon strength—and first brought to Rampart Division. But he'd been quickly transferred over to CTU. Originally, they'd been planning nothing more than a cursory interview, just to keep their records clear. But suddenly Julio's testimony had become very important.

It got off to a pleasant start.

"Who the fuck are you?" the little man said as Kelly entered.

"Good evening," Kelly said. He sat down in this chair the same way he'd sat down with Farid.

"Fuck that," Julio said. He sneered, accentuating the sagginess of his eye. "That bitch told me all he wanted was to ask a question and he'd get out of my face." He was talking about Jack Bauer.

"Well, all I want is to ask a question and I'll get out of your face, too," Kelly said calmly. "I want to know about the man who put you in contact with Farid Koshbin."

Julio sneered at him, squinting with his good eye so that the sunken one glared at him. "You want me to narc. You got to give me something, I give you something."

"So you knew him."

"Maybe. I tell you, you tell me I walk."

Kelly rubbed his jaw with one burned hand, considering. The truth was, CTU hadn't really planned to hold Julio. They'd planned to turn his name over to Immigration and Customs Enforcement and then release him. But Kelly held his pose for another moment to let Julio sweat. Julio stared at Kelly's burned hand, his normally slope-faced expression mixed with disgust and admiration for the agent's stoicism.

"We'll see," Kelly said at last. "Your story's good, I'll let you go."

Now it was Julio's turn to consider the offer, but he didn't have many chips with which to bargain. "Look, homeboy, I don't know the guy's name. Best I can tell you is that he knew some of our people back East." Kelly had read up on MS-13 and knew that 'back East' meant Maryland and Virginia, where the gang was strong. "He dropped the right names to me, I helped him out, you know what I'm saying?"

"You saw him?"

"My cell," Julio said, pointing to his pocket where

his mobile phone would have been if CTU hadn't taken it.

"What did he sound like? Iranian? Hispanic?"

"No, dude, he was a white boy like you."

Kelly nodded, expecting to hear it. "Okay, Julio, you sit tight for a minute."

Kelly left the room and went to Jessi's desk. She nodded before he even got there. "Best Tony could do from where he's at." She pulled up two images on her screen—they were mug shots of two dead men, their faces still covered with dirt stains. The images were low resolution and grainy.

"Can't we get anything clearer?" he asked.

Jessi shrugged. "He's out in the middle of nowhere."

She printed out copies and handed them to Kelly. He returned to Julio's room.

"Recognize these?"

"Shit, my sister's camera takes better pictures. They should buy you a new one."

"If you paid your taxes, we could afford it. Do you recognize them?"

"Yeah, kinda. Looks like two of the ragheads that I brought up. They spent most of the time locked in the back of a truck, you know? But we let 'em out once in a while. Looks kinda like them."

"Okay, Julio, you've been a real hero today. Thanks."

Kelly turned to leave. As he did, Julio shouted, "Hey, so I get to go, right?"

"We'll see."

Walking down the hallway, Kelly thought of the things he had learned. Some of them seemed connected, and some of them seemed random, but all, he was sure, were important. The man who had orchestrated the entry of eight Iranians was white. He worked or spent time on the East Coast, where MS-13 was strong. He had connections with MS-13. The Iranians he had brought over were now dead. The Iranian who was supposed to house them, Babak Farrah, had been angry when they left him, so clearly he wasn't expecting them to go off to commit acts of terror. Militia leader Brett Marks claimed that Farrah was former Iranian intelligence, but according to Farid, he wasn't. Farrah had wanted Farid dead.

And somehow, Kelly knew, this was all connected with the Attorney General's efforts to blackmail Debrah Drexler. Kelly didn't know how he knew, but his investigator's instincts told him it was far from coincidence that Frank Newhouse's name came up so prominently in both schemes. The connection, of course, was Newhouse and the Attorney General. Newhouse and the Attorney General . . . Kelly repeated the phrase over and over, flipping it in his mind like a word jumble that you keep rearranging until it comes close to the solution.

This is what it came down to, always. There were the guns and the tactics and the unbelievable satellites that allowed you to read a note scribbled on the back of someone's hand, but in the end, it always came down to this: someone sitting in a chair, trying (and sometimes failing) to put the pieces together in his head. Kelly forced himself to put away his anxiety and the pain in his hands and bend his thoughts to the various threads of evidence fluttering like a broken spider web in the breeze.

Newhouse had worked for the AG. If Newhouse did work in Maryland, he could have run into MS-13. There was one connection. If Newhouse wanted an alias that no one—not even the CIA and FBI—would track, the Attorney General could arrange it. There was another connection. Frank was working for Justice . . . Frank was also working for the Iranians . . . No, Frank wasn't working for the Iranians. Marks was wrong. Farrah was pissed that the Iranians hadn't stayed and worked for him. The Iranians had been killed . . . before or after the terrorist plan was put into effect? Kelly had to assume they were killed prior to the event, because the event hadn't happened yet. Why bring them into the country and then kill them? Had there been an argument? No. They were killed by the driver of the Ready-Rooter truck. The truck had planned to leave Cal Tech without being noticed. The murders of the Iranians had to be part of that plan. So again, the question: why go to the trouble of sneaking them into the country and then killing them?

Kelly couldn't find a way to reorganize the loose strands. He had to change strategies. Stop thinking about the terrorist threat and Frank Newhouse. Think of it a different way. Think of what was easy to find and what was difficult. The facts that were difficult to uncover were the ones the bad guys feared the most.

Kelly wished he had Jack on the phone, but he wanted to sort out his thoughts first. The facts that were easy to find were, as far as he knew, these: there were terrorists in Los Angeles (Marks had told them so); the terrorists were Iranians; the terrorists had stolen an EMP device from Cal Tech; the terrorists were going to set off a bomb over Kansas.

Kelly reviewed that list, and scratched off one thing. It had not been easy to discover that the terrorists had stolen an EMP device. He looked at his burned hands for a minute—they had learned that only because he had gotten to the condo in time and stopped the bomb. In fact, the bad guys were so determined to keep the EMP clues away from them that they almost blew up two entire floors of a building. And apparently Frank Newhouse had tried to kill his own girlfriend, the only person who'd given them a lead on his alias. If CTU hadn't learned about the EMP theft, what would they know: terrorists in Los Angeles; terrorists were Iranians . . . terrorists planning to set off EMP device over Kansas.

Now how could we have learned about the Kansas strategy so easily without learning of the EMP device itself? Kelly thought. *That information came easily because it came from . . .*

"Oh, shit," Kelly said out loud.

The information on the EMP burst over Kansas had come from Brett Marks.

The information on Frank Newhouse's Iranian connections had come from Brett Marks.

The information on the terrorist cell in Los Angeles had come from Brett Marks.

And every single one of those pieces of information had been wrong.

11:40 P.M. PST
Century City, California

Los Angeles was not famous for its skyline. There was a small cluster of tall buildings downtown, and the Westwood area had another tiny forest of them. But the closer one got to the ocean, the fewer there were, until there were none at all, with only one exception: Century City. This tiny enclave, made up of a few residential blocs, FOX Studios, and the outdoor Century City shopping mall, also included the two massive Twin Towers of the Century City Plaza. These two towers, forty-four stories high, were prominent enough that, on the morning of 9/11, they were considered viable targets for a West Coast follow-up attack by al Qaeda operatives.

A massive plaza served as a foundation for the two massive buildings. The plaza also housed the Shubert Theater, Henry's Grill (home, for those who were interested, of the Annual Bad Hemingway writing competition), and the ABC Network. But all these were only foothills clustered around the mountains that rose into the sky above.

It hadn't taken long for Jack to drive from CTU to Century City. He arrived in time to see the last stragglers from the Shubert Theater easing their way up the parking ramps. He had driven down in the opposite direction. The parking attendants had tried to stop him until he flashed his badge. He had ridden his SUV along the first level, resisting the urge to duck as the low ceiling of the parking structure seemed to drop down to meet the high roof of his vehicle. When he'd reached the elevators he'd stopped, but they were shut down at this time of night. The escalators had stopped working, so he was forced to climb them like stairs until he reached the plaza level. He'd walked across the wide, flat steps to the North Tower and gone inside.

There was a late night security guard there, a young black man in a white uniform shirt, a security guard's badge, and a name tag that said "Darryl."

"Darryl, I'm Special Agent Jack Bauer," Jack said, showing his credentials. "I need to get up to the 44th floor. I'm looking for the office of William Binns."

Darryl looked unsure what to do. "Are you meeting him up there, sir?"

"I hope so."

This told Darryl nothing, of course. "I mean, do you have an appointment? We're not supposed to let anyone up there after hours without an escort."

"Anybody been up to that office? Or that floor?"

Darryl shook his head.

"You can come with me if you want," Jack offered.

Darryl didn't seem to like this, either, but here he was talking to an actual Federal agent. He wasn't about to say no. He came out from behind the handsome marble desk that was his home base, picked up a radio from the counter, and walked toward the elevators. He and Jack both entered.

"Have you ever met Mr. Binns?" Jack asked.

Darryl shook his head. He looked bright for a security guard. "I don't really meet anyone, except some lawyers when they work late, and most of the accountants in March and April. How long have you been a . . . what kind of cop are you?" Darryl asked.

"I'm with the Federal government."

"Like the FBI?" Darryl asked.

"Kind of like that."

"I want to do that someday. I'm doing the police academy next year."

Jack nodded absently. "That's a good place to start."

The elevator stopped and the doors opened to the twenty-third floor. Darryl led him down the hall, past several sets of double doors announcing law firms, to a small set of offices on the east side of the tower. Darryl used his master key to open them and Jack went into the office. He was in a small entryway with a receptionist desk and three chairs. Beyond were three offices, all with window views. Jack flipped the lights, which fluttered and then went on. The offices contained exactly what Jack expected them to contain: nothing. Frank Newhouse hadn't rented these offices to use the space. He'd rented them to get access to the building.

The name on the door said "The Patrick Henry Company." Jack clicked his tongue. "This guy's got a thing for Patrick Henry."

"What's that?" Darryl asked.

Jack shrugged. "You want to be in law enforcement, you can start reading clues with me. This guy, uses the name William Binns. But he had another place under the name Patrick Henry, and this company he's using here is called the Patrick Henry Company. I'm going to have to figure out what that means."

Darryl said off-handedly, "He doesn't like the government."

Jack was surprised. "Yeah? Why do you say that?"

"You know the name, right? Patrick Henry. From American history."

Jack nodded. "He was the 'give me liberty or give me death' guy."

Darryl nodded. "That's right. That's what he was famous for. He was also one of the guys who didn't want to ratify the Constitution."

That stopped Jack in his tracks. "Really?" he asked, genuinely interested.

Darryl nodded even more. "Yeah. He thought the central government was too strong."

"You're a smart guy," Jack said.

Darryl shrugged. "I read. Nights're long, you know? You can only play so much Nintendo."

But Jack wasn't listening anymore. *He thought the central government was too strong.* "I don't believe it," he said in surprise. He reached for his phone. It was ringing by the time he had pulled it from his pocket.

"Jack, Kelly."

"I was just calling you," Jack said.

"Listen, I think I've got this figured. It's been—"

"Brett Marks all along," Jack ended.

Kelly paused. "Yeah. That's pretty goddamned good. You didn't even hear Farid or Julio talk."

"No, but I've got Darryl."

"What?"

"Nothing. Fill me in."

Kelly spent a minute summarizing his conversations with Farid and Julio. With each word, Jack felt his anger and his embarrassment grow. He'd been played. He'd been one step behind on every play. Brett Marks had toyed with him.

"You're got to admire it," Jack said begrudgingly. "They set it up so that there are terrorists in the U.S.

They attack the President and the terrorists get blamed."

"But you know what it means, right?" Kelly added. "It means Brett Marks wanted you to arrest him. He knew you were going to do it. It was the perfect cover for him. On the day the President gets attacked, he's under arrest at CTU."

"They slipped up twice," Jack said. "Someone used Julio's picture on an i.d. That led us to the coyotes earlier than expected. I bet that's why they wanted Farid killed. And the other thing was the fingerprint. If we hadn't found that fingerprint and gotten to Newhouse's girlfriend, we wouldn't know what the hell was going on tonight."

"Jack, Air Force One flies over the city in a little more than an hour."

Jack nodded. "I'll be waiting."

1 2 3 4 5 6 7 8 9
10 11 12 13 14 15 16 17
18 19 20 21 **22** 23 24

....

THE FOLLOWING TAKES PLACE
BETWEEN THE HOURS OF
12 A.M. AND 1 A.M.
PACIFIC STANDARD TIME

....

12:00 A.M. PST
Air Force One

President Barnes was still wearing his tuxedo as he
boarded Air Force One. These fund-raisers exhausted
him, but the war chest could never be too full, especially with that Senator Palmer rising in the polls. He
would have preferred to stay in his hotel room once
the Secret Service had given the all clear for the party
to continue, but even the President had to make a
buck. He'd have to sleep on the plane. There were
early morning meetings in San Diego.

Barnes tugged at his tie as he dropped into the
wide, soft chair in his private study. He'd barely had

time to slip off his shoes before there was a knock at the door. "Come," he growled.

One of his aides poked her head in. "The Attorney General, if you have a minute, Mr. President."

"Send him in."

Quincy entered a moment later. "Mr. President . . ."

"Who's responsible for that disaster earlier, Jim?" Barnes asked. He was too tired to throw a full-fledged fit, but he was still angry. "I spent most of my time at that goddamned thousand-dollar-a-plate dinner explaining why my people shut down flights over Kansas for two hours. Shit, if I could have charged money for the excuses I came up with, we'd be flush for the next two elections."

Quincy didn't look embarrassed. In fact, he seemed energized. "Our guys followed the wrong lead, Mr. President. But they're on the right track. There is a terrorist cell inside the country and they're on it. I think . . . sir, I think concerns over this will push the NAP Act through."

Barnes studied his Attorney General. He wished he had Mitch in the room with him—Rasher was an excellent strategist with a knack for seeing right into the heart of other people's schemes. Barnes, however, had a talent for reading people themselves, and even if he couldn't figure out the details, he sensed what Quincy was up to. "Then this has all been convenient for you, Jim," the President noted.

The Attorney General's face turned the lightest shade of pink. "It's not about me, Mr. President. It's about protecting our country from—"

"Of course it's about you," Barnes said. He spoke with no disdain, no judgment. He spoke in the matter-of-fact tones of one power seeker to another. "It's about putting power into your own hands. Don't deny it! I know, you think once you get more power you'll do more good things. We all do, and maybe we're right. But that comes second. First comes getting the power."

"If you say so, sir."

Barnes took a deep, thoughtful breath and exhaled it slowly. "There's never been a lot of bullshit between us, Jim. This Privacy Act, even the name if it, it's all dressed up to look like a gift to the people, but it's dangerous. Once you break down these walls of privacy, well . . . those walls might never be rebuilt."

"Sir . . ." Quincy hesitated. "Sir, if the NAP Act passes, are you going to veto it?"

Barnes let his head fall back against the cushion of his chair. "Yes, I think I might, Jim."

"I understand, Mr. President."

Barnes seemed eager to change the subject. "Are you flying down to San Diego with us?"

"No, sir," Quincy replied. He knew in that moment that he had to get off the plane and make one more phone call. "I'll be taking a different route."

12:19 A.M. PST
Century City

Jack and Darryl rode the elevator back down to the lobby, then walked to the security station. Behind the desk, Jack saw a row of small, black-and-white screens—monitors hooked up to security cameras all around the building.

"Is all this centralized somewhere?" Jack asked.

"Supposed to be, but the security office isn't working. They had some kind of technical trouble. All we got are these right now."

"Do they show you everything?"

"Every parking level, all the entrances, but not the office floors."

"Can you toggle through the parking areas?"

Darryl sat down at his desk and pressed a button on one of the screens. The image began to change rapidly. "It's four cameras on every level, and six parking levels, so—"

"Wait!" Jack said. "Go back one."

Darryl flipped back. They were looking at P6, the lowest parking level. Like all the security cameras, this one angled down, and showed a driving lane bordered by parking slots and thick support pillars. Peeking out from behind one of these pillars, Jack could just make out the back of a white van.

"Where's that camera?"

"It's on the southwest side, near the elevator. If you go down the elevator, you'll make a left."

"How about if I walk down the driving ramp?"

"Seriously? Then it's straight ahead."

Jack drew his gun.

"Goddamn," Darryl breathed. "Aren't you supposed to be calling for backup or something like that?"

"I wish I could," Jack admitted. "But you can. You just watch those cameras. The minute you see or hear anything, call it in. Got it?"

"Okay."

"One more thing. Do you have a flashlight?"

A few minutes later, Jack took the elevator down to

P5. For the first few seconds, he allowed himself to feel the full measure of his anger. Goddamned idiot! He'd been Marks's dupe from the beginning, from the very goddamned first day! Kelly hadn't said so, but it must have occurred to him, as it had to Jack, that Marks might have pegged him as an undercover agent from the minute he infiltrated the Greater Nation. If Marks was working with Newhouse and Newhouse had the right sources, he would have known about Jack's mission *and* about his demotion, which meant he would have known about the Rafizadehs and the aborted terrorist theory. The militia leader had used that theory, and Jack's own desire to redeem himself, to build his terrorist cover story. He'd given Jack a gift, exactly what he'd wanted, and Jack had fallen for it.

By the time the elevator dinged open at P5, Jack had cooled himself down. He left the elevator, weapon drawn, and jogged quickly across the parking lot until he came to the downward-sloping ramp that led to P6. It was a short drive but a long walk, especially as Jack now moved slowly and carefully. The ramp circled around and leveled out on P6. Jack reached the bottom and pressed himself up against a support column. He listened, but there was no sound. He slipped out from behind his cover and trotted down the lane. Straight ahead, about fifty yards off, he could see the support column and the tail of the white van. Jack slowed as he approached, looking around every few seconds. The parking level was empty except for two or three cars. Parked near the white van were two older model cars—a 1969 Chevy Nova and a 1967 Camaro.

Jack reached the white van and leaned against the

pillar. No sound or movement came from inside. Jack crept along the side of the van—which still had its sign saying Ready-Rooter—and peeked in the passenger window. No one there. He slipped to the back and tested the door. It was unlocked. He opened it, pointing his pistol, but the back of the van was empty.

Jack knew that Newhouse and Marks wouldn't take the elevators. The security guards would see them. He jogged over to the elevators and found the staircase next to them. Six parking levels plus forty-four floors, plus the access way to the roof. Fifty floors was a long way to climb.

At least he wasn't carrying a bomb . . .

12:27 A.M. PST
CTU Headquarters, Los Angeles

"It's been a long night," Ryan Chappelle said. "Let's send all nonessentials home."

Kelly hesitated. "I'm not sure we can do that. We've still got investigations going . . ."

Chappelle flapped his hand in annoyance. "What can't wait? The Iranian bodies will be there in the morning. The Swenson girl is in the hospital. Your two prisoners might as well be released."

"The EMP devices are still out there."

"Yes, but you don't have any leads on them."

"Well, as a matter of fact, we do."

Ryan Chappelle looked at Kelly first in surprise, then in annoyance, then in something on the borderline between mild curiosity and complete dread. "Where's Jack Bauer?"

12:30 A.M. PST
Century City

Jack climbed the stairs as quietly as he could. According to the emergency exit diagrams, there were three other stairwells in the building, but he was betting on this one. It was closest to the vehicle, limiting the distance they had to carry their device, and closest to the elevators in case they needed another exit.

He reached ground level before he started to lose his breath. He'd been up for well over forty hours and he'd been moving nonstop for more than twenty. He felt wide-awake thanks to the adrenaline, but his body wasn't performing at its peak. By the tenth story he was moving slower, the air rattling in his chest as he breathed. He scolded himself to keep motivated. Time was he could hump thirty kilometers with a forty-pound pack before breakfast. Now a few hours without sleep were leaving him weak as a—

Scuffing sounds drifted down the shaft toward him. Someone was moving up above. He listened a little longer, noticing that the scuffing sounds had a rhythm to them: scuff, scuff, stop; scuff, scuff, stop. Someone was lifting something heavy along the steps, then stopping to rest.

Jack hurried his pace, but he moved in rhythm with the scuffing sounds—two big steps and a pause, two big steps and a pause, covering a stairwell in two legs with this pattern.

Fifteenth floor. Jack could see them. Leaning out over
the stair rail and looking up, he could see the shoulders and arms of two men. They would move a few
steps, then stop for a minute. Jack hurried along, using their sounds as cover, and gained two more flights
on them. He was close enough now that he could hear
them whispering to each other.

"Jesus . . . damn . . . christ!" one of them hissed.
"This is ridiculous!"

"Complaining doesn't make it any lighter."

"The elevator's right here!"

"And so's the goddamned camera!"

Jack didn't recognize their voices. He guessed they
were two more of Marks's militia, a couple of left-
overs he'd been saving for his coup de grace.

"Why can't we set it off here?"

The second one seemed more annoyed by his part-
ner than by the long climb. "Didn't you listen? Something about all the metal. It absorbs the electricity or
something. It makes the range less."

"It'd still do something."

"Okay, then you tell Commander Marks."

"Tell me what?"

Jack bristled. That was the voice he was waiting
for. Marks was there. He two-stepped the last flight
of stairs quietly, under cover of the conversation, and
came around the last stairwell to see two men in blue
coveralls standing on the stairs, one above and one below the source of their complaining. It was a metal
tube, shaped oddly like a torpedo standing on its end.
The torpedo was strapped to a wooden base. A small

control panel was built into the side of the device. Beyond the two men, Jack saw Brett Marks.

"Freeze!" he yelled. He laid his gun sights over Marks's chest.

Instead of freezing, one of the men drew his own gun and fired. The gunshots rang like thunder in Jack's ears. But the stairs ruined the militia man's aim and his shots went high as Jack dropped down and returned fire.

"Don't drop it!" Brett Marks yelled, obviously worried about his EMP device. "Get it up here!"

Jack leaned over the railing to look up again. Marks was looking down, his gun ready. He fired as Jack threw himself back against the wall. The rounds sped down the shaft into oblivion.

Jack knew he had to stop them soon. If they reached the roof, they could close off the door and hold it against him. Keeping his back to the wall, he spiraled up the stairs, faster now that he wasn't worried about stealth. The militia men moved slowly, weighed down by their burden. Jack reached the next flight and saw them. Marks leveled his weapon but Jack was ready—he fired, causing Marks to duck for cover. Then Jack paused for aim and put a round through the chest of one of the militia men. He gagged and went down.

The other militia man panicked. Jack saw him reach for the EMP. For a moment, Jack thought the man had lost his grip. Too late, he realized what the man was doing.

So did Marks. "No!" he yelled.

Jack swung his weapon onto the man in the coveralls, who put one hand on the metal railing to maintain his balance while his other hand grabbed a switch and pushed it. Inside the EMP, something thumped like an explosion muffled by walls. At the same time, an intense blast of light blinded Jack, followed by a blood-curdling scream. Jack stumbled backward, panicked that he'd be blind when Marks came at him with another round of gunfire. He blinked, trying to clear the white flash from his sight.

When he opened his eyes, he saw no white flashes. In fact, he saw nothing but darkness. *Complete* darkness, blackness devoid of any light whatsoever. The stairwell lights had all gone out.

1 2 3 4 5 6 7 8 9
10 11 12 13 14 15 16 17
18 19 20 21 22 **23** 24

···

THE FOLLOWING TAKES PLACE
BETWEEN THE HOURS OF
1 A.M. AND 2 A.M.
PACIFIC STANDARD TIME

···

1:00 A.M. PST
Century City

Jack was blind. This wasn't the darkness of nighttime.
He was in the deep darkness of tunnels and spaces under the Earth, where no light ever shone. He flapped
his hand in front of his face but saw nothing, not even
the sense of movement.

Jack fumbled in his pocket for the flashlight he'd
borrowed from the security guard. The flashlight's
battery and wiring were too small to gather up the energy from the EMP, which meant it should still work.
He felt for the switch and slid it forward, grateful
when the beam shot out like a lance to touch the stairs
in front of him. Jack started forward again. Half a

flight up he reached the EMP device itself. The torpedo-shaped object was now burned black and the metal had buckled. Beside the platform lay the man in blue coveralls. His skin looked wrinkled and crisp, as though he'd been cooked from the inside out. Jack knew very little about EMPs, but he guessed it wasn't wise to be too close to the device when it went off, especially if your hand was touching a conductor like the metal guard rails.

A gunshot rang out, followed instantly by a sting like a sharp burn across the top of Jack's hand. He dropped the flashlight and leaped backward into the darkness, landing badly on the stairs and stumbling backward onto the flat of a landing until his back hit the wall. Two more rounds shook the walls, and Jack heard the bullets chip the concrete steps near the flashlight.

Quietly, he crept forward. He grabbed the light in a quick movement and switched it off, then jumped away as more rounds whined and chipped the concrete around him. Flecks of cement stung his face.

"Give it up, Brett!" Jack roared up the shaft. "Your EMP is done now. There's nothing left!"

"There's always freedom!" Marks yelled back. Jack tried to locate him, but couldn't. The militia leader's voice echoed off all the walls, directionless. "All in all, I think I'll stay out of jail."

Jack crept up the stairs, trying to stay quiet, and to move under Marks's voice when he talked. He was sure Marks was doing the same thing—otherwise he wouldn't have talked at all.

"You did better than I thought, Jack. I don't know how you found out about Century City."

"I always said you militia assholes were redneck idiots," Jack replied.

"What does that say about the CTU agent we strung along for six months?"

Jack felt his blood boil. He'd tried to get a rise out of Marks, but Marks had turned the tables on him. He tiptoed up a few more steps, reaching the next landing by feel. Marks didn't speak for a moment, but Jack risked another few steps, so quiet he couldn't hear himself walk. He counted steps until he reached the next landing, floating like a ghost in the darkness. He listened but heard nothing. He must be near the top now. He hadn't heard a door open, so he knew that Marks must be close by.

"You get lost, Jack?" Marks called.

But the voice was practically in Jack's ear! He'd climbed up right next to the militia leader and neither of them had realized it. Jack fired twice.

The muzzle flash illuminated the landing. Jack got the briefest glimpse of Marks's shocked face in the lightning-brief strobe. Marks returned fire. Jack felt a round tug at his shirt near his ribs. He stumbled away, firing twice more blindly. He heard footsteps run up the stairs.

1:09 A.M. PST
CTU Headquarters, Los Angeles

"Everybody just calm down!" Kelly Sharpton yelled. He was standing in the abyss. All around him seemed like primordial chaos—darkness filled with cries of surprise, indignation, and terror. He gathered himself. "Calm down!" he roared in a deep, commanding voice.

The chaos subsided into mere darkness. Kelly heard people shuffling around him. He knew that Jessi was close by, and Nina Myers. But he couldn't see anything.

"It's obviously a blackout," he said into the void.

"Why haven't the backup generators kicked in?" Ryan Chappelle replied. "We're supposed to be immune to power outages from the city."

"I'm going to take a wild guess," Kelly replied, "and say that someone set off an EMP device and we got hit. The EMP will have fried every circuit we've got. Anything that had computer circuitry, or was linked to an antennae array, you can probably write off, including the system that sent signals to our backup generators. But anything that had its own battery power and was independent of the main system will work. So look for flashlights and battery-powered radios. The generators themselves should be working, but we'll have to crank them up by hand."

"What do you know, Jack was right!" Nina Myers yelled.

Yes, he was right, Kelly said. And if his watch had been right, just before everything stopped, Jack had succeeded in doing something . . . because Marks and Newhouse had set off their EMP an hour early.

1:19 A.M. PST
Century City

Jack slid his hand along the wall as he climbed the stairs, moving with painstaking slowness that last flight until his hand touched a steel wall. He groped around until he felt a door handle. He hesitated. Were they waiting for him on the other side? Had they already bolted down some other stairs?

There was only one way to find out. Jack pulled the door open and dived forward. Gunfire pelted the door, the door frame, and the ground all around him. He rolled across the tarmac-like surface of the rooftop, came up to his knees, and rolled again as more gunshots chopped at the ground around him. Rounds were coming off close, and he realized that compared to the utter darkness of the stairwell, the night darkness of Los Angeles provided Marks with enough illumination to see him.

The rooftop of the North Tower was a small forest of utility sheds, ventilation grills, and antennae. Jack dived behind a ventilation shaft for cover. He caught his breath and ejected the magazine from his SigSauer, smacking another into place.

"You're the idiot, Brett!" he yelled into the darkness.

"Why's that, Jack?" Brett Marks asked in amusement. His voice came from somewhere on Jack's right. Jack moved in that direction as silently as he could.

"This stunt is just going to make the Federal government do more of the things you hate. They'll crack down more. They'll take more power for themselves."

"The people have to remember their power, Jack!" Marks shot back. "Either we'll set an example for them to follow, or we'll force the tyrants to become so ruthless the people have to act!"

"The tyrants are elected by the people," Jack pointed out.

"Elected by corporations. Elected by political parties. Not by people." Marks's voice was moving again. Jack had trouble following it through the forest of rooftop structures. "We are the government, Jack.

Me and people like me. We cast the final vote. I intend to make sure the people remember that we have the final veto. We can make this country a real republic, greater than Rome ever was."

Marks had stopped. Now Jack thought he knew where the militia man was hiding, behind a man-sized vent spout curved at the top. "Rome had tyrants. Dictators. That can't be a good example for you," he called out, using his voice to cover his footsteps.

"You really have to get some education, Jack," Marks sneered. "Before it allowed dictators in, Rome was a republic for five hundred years. Kings were not allowed in the city. Tribunes were allowed to serve only two years in office. It wasn't so bad."

Jack caught a glimpse of Marks's silhouette. He rose to his feet and took aim.

Suddenly an arm clamped around his neck from behind and he felt the muzzle of a gun press against the side of his head. "Hello, Jack Bauer," hissed Frank Newhouse. "Drop your gun."

1:28 A.M. PST
Air Force One

Air Force One was wheels up, banking left and leaving the city lights behind them. The President had just closed his eyes in his cabin when there was a knock on the door. He grunted, sat up in his bed, and flicked on the light. "Come."

Avery Taylor stepped into the room. Despite the hour, he looked as crisp and professional as usual. "Mr. President, sorry to disturb you, but I want to keep you informed. There's been a blackout in Los

Angeles. We're currently assessing the risk, but there is some small chance that we'll change our flight plan."

Barnes groaned. "What kind of blackout? Why would it be a danger to us?"

"It shouldn't be, sir, but it's our job . . ."

"I understand, Avery, but unless there's a direct threat to this airplane from a blackout, I want us to take the most direct path. I need to get to San Diego without complications. Understood?"

"Yes, sir."

1:29 A.M. PST
Century City

Newhouse's left arm had closed like a clamp over Bauer's throat, while his right hand held a gun to his head. Jack dropped his gun as ordered. Newhouse laughed in his ear. "How does it feel to be behind the curve every single time?"

"Like this," Jack said.

With his right hand, Jack reached back and snatched at Newhouse's gun, pulling it forward and off his head, pointing the muzzle forward. A round went off right near his head, deafening him. Jack's left hand clamped the hammer side of the gun. At the same time, Jack punched his hands forward and his hips backward into Newhouse, stretching him. Jack snapped the gun from Newhouse's hand, then jabbed his right elbow back into Newhouse's gun, then into his face. He heard Newhouse's nose collapse with a satisfying crunch.

But Newhouse was no weekend warrior. Even as he

dropped from the blow, he kicked Jack's legs out from under him. Jack hit the deck hard and felt Newhouse on top of him in an instant. Newhouse pounded Jack with a hard punch; a second punch came and Jack slipped it. Newhouse howled as his knuckles pounded the tarmac. Jack bucked his hips and rolled, feeling Newhouse grab for the gun as he did. The weapon slipped from Jack's hand and Newhouse rolled over, aiming the gun at him with a grin. He pulled the trigger.

The gun was jammed. Jack dropped an elbow into Newhouse's bloody face. Jack thought that might be the end of him, but Newhouse only grunted. His reached up and dug his fingers into Jack's face and eyes. Jack winced and pulled Newhouse's claws away, and before he knew it Newhouse had kicked him in the chest, sending him sprawling backward.

Jack rolled with the kick and came up to his feet. For a moment he lost Newhouse among the pipes, but a movement on his left caught his attention. Instead of shying away he attacked, hurling himself at the movement and catching Frank off guard. Newhouse staggered backward. Jack grabbed him by the neck and kneed him twice in the stomach. He tried to deliver another knee, but Newhouse caught his leg and dumped him on his back again. Jack felt his left shoulder give. He stabbed upward with his right hand, feeling his fingers sink into the thick jelly of Newhouse's eye. Newhouse squealed and pushed away, straightening his arms. Jack grabbed one of his arms and spun on his back, catching the arm and shoulder between his legs. He pulled Newhouse's arm straight, then arched his back, snapping the arm at the elbow. Newhouse screamed.

Gunfire echoed across the rooftop. Jack rolled away and felt something under his back. He grabbed for it and found his Sig in his hands. He came up firing in the direction of the muzzle flashes. Marks yelped and retreated.

Jack crawled back toward Newhouse, who lay unmoving on the tarmac. In the dark, Jack groped his way to Newhouse's neck and checked for a pulse. There was none. One of Marks's bullets had found the wrong target.

In the darkness, Jack heard a door open and close. Marks was running. Jack took off after him.

Marks had run down the southeast stairwell. Jack opened the door but didn't stand in the frame. There was no gunfire. Jack plunged down into the darkness.

The door swung shut behind him and Jack was in that same pitch black. Now and then he heard shuffling below him, but he didn't try to find it, nor did he light his flashlight.

As he pursued Marks, he tried to anticipate the militia leader's next move. He might just try to escape and go to ground, but he'd also planned long and hard on this plot.

Two EMP devices, Jack reminded himself. They'd stolen two from Cal Tech. Did Marks have a backup plan?

It was likely. Marks had demonstrated the ability to plan for almost every contingency. They'd had two vans at Cal Tech in case surveillance picked them up. They'd used the Iranians as decoys. Marks had even had a plan to throw Babak Farrah at them as an Iranian intelligence officer in case he needed to.

That was Jack's safest bet: Marks had the other EMP

device stowed somewhere, and he'd try to use it now. He would try to get back to the garage and escape.

For Jack, that meant descending over forty flights in total darkness. He started down into the pit.

1 2 3 4 5 6 7 8 9
10 11 12 13 14 15 16 17
18 19 20 21 22 23 **24**

....
THE FOLLOWING TAKES PLACE
BETWEEN THE HOURS OF
2 A.M. AND 3 A.M.
PACIFIC STANDARD TIME
....

2:00 A.M. PST
Century City

Jack's senses had become as attuned to darkness as they could be. But the going was agonizingly slow. At last, somewhere below him, a door opened. As it creaked shut, Jack caught the faintest hint of light—Marks had a flashlight of his own.

Jack risked his own light, and with the flashlight he made better time. He reached P6 and threw the door open, again hesitating in case of gunfire. Then he ran out into the parking area just in time to hear an engine rev and headlights go on. Jack angled toward the headlights. He shut off his own flashlight just in time. A car roared by and muzzle flashes accompanied the sound of shots, but Jack had moved off line and Marks's shots were wild. His car peeled away.

Jack flicked his flashlight on again and ran toward the white van. Near it, he saw that the Chevy Camaro was gone. On a hunch, he ran to the Nova. It was unlocked. He jumped inside. He placed the flashlight on the floor, angled upward, and reached underneath to hotwire the car. The wiring was basic, but the wires themselves were new, and Jack guessed what Marks had planned. The Camaro and the Nova were old cars, with very little wiring that was susceptible to the EMP device. Marks and Newhouse had planned their escape well.

The Nova's engine roared to life and Jack peeled out, headlights illuminating his way through the darkness.

His tires squealed all the way up the circular ramps that led out of the foundation of the building. He scraped the corners several times but ignored it. He needed to catch up to Marks.

At the top of the parking structure he caught him. Marks barreled through the wooden gate and out onto the street, making a hard right turn. Jack followed a hundred yards behind him, but now he flicked off his headlights, hiding himself from Marks.

The streets were black. Not a streetlight or a traffic signal was working. All the buildings were dark. The only artificial light Jack could see was the glow of Marks's headlights ahead of him. There wouldn't have been much traffic at that hour anyway, of course, but now there was none. There were only a few obstacles in the road—cars that had shut down in mid-transit when the EMP went off. Any car that relied on electronics for its functions—onboard computers for ignition, braking, suspension—had shut down. Fortunately for Jack, the streetlights had been, to some degree, replaced by starlight. On any given night in Los Angeles, ambient light wiped out almost all the stars. But tonight the ambient light itself had been wiped out. Jack saw the silhouettes of stalled cars, and sometimes of confounded drivers, as he followed his prey.

Marks turned left onto Little Santa Monica Boulevard and sped west. Jack followed him to the 405 freeway and up the on ramp. The freeway was no different from the surface streets—a few cars stalled here and there. Jack passed one car that seemed to be operational—the driver's headlights were on and he'd stopped to see if someone else needed assistance—but Jack had no time to explain anything to them as he hurtled past at a hundred miles per hour. Marks had somewhere to get to fast.

If Marks knew he was following, the man gave no sign. The militia leader's car sped north on the 405 with no twists or turns and no change of speed. Marks practically flew over the interchange to the eastbound 101, and Jack cruised after him.

Jack's shoulder had begun to throb. It hung lower than his right, and he couldn't lift the arm, which had begun to swell. He also felt a stinging pain in his side. He moved his left hand, painfully, to touch his side where he thought a bullet had passed through his shirt. He felt blood—apparently, the bullet had passed through his flesh as well.

2:20 A.M. PST
Century City

Kelly Sharpton, Nina Myers, Tony Almeida, and a strike team arrived at the Century City Plaza in a Nissan Sentra and a 1972 Chevy station wagon. Every SUV at CTU had been knocked out of commission, but Kelly had managed to commandeer these cars on the street.

They rushed into the darkened lobby, their flashlights probing the ground and finally falling across the face of Darryl the security guard.

"I tried to call," Darryl said. "Was that your guy that was here before? The blond guy?"

"Probably," Kelly said. "Where'd he go?"

Darryl raised his hands. "Where'd anybody go? I heard gunshots up on the roof. I heard gunshots down in the parking structure. But I'm blind as a bat here."

Kelly turned to Nina. "Take half the team and go to the roof. Tony, take the other half and check the parking levels."

"Will do," Nina said. "But it sounds like we missed the action."

"I know," Kelly said. "Whatever he's doing, Jack's on his own."

2:25 A.M. PST
Air Force One

Avery Taylor replaced the handset of the secure telephone and rubbed a hand across his close-shaved head. According to his advance team, the Los Angeles blackout extended in a circle of about thirty miles in diameter, from the Ventura County border south to

San Pedro and Long Beach. East, it had reached past the San Fernando Valley and west the blackout had blanked some of the oil platforms off the coast. There was, essentially, a big black patch where a city was supposed to be. But there was no indication of additional danger.

"Tell the pilot to give us altitude," he decided, "but to maintain his current course."

2:30 A.M. PST
Griffith Park Observatory

Still driving dark, Jack had followed Marks's headlights across the San Fernando Valley on the 101, then down the 110 Freeway to Griffith Park. Near the park Jack had to move in closer, risking exposure because of the twisting and turning streets. But he thought he knew where Marks was headed.

Griffith Observatory was closed for repairs. The entire facility was going through a massive renovation, and although the surrounding park, with its hiking trails and horseback riding, was open to the public, the observatory at the top of the hill was shut down.

Jack found Marks's car abandoned at the bottom of the drive, where the entrance had been blocked by construction vehicles. Jack parked and got out, then began the long, slow climb up the drive. Here, with the starlight, his vision was much better than it had been in the guts of the Century City tower. But he was afraid of an ambush, so he moved slowly, cautiously, searching for Marks as he ascended. It took him nearly fifteen minutes to reach the top of the hill.

Jack trotted up the last stretch of road to the obser-

vatory itself—a grand half-globe perched atop a hill that overlooked the entire city. A lawn-dotted walkway led up to the observatory, although most of the walkway was torn up for renovation at the moment.

In the starlight, Jack saw a shadow move across the broken landscape: Marks. The militia leader reached a mound of something and dragged a tarp away. He hefted something—it looked like a thick, unwieldy bazooka—and trotted toward the domed building.

Jack hurried after him. Nina had said the second weapon taken from Cal Tech was some kind of EMP rifle. He wondered what kind of range it had. He was betting that Marks already knew.

He moved as fast as he could—his shoulder was throbbing now, and every step was agony—among piles of debris along the promenade. He reached the building and rounded it to the far balcony, which gave the best exterior view of the city. He saw Marks' silhouette, but he couldn't help pausing for a half second to notice what he had not noticed atop the Century City tower.

The city had disappeared below him. There should have been endless fields of light stretching off into the distance, gems laid out under a dark blanket of sky. But below there was only darkness, while above—above the Los Angeles basin, for the first time in fifty years, stars shone down in their hundreds of thousands. It was as though the horizon had been flipped—darkness below and lights above. It was, even for a hardened man like Jack, a breathtaking sight.

Marks hefted the electronic rifle. Jack saw a screen light up. As Jack crept up, he saw what looked like a radar screen with a single blip coming into range.

Jack put his gun to the back of Marks's head. "Put the weapon down."

Brett Marks's shoulders stiffened and Jack had that pleasure, so rare in dealing with Marks, of seeing the man totally surprised. But Marks didn't put the HERF gun down.

"You are persistent, Jack. What you lack in brains you make up for in determination."

"I'm not going to say it again."

"Or you'll kill me," Marks said calmly. "Who would you be killing me for, Jack? On whose behalf?" He nodded toward the small screen on the weapon in his hands. "For the people on that plane? You know, at least one of them was willing to sell the rights of the people he represents just to get more power. He was also willing to scare the hell out of the entire country to convince them to give up those rights."

"You helped them do it," Jack pointed out.

"Yeah, I did. But I never claimed to lead the country. I only stand up for *my* rights. When are the rest of the people in this country going to stand up for theirs?"

"They're not as insane as you are," Jack said wearily. The Sig felt heavy in his one good hand.

"They're not as aware as I am. You know, society always punishes the enlightened. I'm telling you, Jack, we are the victims of crimes and we don't even know it."

While he talked, his hand moved slowly to the side of the HERF gun, toward a switch. "The people are too weak to help themselves. They're getting what they deserve. I just think the people on that plane should get what they deserve, too."

"So should you," Jack said.

Marks reached for the switch. Jack pulled the trigger of his SigSauer. The bullet passed through Brett Marks's skull and shot out into the distance. His body jerked backward as he pulled the trigger on the HERF gun. The weapon emitted a high-pitched whine that died away as it clattered to the ground.

Invisible, a stream of focused high-energy radio waves sped up into the night as Air Force One passed overhead. On the plane, the President of the United States slept soundly.

In the seats to the rear of the plane, Attorney General James Quincy pondered his next move, sure now that the New American Privacy Act would pass into law.

Though neither of them would ever know it, the destructive radio wave streaked past the jet, missing Air Force One by five hundred yards on its way up into the atmosphere, where it sped harmless into space. Air Force One cruised past Los Angeles on its uneventful journey to San Diego.

On the hillside at Griffith Observatory, Jack Bauer fell to his knees. He was losing blood from the wound in his side. His left shoulder hung useless at his side. He looked out from the hillside onto the city, currently lost in the void. Out there, millions of people lay under a blanket of darkness, some fearful, some angry; some good, some bad; but all of them, every last one, in need of protection against those who thought nothing of slaughtering them by the hundreds.

Jack Bauer knew who he was fighting for. He was fighting for them.

2:59:59 . . .

AN ENTIRE
INTERACTIVE SEASON

24™

THE GAME

THE COUNTDOWN BEGINS
FALL 2005

INTERROGATE ENEMIES, USE MODERN DAY CTU TECHNOLOGY AND BEAT THE CLOCK TO SAVE THE DAY!

EXPERIENCE "ONE OF THOSE DAYS" AS JACK BAUER

GET INTEL AND ASSISTANCE FROM THE ENTIRE CTU TEAM

PlayStation.2

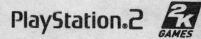